TOOL & DIE

TOOL & DIE

A
Home Repair Is Homicide
Mystery

SARAH GRAVES

B A N T A M   B O O K S
NEW YORK TORONTO LONDON SYDNEY AUCKLAND

TOOL & DIE
A Bantam Book/January 2005

Published by
Bantam Dell
A division of Random House, Inc.
New York, New York

This is a work of fiction. Names, characters, places, and incidents either are the product
of the author's imagination or are used fictitiously. Any resemblance to actual persons,
living or dead, events, or locales is entirely coincidental.

Library of Congress Cataloging in Publication Data
Graves, Sarah.
Tool & die / Sarah Graves.
p.   cm. – (A home repair is homicide mystery)
ISBN 0-553-80309-3
1. Tiptree, Jacobia (Fictitious character)–Fiction. 2. White, Ellie (Fictitious character)–
Fiction. 3. Women detectives–Maine–Eastport–Fiction. 4. Dwellings–Maintenance
and repair–Fiction. 5. Female friendship–Fiction. 6. Eastport (Me.)–Fiction. I. Title:
Tool and die. II. Title.

PS3557.R2897T66 2005b
813'.6–dc22
2004056632

Manufactured in the United States of America
Published simultaneously in Canada

10 9 8 7 6 5 4 3 2 1
BVG

TOOL & DIE

Chapter 1

It was a bright June afternoon in downeast Maine, and my friend Ellie White and I were on our way to visit a large angry man with a criminal history. His name was Jim Diamond and we just wanted to ask him a question.

But his answer—plus what he said *after* he answered—could put him behind bars again, and he would know that because I meant to tell him about it.

So I was nervous, a little.

As a rule I try to avoid angry persons with criminal pasts. For one thing I spend most of my time fixing up a big old house; thus my days are already fraught with potential injury. But Jim Diamond's ex-wife had been getting anonymous threats and I had an urgent personal reason for trying to have them stopped.

Job one was finding out for certain that Diamond was the culprit, as I suspected. Once he admitted it, I intended to assure him that if he didn't agree to cutting it out *pronto,* my next visit would be to his probation officer.

Hey, it *might* work, I told myself for the dozenth time. He could just lie about his guilt, but I didn't expect this. Small-time troublemakers generally don't, once they know somebody's got their number.

And even if he tried, I was confident that I could detect it. Back in the big city when I was a hotshot money manager I'd done business with fellows so corrupt, their code of conduct consisted almost entirely of the seven deadly sins.

As a result I was sure I could smell a rat if one presented itself—yet another reason I'd wanted to check out Jim Diamond in person: to get a good whiff.

But my second thoughts were mounting like the miles on the odometer as Ellie and I sped down Route 1 in the dandy little car I'd bought from a friend the previous autumn. It was an old Fiat 124 Sport Spyder with a black cloth top, apricot paint job, and five speeds forward, plus a professionally installed infant car seat.

The Fiat also had lots more engine than it required for its small size; that fifth speed could be very interesting. And now that we were on the road I hoped fervently that we wouldn't need every bit of power the little car possessed, to make our escape.

Ellie by contrast seemed entirely unworried, which for her was pretty much par for the course. Ellie would worry when pieces of sky actually began hitting the ground, and shattering there into tiny cloud-splotched pieces. Relaxing in the bucket seat beside me she let her head fall back onto the headrest, putting her face up into the sunshine dappled by summer leaves and by the ancient evergreens towering at either side of the road.

"Oh, that feels lovely," she murmured.

It did, too, and especially by comparison. Just a few weeks earlier we'd endured a three-day visitation of sleet, which to my mind is only a little less trying than a visitation of boils, but the weather was standard for what I thought must've been the most extended winter in Maine history.

"I hope Jim doesn't have a gun," I said, zipping through the S turns of the narrow two-lane road while mentally thumbing my nose at the massive recreational vehicles lumbering past us in the other direction. It was the first big week of Maine's tourist season.

Ellie turned, wrinkling her freckled nose at me in surprise. For a trip with the top down she had pinned her hair into a red-gold twist. Curly wisps escaped prettily all around her head.

"Jacobia, you know he won't," she told me. "We've been over that already. Besides, it's illegal for an ex-convict to have a gun," she finished blithely.

This I thought ignored an important fact about how Jim Diamond got to be a convict in the first place. But it was true, we'd researched the guy very carefully in the firearms department, not wanting to blunder unwittingly into any high-caliber developments. Between my husband Wade's friends and Ellie's husband George's, we'd been in touch with just about anyone who might have sold or given Jim Diamond a deadly weapon, and nobody had.

So unless he'd found one by the side of the road somewhere—I happened to know that he'd come out of jail owning little more than the clothes he was wearing when he was arrested—Jim would be unarmed.

And anyway, I wasn't about to turn back.

We sped over the Harmonyville Bridge, the wide mouth of the river below us tumbling and foaming with the force of the tide rushing into it. To our left the river opened into Passamaquoddy Bay, deep blue with a little red scallop dragger puttering out as we passed and gulls drawing white V shapes on the azure sky.

"Besides, we're not going to argue with him," Ellie added. "We're just going to blind him with science."

The science in this case being a simple equation: he talks to us = we *don't* talk to his probation officer. Assuming he owned up to being a bullying rascal, I mean, and promised to quit.

Still I couldn't seem to shake the notion that the whole thing might turn

GOTTA HAVE IT

*A basic tool kit = a hammer, a
pair of pliers, two screwdrivers
(one slot-head and one Phillips
head), a small crescent wrench, a
tape measure, and a box of Band-
Aid plastic strips in assorted sizes.*

out to be far more complicated than that. After all, Diamond hadn't been
very susceptible to the "do it = go to jail" equation in the first place, had he?

But I really needed those threats stopped, and the police had been no
help in doing anything about them. So I pressed the gas pedal down a little
harder as we entered the Moosehorn Wildlife Refuge.

Atop a tall wooden platform a hundred yards from the road, a bald eagle
swiveled its enormous white head slowly, gazing down at us from a nest
big enough to belong to a pterodactyl. The Fiat's engine growled as if it,
too, were some species of predatory wildlife when I downshifted for the
next set of curves.

"And," Ellie pronounced as if this settled everything, "it's a fine day for
a ride."

Right. Probably this visit would turn out fine, as well. I only wished I didn't suddenly have such a bad feeling about it.

"Yes," I replied, keeping my voice light. No sense alarming anyone else. "Yes, it certainly is."

Then I just concentrated on the road, its blacktop heavily rutted and potholed from the steady traffic of massive logging trucks and eighteen-wheelers alternating with the tourists' RVs.

With us in the car that day was Ellie's daughter Leonora, who unlike the car seat she rode in had not been professionally installed, arriving instead in the amateur way about seven months earlier. We'd also brought my father, who had once been an angry man himself and said he could remember how, and my son Sam's ex-girlfriend Maggie to care for Leonora in an emergency.

Not that I really expected one, despite my misgivings. I wouldn't have brought any of them along, not even Ellie, if I had truly believed the scene with Jim Diamond would get ugly.

No, it would be unpleasant but perfectly manageable if all went as planned, and as far as I knew there was absolutely no reason why it shouldn't. Or at any rate that was what I went on telling myself for another ten miles.

The road widened as we reached the town of Whiting, passing the tiny general store with its pair of extra gas pumps: one for diesel, one for kerosene. Little houses, each with a garden plot neatly planted in peas and potatoes, dotted the pale green slopes around the white clapboard two-room school.

"Maggie, do we need to stop?" I asked over my shoulder. By which I meant did Leonora need changing, feeding, or to have any item of her complicated costume deleted or adjusted?

Strapped into her car seat, the baby currently wore a pink long-sleeved cotton romper, a floppy sun hat, a pair of crocheted booties made to look like white high-top sneakers, and a tent of mosquito netting to protect her from flying insects.

"No, she's fine," Maggie replied. "I put more sunscreen on her hands just a little while ago."

Wearing a green tailored shirt and tan cargo shorts, Maggie met my glance from her cramped perch on the Fiat's vestigial backseat. At nineteen, with masses of dark wavy hair pulled back in a braid, deep brown eyes full of soulful intelligence, and the high lip and cheek color that cannot be found in any cosmetics bottle, she was the kind of big, beautiful girl that is so unfashionable nowadays.

An ache of sympathy for her mingled with a pulse of renewed anger at my son. Sam had broken up with Maggie for perhaps the tenth time a few weeks earlier, and she still felt this latest rejection keenly.

Probably he wouldn't have approved of my spending so much time with her, either. But, I thought stubbornly, just because he broke up with her didn't mean I had to.

Don't worry, I mouthed at her—in the moment when I glanced at her, she had looked even more full of foreboding than I felt—then watched in the mirror as she squared her shoulders bravely under the burden of my son's latest display of fickleness.

Or anyway that's what I thought she was being brave about as we turned left toward Lubec, on the last leg of our journey. More houses dotted the hills rolling ponderously toward the sea; old-style clapboard cottages with still-intact barns and pastures were outnumbered by prefabs, modest ranch homes, and a few kit-built log dwellings.

Here and there between them, dark shells of long-abandoned structures hunkered like warnings of what happens when you don't keep your maintenance schedule current.

"Oh, look at that one!" I couldn't help exclaiming as we passed an ancient farmhouse, its outbuildings fallen to heaps of lumber.

A pang pierced me at the sight of a once-bright exterior, now a mess of empty windows, rotted clapboards, and snapped roofbeams all collapsed onto a hip-sprung front porch.

"Don't even dream about it," Ellie said warningly. In her view the only thing sillier than owning one broken-down old house was the possibility of buying another.

"But you could turn it into..."

A shimmering picture of what the old farmhouse would be if someone restored it rose up in my mind, sort of the way I've heard that images of water-containing oases may rise in the desert to lure travelers: lovely and false.

"The only thing that old place needs to be turned into is toothpicks," Ellie declared ruthlessly.

Besides, I already had one old house to care for and it didn't seem to me that I even was doing a very good job of that. At the moment for instance I was playing hooky from a pile of unpainted shutters....

Soon, I promised them mentally, stepping on the gas again.

"I just hope Jim's home," Ellie said as we flew past the Quaker meeting-house, a roadside stand advertising fresh clams and lobsters, and a shed with a cardboard sign tacked to a fence out front, offering free kittens.

"Right," I said, still not wanting to let on the extent of my growing doubts. For one thing at this point I couldn't think of a good excuse for bailing out.

And for another, probably there wasn't any. Besides, we were almost there; in a few moments the acres of field and forest showed signs of becoming outskirts and soon after that we reached the village of Lubec, perched at the mouth of Passamaquoddy Bay.

Entering town we passed through a neighborhood of well-kept houses, bed-and-breakfasts lodged in venerable old sea captains' mansions, and jewellike gardens brimming with early perennials. Downhill lay the water and the long curving International Bridge leading toward the Canadian island of Campobello.

A line of cars, RVs, and campers all bearing out-of-state license plates waited at the busy customs kiosks. Bypassing them we arrived in the downtown district, a single street lined with two-story frame buildings some of which dated back to the nineteenth century.

According to the building permits posted on them, many would soon be under repair; like the rest of the downeast Maine coast, Lubec had become a mecca for waterfront-hungry bargain hunters.

Glazing compound, linseed oil, putty knife, I thought as I gazed at them. Coveting their antique beauty, you could almost believe it wouldn't half kill you, trying to fix some of them up.

But that was an illusion for the new owners to labor under, not me, so with a stab of regret I returned to the task at hand: finding Jim Diamond. We had directions to the place he lived in, but no actual address.

"It should be right here somewhere." Ellie peered up at the windows above the storefronts.

"Try looking for a sign that says 'Rooms,' " my father said from the Fiat's backseat. It was barely big enough to contain two people, and with Maggie and the baby both in there beside him he'd been jammed. But with the car top down at least he could sit up straight, and as he said, he'd been in tight places before.

"I'd forgotten how pretty it is," Maggie murmured, though her tone suggested that she would prefer to be anywhere else.

It was pretty, too: salty and sun-washed, the light slanting in through a thin fog so it seemed the water glittered at us from behind a gauzy veil. In and around the refreshingly idiosyncratic downtown buildings, new paint, big planters of flowers, and colorful window displays brightened places where painters, jewelers, and other handicraft folks had taken advantage of the cheap rents to start interesting, precariously financed shops.

In short, Lubec was lovely and authentically coast-of-Maine atmospheric, if not always exactly bustling; it was one of the last pure, unspoiled places, I thought. A bell buoy clanged lonesomely from somewhere out beyond where the fog veil shrouded the far end of the bridge. "So here we are," I said uncertainly, pulling the Fiat to the curb.

A few tourists strolled the business district, which besides the art shops, the public library, and a pharmacy, included an ice-cream parlor with umbrella-topped tables out front. At the end of the street was the harbor with a pier and some floating docks.

"Come on, baby," Maggie said, climbing out of the car and unstrapping Leonora while my father sat looking around. "Let's go get an ice cream."

"Your son," Ellie said quietly to me when they had gone, "is an idiot."

"Yeah, tell me about it," I replied. But that wasn't my big problem right this minute.

I peered around some more. The tourists looked stunned, as if set without warning on another planet. Never mind about the authentic craft items on offer; where were all the T-shirt shops that multiplied like rabbits in other tourist towns, and the fast-food joints, trinket emporiums, poster shops, and other clever devices for separating them from their money that any other self-respecting vacation destination had?

Not here, where the nearest stoplight was forty miles north or a hundred south. Oh, there was plenty to do, see, and buy, but like the rest of the coastal communities in this remote area of Maine, the place wasn't constructed artificially for your retail-oriented viewing pleasure, merely to shake the cash out of your pockets. Lubec was *real.*

Meanwhile, the only thing I wanted to view was the front door of the creep I'd come all this way to question. That, or the road home.

Maggie came back to the car while we still sat in it. "There it is," she said, pointing. "Maybe," she added doubtfully, as if thinking better of her original certainty.

I followed her gesture. In one of the upper-story windows of a building I had thought was empty, a small yellowed sign was taped to the glass.

Sure enough: ROOMS, the discouraged-looking sign read. "Need some backup?" my father asked mildly.

He was a lean, clean old man with pale blue eyes, thinning gray hair pulled back into a ponytail fastened with a leather thong, and the placid expression of a person who has recently had several serious federal charges against him summarily dismissed. Until a few months earlier he'd been the kind of long-term fugitive whose capture makes the newspapers.

But not anymore. "I *was* going to leave the baby with you," Ellie began to him. "But as long as Maggie's with us..."

Having missed most of my childhood, my father adored taking care of Leonora. Aside from Maggie, he was one of the few sitters Ellie trusted for more than a few minutes.

"Never mind," I told him, getting out of the car and gazing up at my destination uneasily.

"I'd rather you stuck to watching from a distance. You're both pulling lookout duty on this little mission," I added.

Now that we were here, the chances of Jim Diamond's actually having a gun—or a knife, club, or other murderous weapon of opportunity, and the impulse to use it—loomed suddenly higher on my list of possible disasters.

"In fact, how about staying in the car?" In a sure sign of my ambivalence I hadn't even shut off the Fiat's ignition.

"You keep it running," I told Ellie, "and you come get me if I wave at you from up there," I added to my father.

Neither of them seemed unnerved by the sight of the window with the sign in it, partly open and so empty-looking...

So oddly vacant-appearing. But after following my gaze my father looked back at me with his pale blue eyes, and in them I saw my own thoughts as clearly as if I were reading them from a teleprompter.

The place didn't look right. And you couldn't fool him; guys who have been on the run thirty years don't fool very easily, and they don't underestimate the potential for imminent disaster, either.

He got out of the car by uncoiling his body and swinging one leg over the side, then the other, moving to stand in the shade of the ice-cream parlor's green-striped awning. From that vantage point the sunlight didn't glint in the glass across the street, spoiling his view.

"If you do get in, Jake, go right over to that front window," he said. "That way I'll be able to see you."

He didn't say to be careful. He already knew I would do that. It was a habit I'd inherited from him, one that had served us both pretty well one way and another. I crossed the street.

The downstairs front door of the rooming house was sandwiched between a storefront that used to be a marine-supply place and one that was being remodeled as a bookstore: old smells of engine oil and bait tanks on one side, fresh varnish on the other.

The door was unlocked. I went in, passing two rusting metal mailboxes. No names were on the boxes, but a reek of something cooked way past well-done now mingled with that of the bait tanks and paint.

So somebody lived here. "Hello?" I called up the stairs.

No answer. But now I could hear music, Led Zeppelin repeating the age-old refrain about the stairway to heaven.

It wasn't the stairway rising up ahead of me, that was for sure. Cracked treads, bare risers wormholed with the marks of old nails and a general air of deep, bone-weary discouragement pervaded the place. Even the paint peeled off the scarred woodwork in thick curling strips, as if desperate to escape.

A bare bulb hung at the top of the stairs. I climbed toward it, hearing the risers squeak under my feet.

Finishing nails, hardwood shims, 3-IN-1 oil, I thought automatically. Fixing up and maintaining old houses had become my specialty in recent years; it was why ruined places like the ones we'd seen on the way here always caught my interest.

And in a roundabout way, why I was here now.

Pausing on the second-floor landing, I confronted a pair of doors. One had three padlocks, as if you couldn't have bashed it in with your shoulder, the frame looked so flimsy. *Hinges, latch plate, wood screws, one-by-eights,* I thought.

The other door stood ajar. The burned smell was coming from somewhere behind it; also the music.

The window in the second-floor landing was open as well; it was the only way to get any cross-ventilation in what was essentially a railroad flat. Or maybe somebody had left it open fifty years ago and no one ever bothered to close it.

"Hello?" I called again, wondering if anyone was home.

By now I almost hoped no one was. After all, the door *was* open. A conversation might be helpful but a quiet look around could probably tell me what I wanted to know, too.

If I found anything that looked like the first draft of a threat note, for instance, I could just skip the rest of the plan and start working on getting Jim Diamond sent back to jail.

I put my head inside the doorway. "Hello? Jim?"

A muffled sound came from within, startling me. The volume on the music cranked up suddenly.

"Bye-eye-ying a stay-er-way . . ."

Jim didn't want company, I guessed. Disappointed now that he'd turned out to be there at all, I pushed the door open wider.

"Look, I just want to ask a . . ."

Inside, a short plaster-peeling hallway led to a tiny kitchen, and in the other direction to a front room overlooking the street. The music came from there.

Nervously I followed the hall, making my way between bags of recyclable bottles and cans, a telephone—no dial tone—and a plastic hamper piled high with clothes.

Men's clothes: raggedy shirts, jeans, and underwear. Past them was the living room with a small TV on a milk crate, a worn brown recliner, and a massive boom box with a CD player in it.

"Heh-*vunnnnn,*" Robert Plant finished, bless his repetitive little heart. I crossed toward the partly open window upon which the yellowing sign hung, secured by ancient transparent tape.

Before I got there something behind me moved stealthily; I yelped, staggering and nearly falling over the old recliner. But it was only a cat, knocking down an empty beer can while leaping from the top of the dusty boom box to the top of the dusty TV. As its paws brushed past the boom box control knobs, the volume went up another skull-cracking notch.

I reached out and switched the thing off, my heart still in my throat. "Scat," I hissed at the animal now scampering behind an overturned wooden chair.

Prrr-utt, it replied insolently, and began washing its paw, oblivious to the mess of used paper plates, dirty coffee cups and plastic utensils, and more piles of old clothes.

All this place needed was an embroidered sampler on the wall: HOVEL SWEET HOVEL. Taking a shallow breath, I strode to the window and gave the high sign to my father, standing across the street.

Because nobody was here. The window seemed ready to fall so I propped it with still another empty beer can, noticing as I did it how loose the sash was in its wooden frame.

Felt strips, weather-stripping nails...

Stop that, I instructed myself. Maybe he'd just gone out for a minute, leaving the door ajar so the cat could go in and out, too. He could come back at any time, but if he did my father and Ellie would see him.

Meanwhile, whatever was burning in the kitchen smelled like canned cat food simmering to a crisp. Atop that smell floated yet another strong aroma, warm and unpleasant.

I waved down again to my father and Ellie: *All quiet.* Maggie had rejoined them, carrying the baby in one arm and an ice cream in her other hand.

Vanilla, it looked like. Ellie took the baby so that Maggie could manage the dripping cone, as I turned back to the room. The new smell was familiar; unpleasantly so. Like...

Like the smell of blood. Something moved behind me again.

"Hey, cat. I said beat it."

A warm weight fell heavily onto my shoulder. I glanced at it and let out a shriek so loud they must've heard it on Campobello, nearly jumping reflexively in fright right out that window.

Because it was a hand. A big bloody hand, attached to a big hairy arm. A *man's* arm.

Scrambling away, I felt the hand fall off my shoulder. Then something heavy hit the floor. The hairy arm's owner, I figured, and when I turned I saw I was right.

He sprawled on his back, big and surly-looking even as he lay there unconscious. From the description his ex-wife had given us, I was pretty sure I was looking at Jim Diamond.

By then my father and Ellie had made it upstairs and were rushing down the hall toward me, Ellie bringing up the rear with the baby still in her arms.

"Stay there," my father told Ellie. She managed a glimpse, then hastily shielded the baby's eyes with her hand and backed away.

"Call nine-one-one," I yelled after her.

"Phone's out," she said. "I'll use the one in the ice-cream parlor."

Her footsteps hurried down the creaky stairs as I crouched over Diamond's body. From this angle I could see that he had been hit on the head, the deep dent in the back of his skull showing all the way around nearly to his ear.

"What do we do for him?" my father asked.

My ex-husband had been a brain surgeon and my dad knew I'd learned a few head-injury first-aid tips while I was married. Preventive ones, too, like never marry a brain surgeon. That way you will be vastly less likely to inflict head injuries.

But now was no time to nurse a grudge; instead, it was time to nurse this guy. Unfortunately my expertise extended only to the kinds of accidents active youngsters may suffer: the mildly bonked noggins, superficial scalp wounds, and so on.

Also it seemed that the window of opportunity for fix-it measures was closing fast, if it hadn't shut and locked itself already. I looked closer, hoping I was wrong.

But my first impression had been accurate. The man lying on the floor had half his skull caved in.

I glanced around. Near that overturned chair, a black iron skillet lay behind the milk crate that held up the TV. A few dark hairs clung suggestively to the bottom of the skillet, clueing me to what someone had used as a clobbering tool.

"I don't know what to do," I told my father helplessly. "I just know this is bad. He needs an ambulance *fast*."

Because in addition to being large, the injury had obviously happened quite some while ago. Head wounds bleed, and this one had been a gusher. A large dark pool behind the recliner was the marker for where he had originally fallen.

But the blood there was mostly coagulated, which meant he'd been lying semiconscious for hours, maybe even a whole day.

A siren howled distantly, coming closer. As if at the sound Jim Diamond took a deep, hitching breath. When the siren shut off he took another. The third one came as the EMTs rushed in, and then he didn't take any more.

We moved back to let the emergency people get at him. They did what they could to stabilize him, got him loaded and belted onto a backboard efficiently, and hauled him out of there.

So that part was over. But we still didn't know the answer to the question we'd come all the way here to ask, so when one of the Lubec cops came up to me I stared at Ellie over his shoulder.

She took the hint and handed Leonora to my father.

"You know the guy?" the cop wanted to know from me.

Swiftly, Ellie began moving around the hideous little flat, looking at all its contents without touching anything, giving it a good once-over without appearing particularly interested.

Watching her, I found myself suppressing an appreciative smile despite the situation. It wasn't the first crime scene we'd ever come upon; since I'd moved to Eastport, Maine, a few years earlier, Ellie and I had snooped into a number of local murders, and she was a champ at picking up small, meaningful details.

Or the absence of them. "No," I replied to the cop. "We just came here to give him a message."

With any luck, what we wanted would be out in plain sight. *Notebook*, I thought at Ellie, although she knew. *A pen, or even a sample of his handwriting.*

Because I wanted to be able to assure his ex-wife that the threats were over, even if it was for a reason that in spite of everything I thought she wouldn't welcome.

"His ex has a restraining order against him so they can't communicate directly," I added. "And his phone's out."

The cop looked unimpressed. "Yeah? So what was the message?"

I searched my mind for something plausible. "Their daughter wanted to see him about something but she hasn't been able to get hold of him, either."

My father's lip twitched. *Yeah,* I thought at him, *I can feel my nose growing.* But considering Diamond's condition I already thought his ex-wife could be in big trouble.

And I didn't want to make it worse. "I mean," I blundered on, "it was a nice day, we were planning to take a ride anyway, so . . ."

The cop seemed to find this tissue of lies believable enough. He nodded, accepting my string of whoppers as Ellie moved from the living room to the kitchen, where whatever it was still emitted that dreadful odor.

Something on the stove. "Lucky this was turned way down or there'd have been a fire," Ellie said. "Okay if I turn it off?"

"Yeah," the cop told her, snapping his notebook shut. He'd already gotten our names and so on from my dad. But then another thought hit him. "That your little car outside?" he asked me.

I allowed as how it was. Maggie still stood by it, looking up anxiously. Squad cars had boxed in both ends of the street, and apparently the cops weren't letting her into the building.

"That you here visiting in it yesterday?" the cop asked. "Reason I noticed, it's sitting in a no-parking zone," he added. "It was then, too."

At which I carefully did not burst out laughing; Lubec was a pleasant place, but even in tourist season it didn't exactly have a traffic problem.

No-parking zone, indeed. The truth didn't even occur to me. I assured the cop that he must've seen a different car belonging to another visitor to Lubec and promised to move mine.

"See anyone else when you got here?" he asked.

In the apartment, he meant, or on the stairs or loitering around outside. "No. I didn't even know *he* was here until he fell on me."

Ellie slipped out of the kitchen to look around in the bedroom. Better her than me; except for Ellie herself, I didn't know anyone whose bedroom was tidy on short notice. I had a hunch this one wouldn't be precisely springtime fresh, either.

"The door was open," I added, so the cop wouldn't think I'd broken in.

"What I don't understand," my father offered, frowning, "is how he managed to stand up at all, he was so..."

From the blood smears on my T-shirt he'd figured out that at some point recently, Jim Diamond had been upright. And now that the shock had begun fading I recalled again what the back of Diamond's head had looked like.

And let's just say it hadn't resembled anything with bones in it. Or thought processes, either. You didn't have to be a brain surgeon—or the ex-wife of one—to know that much.

"Trauma victims can do funny things," the cop replied cheerfully. "Even the real train wrecks can surprise you."

Which was putting it mildly. For an instant the injured man had towered over me like something resurrected out of the nearest graveyard. All he'd needed was a sound track to make the apartment resemble a stage set from *Night of the Living Dead.*

"I don't know why some of 'em wake up like that at the end," the cop added, "but they do."

Remembering, I felt myself sway a little. My father looked sharply at me. *You okay?*

I nodded at him, spoke to the cop. "I'm not *completely* sure if this was even really the guy I was looking for. Jim Diamond?"

The cop grimaced. "Oh, yeah. It was him, all right. No real surprise, either, the kind of pals that guy had."

Which gave me a moment of hope. "You mean you think you know who might have done this to him?"

He paused. "Well, not really," he admitted. "Nobody in the gang he hung with has a history of crimes against persons."

Darn. It was what I'd heard about Jim Diamond also, and one reason why I'd decided after all to risk bearding him in his den.

Diamond wasn't a basher. But now he'd become the bashee. "State cops'll probably have more questions," the cop informed us.

That cheered me briefly, since it meant that at the moment he didn't have any more himself. I wanted out of this apartment with its smells of burnt food and old blood.

I wanted it bad. "We'll stay available," I promised him, and was about to find Ellie and give her another eyebrow-wiggle, this one meaning *let's vamoose.*

But just then the cop's radio sputtered and he stepped out of the apartment to hear it, as if maybe it was going to transmit a top-secret national-security bulletin.

Ellie was exiting the bedroom when he returned, and he gave her a dark look. But she moved past him to take the baby from my father's arms, and I saw the cop deciding not to comment.

Instead he kept the "Okay, let's wrap it up" expression on his face; after all, Ellie appeared harmless enough.

Little did he know. "You can tell your friend she's not an ex anymore," he said as he put the radio back into its holster.

Bella Diamond, he meant; Jim's ex-wife. She wasn't a friend, exactly,

just my housekeeper and the person whose worries we had come all this
way to put an end to.

Well, they were ended now ... I hoped.

I put my face to the window for some air. Down in the street a gaggle of
onlookers had gathered, a few of the tourists taking pictures of the squad
car and blood drops where the ambulance had been: What I Saw on My
Maine Vacation.

"Guy died on the way to the ER," the cop explained. " 'S'what the radio
call was. Guess that makes your friend a widow."

I hoped that was all it made Bella. And in any case I didn't want to be
the one breaking the news to her. "She'll get official notification?"

He looked at me impatiently. "Sure she will. State cops'll tell her. One of
the things I need to do, notify 'em right away."

His face said he had many other tasks to accomplish as well, and that
standing around gabbing with me wasn't one of them.

"Knowing Jim, though," he finished, "she'll probably just go out and
celebrate."

Or maybe not; like head-injury victims, ex-wives did funny things.
Glancing down at that bloody skillet, I only hoped this ex hadn't done
something a little funnier than usual.

Outside, the sky had darkened in the half hour since I had entered the
apartment, the fog thickening into a cold, optimism-dampening drizzle that
matched my mood.

Not that Diamond wouldn't have been dead no matter who found him.
But as I've mentioned, in the past couple of years dead guys had gotten
into the habit of showing up on my doorstep, or me on theirs. And before
I'd even gotten to Diamond's apartment I'd had the feeling he could be
trouble.

So I was in an unhappy frame of mind when, after raising the canvas
top, I aimed the Fiat back toward Eastport with Ellie, the baby, Maggie,
and my father all jammed into the car with me.

"May I drive?" Maggie asked when we pulled to the gas pumps in Whiting. She looked pale and miserable, as if she needed a task to distract her from what had happened. And she had borrowed the car many times so she knew how to handle it.

The thought even crossed my mind that she'd been out in it the day before. But of course there was no connection; Maggie didn't even know Jim Diamond, or Bella either.

Still . . . "Maggie, you weren't in Lubec yesterday, were you?"

"Me?" She looked startled. "No, why?"

"Never mind." I was really tempted to let her take the wheel. It would have been more comfortable for her than the backseat, and I felt tired. But at the moment I also needed to be in control.

"Sorry," I told her, hooking the gas nozzle back up to the pump. "You can drive another time, okay?"

It seemed even smaller inside with the top up. Still, there was no hope of putting it down again on this trip. Moments later the skies opened abruptly, hammering the taut black canvas with a good old-fashioned summer downpour.

Also it was leaky black canvas, another unhappy surprise.

A drop of cold water hit the back of my neck, then two more. Ellie found the roll of adhesive tape I kept in the glove box, because it's amazing what you can fix with enough adhesive tape.

But not black canvas convertible tops. She tore off a strip and pressed it to the wet spot over my head. Promptly it fell off and slid irretrievably down the back of my shirt.

"Never mind," I said glumly. "But don't lose the rest of the roll, please."

Another cold drop hit my neck. "Something tells me I might be needing it to hold myself together before this is all over."

I was hoping she'd contradict me. But Ellie only sighed and nodded agreement. "Me, too," she said. She sounded worried.

Because maybe the sky wasn't actually falling, but with the rain thundering down so hard that the drops were bouncing up off the pavement again, it was doing a pretty great imitation of it.

And to think, I ruminated as we sped through the cloudburst, that only a few days earlier I'd believed my worst problem—

—other than my son Sam, his girlfriend Maggie, and Bella Diamond, who even without a murdered ex-husband had turned out to be the house-keeper from hell—

—was a moose on the loose.

Chapter 2

T he whole thing began on another bright morning a couple of days before we found Jim Diamond clobbered in his apartment. On that day I'd been feeling lighthearted even though an unpleasant chore lurked gremlinlike on my to-do list.

Which of course was a part of the problem. If I'd suspected in advance even a little bit of what I was in for, I'd have taken preventive measures.

Rocket launchers, say, or a moat full of alligators. Twelve-foot spikes, their tips smeared with exotic poison, backed by a razor-wire fence so sharp it could trim your toenails all the way up to your . . .

Well, you get the idea. But instead birds were singing and the dew-spangled lilacs were doing their perfume thing, richly intoxicating. A salt breeze off the bay blew in through the open kitchen window, sweet as a kiss.

The whole situation was so invigorating, in fact, that I'd gotten a start on two projects I'd been avoiding for months: I'd taken the screen off that open window so I could repair it. And I was painting the shutters I'd bought secondhand to replace the ones demolished in a gale the previous February.

I'd been up in my third-floor workroom where I had finished priming two pairs of the shutters, decided to come downstairs for a break, and was getting ready to clean my paintbrush at the sink in my one-hundred-and-eighty-one-year-old house in Eastport, Maine. Humming cheerfully in the big barnlike kitchen with its high tin ceiling, worn hardwood floor, and pine wainscoting, I had just turned on the faucet over the old soapstone basin when suddenly from that wide-open window behind me came a sound.

A *loud* sound, like...

Buh-wha-a-a-t!

Dropping the paintbrush in a splatter of paint, I whirled to confront a full-size moose head complete with a very respectable rack of moose antlers, attached to a full-size moose.

A *live* moose. The creature's huge yellow teeth chomped down onto the last of six red Martha Washington geraniums I had planted in the kitchen window box only a few hours earlier, and began chewing.

"Muh-muh-moose," I managed faintly. Nothing remained of the other five geraniums but short green stumps.

The moose rolled his eye at me, chewing pensively on a mouthful of Martha Washingtons. A single red blossom clung wetly to one of his enormous nostrils.

Bwha-a-t! he remarked again, spraying geranium cud all over my clean kitchen.

"Scram!" I quavered, glancing around for something large enough to discourage the creature.

Like maybe one of those rocket launchers. But none were in sight and when I looked back again, neither was the moose.

Hurrying to the window I skidded hard on moose cud, flailed wildly, and avoided a pratfall only by slamming into the refrigerator and wrapping my arms around it. This set the antique crystal lemonade pitcher I'd bought at a church sale and put up there for safekeeping teetering dangerously, as the cat perched next to it showed no interest whatsoever in saving it.

She just looked intensely bored, and when I'd rescued the pitcher and made it to the window to peer out, all I saw of the moose was his tail twitching casually as his big brown rear end vanished among the trees and bushes at the back of the yard.

Then he was gone, leaving my previously spotless kitchen heavily splattered with geranium cud. Oh, and by that paintbrush, too. In my confusion I'd apparently grabbed it again, waving it around rather wildly and indiscriminately.

As a result any surface not fire-hosed with moose cud was now heavily anointed with white latex paint. And the combination was not one your average home decorator would approve.

Even your average zookeeper couldn't find much to approve about this mess, I thought as I gazed forlornly at it. And at the moment I couldn't think of a good way of cleaning it up, either, except possibly with a blowtorch.

Mee-yow-row-wowl, the cat remarked. She was a cross-eyed Siamese named Cat Dancing who thought any troubles the humans got into were their own fault, and by the way, was it suppertime yet? Also she regarded herself as too refined to chase a mouse, much less a moose.

"Oh, hush up," I told the cat irritably, thinking about cat prints tracked inevitably through a combination of moose cud and latex paint. "And you'd better stay up there if you know what's good for you."

Urmph, Cat replied, which in cat lingo I happened to know meant *"Oh, stick a sock in it."*

Just then Ellie came in with the baby strapped to her back and my two dogs, Monday and Prill, straining at the ends of their leashes.

"Hi," Ellie greeted me, not even breathing hard. "What's new?"

She'd been out for her usual two-mile morning walk, which she took to

maintain her already-lithe figure and believed was made even more health-
fully effective by the addition of a twenty-pound baby and nearly two hundred pounds of rambunctious canine.

"Ellie, don't—"

But it was too late. She'd dropped the leashes before she'd had a look at
the kitchen. Instantly both dogs got the scent of the moose. They began
bouncing off the walls like a couple of balls in a canine-themed pinball machine gone mad.

I slammed the hall door and the one to the ell of the house, then the one
leading through the butler's pantry to the dining room, and finally the
kitchen window.

"Jake," Ellie asked, peering around, "what on earth happened in here?"

Meanwhile Monday, the Labrador retriever, had snuffled up a snootful
of moose-flavored geranium cud. She stood stock-still as an odd look came
onto her doggy features. Then—*ker-schnoof!*—she sneezed it out again in a
paint-infused aerosol that went absolutely everywhere instead of just
nearly everywhere, the way it had been before.

"And what," Ellie added, her nose beginning to wrinkle, "is that *smell?*"
Because morning moose breath, as it turns out, isn't exactly minty-fresh.

Prill, the red Doberman, didn't sniff at all, instead deciding instantly
that whatever had been in here, she didn't like it. She hit the floor running,
heading for the window where the scent was apparently strongest, struck a
patch of paint, and slid forward on all fours, barking furiously and spreading paint in a long thick smear all the way to the washing machine.

Hitting it with a thud didn't discourage the big red dog one bit. Instead
Prill scrambled back, took a running jump that carried her onto the top of
the machine, and would have gone right on out through the window glass
had I not remembered the magic words.

"Prill! Time to eat!"

The dog stopped short, realized where she was, and began to whimper.
Jumping up was one thing, her sad look seemed to say.

Jumping down was something else again.

Yowrl, Cat Dancing commented from atop the refrigerator. In cat lingo, that meant *ha ha ha.*

Wuff? Prill asked softly and a little embarrassedly, seeming all at once to feel very nearly as foolish as she looked, perched there atop a major household appliance.

"Oh, for heaven's sake, you big goof," I said impatiently. "Ellie, give me a hand, here, will you please? And you," I added to the dog now eyeing me imploringly, "don't you move a goddamned inch."

Then I remembered Leonora, who laughed happily from inside Ellie's baby carrier. A cheerful little soul, Lee gazed around my kitchen with the goggle-eyed glee that pretty much symbolized her whole personality except when she was hungry.

"I mean a gosh-darned inch," I amended. It had been twenty years since I'd had my own baby around the house.

"Don't worry, she already says worse." Ellie put her arms around Prill's hind legs. "George took her down to the fish pier the other day to meet some of his buddies. Some of the mackerel they were pulling in, he says, were as big as the baby. Anyway, she came home cussing a blue streak."

Knowing the daily habits of some of George's buddies, I was surprised little Lee hadn't come home demanding to drink beer and smoke cigars. Still...

"Ellie, are you sure that baby was cussing?" A small round spit bubble appeared, glistening on the infant's rosebud lips.

For her walk that day Ellie wore a pale blue sundress with yellow sunflowers on it, a pink canvas sun hat whose floppy brim framed her delicately featured face, and a green cotton cardigan whose pockets were stuffed with all the baby items that didn't fit in the baby backpack.

"Well," Ellie admitted, "maybe not. At her age, I guess just about anything can sound like anything else."

On Ellie's feet were a pair of big brown Earth shoes that didn't make her legs look fat, mostly because nothing could make Ellie's legs look fat. With pale green eyes, red hair escaping in wisps from a purple hair ribbon, and freckles the color of gold dust sprinkled across her nose, my best friend was as fragile-appearing as a fairy princess out of a storybook, and as tough as shoe leather.

"At first George thought she was actually saying words," she went on. "And wasn't he some proud, though?"

Ellie's husband George Valentine was the man you called when you had a bird's nest in your chimney, raccoons in your attic, or foxes building a den behind your garden shed, from which shelter they were planning to feast all winter on neighborhood pets.

I wondered if I could get him to deal with a moose.

"But then he figured out what those babblings sounded like," Ellie went on, "and hit the roof."

"Maybe that's what made it leak," I replied.

George and my own husband, Wade Sorenson, were reshingling the roof of George and Ellie's house when they weren't both out working other jobs.

"Maybe." Ellie laughed as we maneuvered a frightened Prill to the edge of the washing machine. "Anyway, he won't let the guys cuss around Lee anymore, and he already wouldn't let them breathe on her in case they had colds."

All of which warmed my heart. After several childless years, Ellie and George had gotten used to being footloose and fancy-free, so I'd wondered how they would adjust to having a baby. But Leonora had instantly become their sun, moon, and stars; neither could bear to be away from her for long, and it was a contest as to which of them doted more upon her.

"Oof," I said as we lifted the unhappy dog, me at the front of the frightened animal and Ellie at the other end.

Glrp, said Prill, stiffening anxiously as we raised her up off the washing machine.

"There," Ellie exhaled, dusting her hands together as we finished setting the creature securely back down onto the floor.

Chagrined, Prill went to her water bowl and drank thirstily, as if to say this was all she'd meant to do in the first place, and how did she ever get up onto that awful contraption, anyway?

Murp, Cat pronounced disappointedly, and went back to sleep.

Whereupon I didn't have the heart to scold Prill; after all, I hadn't exactly distinguished myself with my own reaction to the moose, had I? Instead I put both dogs out in the ell where they couldn't create more mayhem.

"A *moose?*" Ellie repeated in astonishment as I explained what had happened. "You're sure it was a real, live moose?"

"Well, it wasn't a stuffed one. Believe me, after seeing it I can definitely tell the difference. *And* after smelling it."

Just then George himself arrived. He was a small, dark-haired man with a five o'clock shadow already shading his stubborn jaw and the creases in his knuckles permanently stained by the many varieties of hard, dirty work he did in Eastport year-round. Today he wore an old white T-shirt, faded jeans, and battered leather boots.

He bent to embrace Ellie and kiss the baby, then sniffed the air. "Phew, what's that?"

He didn't wait for an answer, instead heading to the cellar where Wade had stashed a carton of roofing nails; when George was on a mission you got in front of him at your peril. But his question made me even more aware of the green, richly weedy aroma in the room, mingled with something I can't fully describe without being indelicate. Suffice it to say the atmosphere in my kitchen was as rank as a cow barn that for some reason has been situated in the middle of a swamp.

"So yes," I told Ellie, "I'm sure that it was a moose."

Once George had retrieved the nails and departed, Ellie and I met again to confer at the kitchen table. We'd put Leonora down for a nap in the crib I kept ready for her in what had been the downstairs maid's room, back in the time when my house was lived in by people who actually had maids.

In those days, when water came from hand pumps and heat came from woodstoves that had to be tended in a filthy, never-ending round of back-breaking work, all the backs that got broken around here belonged to servants.

Nowadays, the back belonged to me. Or it had until recently; fear touched my heart as I remembered that I wasn't alone in the household-help department at the moment. Also, the prospect of the unpleasant chore looming over me had just gotten worse.

"A big," I emphasized, "moose." I leaned down to wipe at yet another stubborn paint splotch.

It didn't come off. The finish on the nineteenth-century kitchen floor was so thin—and let's face it, in places so nonexistent—that the paint had quickly sunk in. Somehow the smears had also reached the cabinets, the stove and countertops, and the ceiling that Monday had apparently managed to hit with her explosive sneeze.

In short, you couldn't have spread that paint around better if you'd shot it from a shotgun at about a hundred yards, which was how far I wanted to be from the situation, minimum.

Because given enough elbow grease and the same determination as that famous old Greek guy used to sanitize the Augean stable, I could've cleaned the kitchen up myself. Trouble was, I wouldn't be doing it myself because for the first time since I'd moved to Maine seven years earlier, I had household help.

Actual paid-by-the-hour help, I mean, not the kind Ellie always gave so cheerfully and willingly. And the help was due to arrive in . . .

Good heavens, only about thirty minutes. As if to emphasize this fact, the hall clock chimed the half hour. Ellie looked up, catching my thought. "Uh-oh."

"Yep. Bella's coming," I said hopelessly. "*Soon.* And when she gets a look at this place, she'll go absolutely bananas."

"Right," Ellie agreed, instantly reaching out to scrub at the front of a kitchen cabinet.

But a mixture of moose cud and latex is apparently the stuff they should use to glue ceramic tiles onto the walls in bathtub enclosures. In ten minutes it had dried to the durability of epoxy; now the only way it was coming off was with a hammer and chisel.

Assuming I didn't really go out and rent a blowtorch, a plan that was starting to look more tempting by the minute. Even the most determined domestic helper wouldn't be able to clean a house if it was actually on fire.

I hoped.

"So it's true," Ellie said, changing the subject. "There is really a moose running around town."

I just stared at her. "You mean you *knew*?"

Here I should explain that Eastport is located on an island, which funnily enough is actually called Moose Island, seven miles off the coast of Maine and so far downeast that it is almost in Canada. Two miles wide, seven miles long, three hours from Bangor and light-years from anywhere else, Eastport is reachable by car over a causeway, although at low tide you could probably just wade across the clam flats.

Which it seemed our moose must have done, wandering from the thousands of acres of wild, wooded mainland on the other side of the channel. Something about Eastport had attracted it, possibly, or maybe it just got lost.

And now at least according to Ellie it seemed other people had seen it, too.

"Deke Meekins from the marine store said he nearly walked right into it this morning, putting kayaks in the water for some tourists," she reported, glancing nervously at the back door.

This made me feel better, suggesting as it did that I wasn't the only one frightened of my soon-to-arrive housekeeper.

"I saw Deke while I was out on my walk," Ellie went on, "and he said the moose was standing on the beach at the foot of Clark Street, having a drink out of the freshwater spring by the ruins of the old sardine cannery."

She got out two cups as the coffeemaker finished spitting and chuffing. In my old house there is no such thing as a level surface, so no matter where you put it, that coffeemaker always sounds like the steam boiler on a locomotive.

"Deke said it was quite a sight," Ellie added, getting out the cream and sugar, "with the seagulls out there taking morning baths in the freshwater pools, and this moose among them."

My heart softened briefly as I pictured this. But then the reality of what I was facing washed over me again.

"Ellie, we've got to..." I gestured desperately. The task I'd been dreading was already bad enough without the moose mess. "We can't just *sit* here. She's going to..."

Ellie poured the fragrant coffee. "Yes, I suppose she is. Any minute, too," she added uncomfortingly.

"But what do you suggest? I guess we could lock the door," she continued, "and pretend we're not here, except that you decided to give her a key of her own in the first place."

Drat, so I had. Because what good is a housecleaner if you actually have to *be* in the house all the time that he or she is cleaning? Or so I'd believed back in the days before I'd gotten to know Bella Diamond.

"Go on, drink your coffee," Ellie told me. "Think of it this way: What's the worst she can do?"

"Egad." At her question I nearly choked on a swallow of the hot liquid. "She can break up my marriage, alienate my son, hurt my dad's feelings, and destroy my life. *That's* what she can—"

"Wah!" In the maid's room, the baby woke up and emitted the short, piercing yell she used as a distress signal whenever she forgot all the colorful profanity her dad's friends had taught her.

Ellie went to check, came back carrying the infant. "I guess I shouldn't have bothered putting her down. I almost forgot we've got to go to a pediatrician's appointment. It's just a regular checkup, but...oh, Jake, I'm so sorry to leave you with all this!"

"Never mind." I went to the door with her. "No sense both of us dealing with Bella's wrath. I've got to talk to her, anyway."

It was the confrontation I'd been fretting over. "So this'll just give me a good excuse to..."

But then I stopped, hearing myself. "An excuse to talk with my own employee; how gutless is that? You'd think that she was a hurricane about to make landfall."

But Ellie wasn't fooled. She'd met Bella, too. "That's fine to say now, Jake, but you just wait. She may not be a hurricane, but she's definitely a force to be reckoned with. Don't underestimate her."

Not a good thought; too bad it was so chillingly accurate. Certainly it hadn't taken long for Bella to blow an ill wind through my house.

Outside, I followed Ellie down the porch steps, avoiding the rotten one that had been threatening me with a broken ankle for months. *Two-by-eights,* I thought automatically; *a hammer, nails, and a bucket of porch paint.*

Then I paused, captured abruptly by an island summer day as fresh as a newly finished watercolor. Maple leaves gleamed in the lemony sunshine. Late tulips massed amidst the last of the yellow daffodils in the dooryards of graceful old wooden houses up and down Key Street. Fat purple lilac blooms basked in the soft June warmth, and in the shade by the porch the last of the hyacinths clustered shyly between lush green patches of moss.

A snarl of engines made me look up. Above, a pair of vintage biplanes from the aviator's club at Quoddy Airfield drew lazy 8s on the paintbox blue sky. The long white banners ribboning behind them read WELCOME TO EASTPORT!

Meanwhile my house loomed comfortingly behind me, an 1823 white clapboard Federal with three full floors, a two-story ell, forty-eight tall green double-hung windows, and three red brick chimneys. Despite missing shutters, decrepit porch steps, and the many other repair challenges the massive old dwelling continued regularly to present, my home was as fundamentally solid now as it had been for nearly two hundred years.

And that encouraged me. But Ellie's next comment didn't.

"Don't let Bella push you around," she warned as she and Leonora departed. "Or mark my words, the next couple of weeks will be hell on wheels."

Which they were anyway, but not for the reason either of us thought.

Back in the house, I turned away from the moose mess and instead decided to fix a fritzed light switch in the hall while I awaited Bella. That way, there was a chance that I might be electrocuted before she arrived.

Although not a very good chance, since I did shut down the circuit breaker in the cellar before I began. After that it was only a matter of removing the switch plate, pulling the old switch and removing the screws holding the wires to the contacts, attaching a new one, and shoving it back into the wall before replacing the switch plate to complete the procedure.

So while I worked I had plenty of opportunity to think about (a) how hugely reluctant I was to confront my errant housekeeper, and (b) why I had to.

The main reason being that the night before, my husband Wade Sorenson had waited until after dinner and then—astonishingly, for him—laid down the law.

"Jake, she follows me around the house with a whisk broom, waiting for me to shed skin cells. Or hair follicles. Whatever."

Wade took a deep breath. "When I get home from work I never know what to expect. What I do know is that I practically have to strip down to my birthday suit before I come in, or she gives me the evil eye."

The evil eye wasn't what I gave him when he stripped down to his birthday suit. But he was serious, so I'd kept quiet.

And in the next moments I'd realized just how very serious he was. "Wade..."

He'd put a hand up, stopping me. "She takes the beer bottle out of my hand, rinses it, and cleans the label off to put it in the recycling bin before I've even finished drinking out of it."

After a swallow of wine he continued. "She goes into my workshop and sweeps the wood shavings off the floor. I was," he emphasized, "*saving* those wood shavings."

Broad at the shoulder and narrow at the hip, Wade had blond brush-cut hair, blue eyes, and a square, solid jaw whose muscles flexed just the tiniest bit when he was angry.

The muscles were flexing. "I know, it was fun for you to have a house-keeper, Jake. And I enjoyed it, too. I thought it was wonderful. At first."

Sure, who wouldn't? After I won a full month of her services at the same church fair where I had bought the crystal lemonade pitcher, Bella had arrived and cleaned the house so thoroughly you could see what color the woodwork was, except in the places where she had scrubbed every bit of the paint off.

"I even liked it when she laundered all the curtains, washed the windows, and steam-cleaned every one of the rugs," he went on inexorably. "Though I believe I might have preferred that she not do it all in one day," he added.

Sorrowfully, I had to agree. Between bleach for the curtains and ammonia for the windows, not to mention chemicals that boiled in steaming jets from the nozzles of the rug-cleaning machine, we were all nearly gassed right out of the place.

"But Jake," Wade said, "this morning she walked into the bathroom without knocking, took my razor away from me, and dipped it in some evil-looking antiseptic solution. And when she did it I hadn't even gotten done shaving!"

"Oh, Wade," I moaned. "I'm very sorry. That is really too much to bear."

"Yes, it is," he agreed firmly, looking down at his hands. They were big, calloused hands, permanently stained and work–battered. "I hate to say it, but it was the last straw." His tone brooked no.

Wade is Eastport's harbor pilot, which means he guides freighters in through the treacherous rocks, channels, tides, and currents with which our harbor is so plentifully furnished. When he isn't doing that, he restores old firearms in his workshop, upstairs in the ell of my old house. And in his spare time he does things like help reshingle George and Ellie's place.

"But that's not all she's been doing," Wade went on, looking regretful but determined.

Very determined. "She's been into Sam's room. She put his sneaker collection through the washer. *And* his baseball caps."

Horror pierced me. "Wade, you can't wash a baseball cap! It won't stand up to the..."

"Yeah." Wade looked grim. "The sneakers are bad enough. It takes a kid years to get a nice, grotty patina on a sneaker, not to mention the holes which I'm afraid she has mended neatly, and the laces which she replaced. But the caps..."

Sam owned a baseball cap from every major-league game he had attended throughout his life. And a ball game was his father's way of bonding with Sam—to my ex-husband, the phrase *personal relationship* might as well've been written in Urdu—so by now Sam had a substantial and possibly even a valuable collection.

And anyway, it was valuable to him. "The bills on those caps didn't take well to the hot water," Wade reported unhappily.

Oh, lord. "They can be restiffened. I can open 'em up, put in new linings," he'd gone on. "I think I can, anyway. Lucky the colors didn't run. But at the moment the whole bunch of them," he finished ruefully, "need baseball-cap Viagra."

Fortunately Sam hadn't noticed them yet. A sophomore at the University of Maine in nearby Machias, my son was home from college but had already begun a summer project at the local boat school, so his eye for details around his room wasn't as sharp as usual.

Also, he had a new girlfriend soaking up his spare time and concentration. I drank some wine, unsure whether I was unhappier about the caps or about the girlfriend. I knew how angry Sam was going to be about the precious headgear.

But Sam's new romance was becoming a worrisome problem, too. Then I looked at Wade's face, so gently insistent. He was being awfully nice about this. And suddenly I was afraid I knew why.

"*That's* not all, either, is it?" I asked.

He shook his head. "I'm not even so sure I should tell you this part."

His general habit is to repeat the good things and shut up about the bad. "But the other morning," he continued, "I overheard her telling your father that if she'd known there was going to be a dirty old man around here, she might not have taken the job."

I gasped as Wade added, "I think he dropped a cigarette ash on the cellar floor. That's probably what got her going."

"You're kidding," I managed. "I mean you're *not* kidding, are you? Bella really said that?"

The only person allowed to smoke cigarettes in my house is my father, and then only in the cellar. But the point is, he *was* allowed to smoke down there, he is as much a part of our family as Sam or Wade or I am, and I didn't know what the heck she was doing in the cellar, anyway.

A hot little flame of fury sprang to life in my heart. "What did *he* say?"

Wade chuckled. "He called her a sourpuss. He said if he'd known she was going to be around here *he* certainly wouldn't be, and he asked if there wasn't a lemon around somewhere that needed a good sucking, preferably at someone else's house."

Which meant my dad had managed to give as good as he got. But I still didn't like the sound of it, suggesting as it did the very thing I tended chronically to worry about: that if he were provoked sufficiently, the old man might just take off.

And not only the *old* man. "Jake," Wade said.

Here it came. I braced myself. I could straighten things out with my father, who'd dealt with much worse and was a tougher old bird than any housekeeper could possibly be. But . . .

"Jake," Wade repeated quietly, "if Bella's going to stay for another couple of weeks and things with her don't change, I might just think of locking up the shop and taking a sabbatical down to the house on Liberty Street."

My heart plummeted. "That way," he went on, "you can still have what you want, and I can have . . ."

A moment's peace, he didn't have to finish. Wade had kept his own little house when we got married, on a bluff overlooking the bay. Every so often he went down there to smoke cigars, drink brandy, and play poker with his firearms-collecting buddies.

I didn't mind. For one thing I didn't particularly want a coffee can full of cigar stubs on the dining room table. But Wade had never fled to the Liberty Street house to escape something at *this* one.

Until now. "Maybe I should fire her," I said. "After all, the house is already so clean you could build microchips in it."

In the flickering gleam of the candles on the table, the vintage champagne brocade curtains shone spotlessly and the windows gleamed against the deepening evening. The tiled hearth glimmered before a stack of white birch logs, the mantelpiece sparkled as if newly painted, and even the gold-medallion wallpaper had been gone over with a damp cloth so its antique design stood out crisply against the background of faded cream.

"I did have a few other things for her to do. She said she liked gardening as much as indoor chores, and the yard needs a spring cleaning."

Which was putting it mildly. "But," I went on, "she can't be disrupting this household, your life, or Sam's belongings. And she certainly can't go on insulting my father."

The consequences of firing Bella wouldn't only be unhappy for me. Probably everyone else in Eastport already knew about her peculiarities and wouldn't hire her. Still . . .

"She just isn't worth everyone being upset around here. And especially not you."

Wade would cheerfully have done the housework and gardening, his share and more. But at the moment the port was busy and so was the gun business, and when you're self-employed like Wade you've got to make hay while the sun shines.

Besides, once George Valentine's roof was completed, George would be coming here to help Wade scrape and paint this place.

Wade rubbed his chin. A patch on his left jawline was still stubbly from where Bella had taken his razor away from him.

"No," he said thoughtfully, "I don't think you have to go that far. I think you should talk to her. Lay out the situation, make sure she knows she's the employee around here, not you." A grin creased his face. "Although I realize it's not going to be as easy as it sounds, considering that it's Bella."

I felt my shoulders slump heavily at the prospect. So far my conversations with her had been like juggling chain saws, dancing in quicksand, or both.

Mostly both. "Don't worry," I said, not sounding convincing even to myself. "After I talk to Bella, I'll go leap a few tall buildings in a single bound. One each, I mean. A bound for each building."

Or a build for each bounding. Whichever; I'd been slugging the wine down pretty steadily since our conversation began.

Because mostly Wade's reaction to this kind of inconvenience was a shrug of indifference. He'd grown up here in Eastport in a knockabout family whose notion of riches was a couple of nickels rubbing together; he understood real hardship.

So to him, household annoyances were mere speed bumps on the highway of life. But once in a long while something was important enough for him to make a fuss over, and then he stood his ground.

Which was how I knew I would have to rein in my unruly housekeeper, fast. Wade hadn't *exactly* delivered an ultimatum; he never did. But he'd just made it *very* clear that if I didn't summon up a little spinal fortitude, consequences would follow.

Mostly the consequences would consist of me feeling that I'd disappointed him. That plus the notion that I hadn't stood up for my dad when the chips were down.

And along with anything at all having to do with failing my son Sam, these were the things that could sit me bolt upright out of a sound sleep at night, sweating and shaking.

"I could talk to her if you want me to," Wade offered kindly after a moment.

Wade once stepped into a fight on the street in front of Eastport's Mexican restaurant, La Sardina. The two brawlers were (a) bigger than Wade, (b) meaner than Wade, and (c) brandishing sharp knives. But not much later the three of them were sitting inside at the bar together, drinking Dos Equis and debating whether the Sox had a chance at the pennant.

He never told me exactly how he did it, and I never asked. I just knew that for a strong, silent Eastport guy, my husband had a way with words and in a crunch he was willing to use it.

But... "No, thanks," I said after a minute.

I looked around at the remains of the dinner he'd come home and cooked: fresh grilled salmon with mustard mayonnaise, wild rice with scallions and baby mushrooms, and a salad of romaine lettuce and plum tomatoes with Wade's special homemade dressing.

It was one of the few evenings off he'd had in weeks. "Bella's my responsibility," I said. "I'll take care of it."

"Your choice," he conceded, then began clearing the plates.

"Don't do that," I protested, jumping up, too. "You cooked. The least I can do is the dishes."

Leaning down, Wade touched his head to mine, pressing his forearms to my shoulders while holding a plate in each big hand.

"Tell you what," he said into my ear, his voice starting up a delightful little rumble somewhere in my chest. "We'll do 'em together. Later we'll go out, look at the stars, take another bottle of wine along with us, and maybe fool around a little."

He kissed my earlobe tenderly. "That suit you?"

Oh, boy, did it ever.

Chapter 3

H ello? Anyone home?"

Bella Diamond's distinctive voice, like a cross between a broken harmonica and a rusty hinge, startled me from my memory of the previous evening.

"Here," I called from the kitchen, a room that in my house had an air of comfortable dishevelment at the best of times.

This wasn't one of them. The housekeeper appeared in the doorway. "Good morning," she began, and then her jaw dropped.

On Bella it wasn't a pretty sight. "What's gone on in here?" she demanded, her tone turned high and breathy as if she'd just witnessed a bad highway accident.

Except for the lack of blood it was what that kitchen most resembled. "Bella," I faltered, "it's not really as bad as . . ."

But it was no use. "Oh," she moaned, stricken.

A short, stout woman with dyed red hair skinned back into a tight ponytail, she wore as usual a pair of old jeans and a faded sweatshirt over beat-up penny loafers. Protruding blue eyes, big teeth, and a grayish complexion completed the picture. As Sam said when he first met her, she was no oil painting, and although of course I'd forbidden him to repeat this I had to agree.

"Well!" she huffed, making a beeline for the broom closet.

"Bella," I said again, hopelessness rising in me. "Listen, this can all wait. Bella, I want you to sit down here and . . ."

A clatter of scrub brushes, mops, and buckets came from the closet, along with a wheezing sound that I was pretty sure was Bella, hyperventilating.

She emerged looking even more agitated than before. "Wait? But it can't *wait*. How can you . . . I've got to . . . oh! Where's that bottle of Lysol?"

She dove for the cabinet under the sink where I kept all the bottles of cleaning solutions, along with many of the household tools that belonged in the toolbox but never got there.

"Heat some water, Missus," she gasped. "It's an emergency. Get that big kettle, the one for the lobsters, and—"

"Bella!" My fist slammed onto the kitchen table. This was ridiculous; in the old days I'd brazenly faced down Wall Street pirates of commerce so black-hearted, their private Lear jets all should've been emblazoned with skulls and crossbones.

"Bella," I repeated, "you stop it *right now!*"

She paused, blue eyes bulging. "But . . . but I can't!"

"Sit!" I commanded.

Abruptly, both dogs dropped their rumps to the floor as if by involuntary reflex. Startled, Bella sat too, every muscle in her body still visibly twitching to leap on the task at hand and wrestle it into germ-free submission.

"I'm sorry you had to walk in on this, Bella," I said. "I agree, it's a terrible mess. But you and I need to have a talk."

Her expression turned cautious. "You work for me," I went on, pressing my advantage while I still had even the most tenuous grasp on it. "You can't clean this kitchen unless I want you to. And right now I *don't* want you to. Understood?"

Bella blinked slowly. "Yes, ma'am," she answered.

"And stop calling me ma'am. It annoys the hell out of me. My name is Jacobia Tiptree, most people call me Jake, and that's what you'll call me from now on. We're going to have rules around here and that's the first one. Are you with me so far?"

She nodded, eyes wide, which on Bella was saying something. When she looked straight at you it was as if any minute those big blue peepers of hers might decide to pop right out on stalks.

But there was something oddly appealing about her, too; the uncamouflaged honesty of her rough appearance for one thing, and the way she held her head up so high in spite of it, for another.

I poured her a cup of coffee and set it in front of her; she recoiled as if it were poison. Someone had apparently instructed her at some time or another that household employees do not have refreshments with employers, and the warning had stuck.

"Oh, drink that," I snapped at her. "And have a sweet roll."

I put one on a plate before her. "This isn't the White House and you're not going to get arrested for breaking protocol."

Hesitantly, she nibbled the roll, then bit into it. With a pang I realized she was hungry.

"I'm having some fruit and I can't eat all of it," I told her. "So do me a favor, eat half an orange or it'll just go to waste."

I spoke sternly. Bella nodded obediently and began peeling the orange I got out, then dividing it into sections. Her hands were shaking, whether from hunger or nerves I couldn't tell.

But suddenly I realized I hadn't been doing *her* any favors, either, letting her walk all over me. Sam had said Bella was so hygienic he thought she must have Clorox running in her veins; as I watched her now, though, it struck me that something more was going on here besides extreme cleanliness.

Something like fear. I'd been so fixed on her hyperactivity, I'd missed it, but now I noticed the darting glances, her anxious breathing, and her hands, so sweaty that they left a puckery spot on her paper napkin.

Along with this new insight though, I got the strong feeling that if I asked her straight out what the trouble was, she might flee. So instead I returned to the subject of her employment.

"You and I never did talk precisely about your duties," I began gently. "And so I think it's possible we might've gotten off on the wrong foot."

"I'm sure I've tried to keep things clean." She bridled as if insulted. "If there's anything I've neglected I'm sure you only need to—"

"No," I interrupted. "It's not that. You're not neglecting anything, Bella. It's the opposite. You're doing too much."

Confused, she frowned down at the crumbs of her sweet roll as if they might spell out an answer. "The girls at the agency told me to do my best, and I have."

Oh, dear. The whole idea of having household help had never come easily to me. In fact if the Gopher Baroque home employment agency hadn't contributed Bella's services as the grand prize at the church raffle, I'd never have hired anyone.

"I know you have," I assured her. "Of course you've done your best, and I appreciate it. But you're overcompensating."

She looked blank. Clearly the psychological approach wasn't going to work either. I tried another tack. "Bella, have you ever heard the phrase 'too much of a good thing'?"

"No," she said flatly. "You eating the rest of that orange?"

I pushed it across the table at her. "Here. And thank you, you've just come up with rule number two. A person can't work on an empty stomach, so the first thing you're going to do when you get here every morning is eat breakfast."

Black coffee, I figured from the way her hands trembled, was probably the only thing she'd swallowed recently.

"I'm the boss, Bella," I added firmly when she made as if to protest. "And from now on the morning meal is a condition of your continued employment."

She looked down again. The orange sections had vanished, but I was perilously close to patronizing her and that would've been a disaster, too.

"It's not what I want to talk to you about, however," I went on, putting a note of steel back into my voice.

It struck me now also that there was a reason why the home-help agency had sent Bella. As opposed, I mean, to someone else. And because at the moment she wasn't driving me crazy, I was able to think it out.

Gopher Baroque had wanted to donate something to the church raffle. Doing so was just good public relations. But unless you were biblically good, you didn't give your most valuable products or services away. You gave what you could afford.

Or even better, what you couldn't use. So the Gopher Baroque housekeeping agency had packaged up the services of somebody they couldn't employ any *other* way, and called it a prize.

Silently, Bella ate the sweet-roll crumbs off her plate one by one. I resisted the urge to make her a sandwich, and went on with my lecture.

"Rule three is that from now on," I told her, "you are not to work so hard. We have several weeks of your assignment still to go, you know, and that's plenty of time to do all the things you think should be done."

Or that I think should be, I added silently. "They needn't be done all at once, though, and I don't want them to be."

Bella nodded, head bowed.

"And just to make sure there isn't any confusion, as of today you are to do only the tasks I ask of you, in the order I ask you to do them. Is that clear, too?"

Another nod, less emphatic than the first.

SAFE HOUSE

A basic safety kit = work gloves,
safety glasses, a dust mask,
muff-style hearing protectors,
and sturdy shoes.

"Mr. Sorenson's workshop is entirely off-limits," I added sternly.

"I uh-understand," Bella said. Her shoulders made convulsive little hitching movements. "Whatever you say, Missus—um, I mean Jake. Because...because..."

Oh, good heavens, she was weeping. "Bella, please don't. I'm so sorry, I didn't mean to offend you or hurt your feelings..."

She looked up, her eyes streaming. "It's not that! I ain't offended. I knew this had to be coming soon. And anyway, if your boss can't yell at you, well then, I don't know who can."

No one, I thought firmly. But that was an argument for some other time.

"Now, Bella, I wasn't yelling at you, I was only—"

"Oh, yes, you were!" Another flood of sobs burst from her. I hurried for a tissue and she grabbed it, pressing it to her face. "And my god, who wouldn't be?" she demanded. "I deserve it!"

A long, honking blow; then: "It's got to be more'n a person can fairly stand, getting cleaned around as if the place was full of plague germs." She drew a shuddery breath. "I swear your husband must've wanted to smack me the other morning when I asked him to pick up his feet so I could sweep while he was reading the newspaper."

Indeed, he certainly must have. I gave a moment of thanks for the Zenlike calm with which Wade approached the world in general, and fuss-budgets like Bella in particular.

"But Bella, if you know this . . ."

"And then there's the dogs," she went on. "I bathed 'em both while you were out one day, and now neither one of 'em 'll come near me, even for a biscuit."

Which solved one mystery, anyway. The day before, I'd taken my own bath, but when I went to let the water out of the tub I found the drain so clogged, I practically needed nitroglycerine to get it running again.

Dog hair, of course. The other mystery was how Bella had gotten Prill into the bathtub at all. But I decided to leave that question alone, too.

"Bella, if you understand how uncomfortable your efforts were making everyone, why did you continue?"

"I told you, I can't help it!" she wailed. Her huge eyes brimmed with despair. "And it's getting worse. The agency sent me to two families before you, and you are the only ones as managed to keep me on for more than a day."

Noticing her distress, the dogs began whining. Bella glanced down at them; Monday was relatively paint-free but still might have a fair amount of moose cud ready for sneezing, while Prill was more white than red.

At the sight Bella gasped, then caught herself. "You ain't told me to clean them dogs up, have you?" she inquired cannily.

"No, Bella, I haven't. And I'm so pleased you thought to ask before taking the job upon yourself."

I got up. "But now that you have asked, why don't we do it together,
and while we work you can tell me how this compulsion for cleaning happened to develop."

"It didn't develop," she replied. "It came upon me. Month ago, all of a
sudden, like. Here, doggy, now I ain't going to hurt you," she added,
crouching near Monday.

The black Lab eyed Bella for signs of scrub brushes or dog shampoo.
Noticing none, she romped up happily and favored Bella with a big wet
doggy kiss.

"Argh!" Bella said, reeling back with distaste. But then she thought better of it.

"Well," she allowed to the animal, "I guess you probably got no worse
bugs than I have, when you get right down to it."

Which I thought was progress. "So one day you were being as tidy as
anyone else and the next day you couldn't stop cleaning?"

She nodded, examining Monday carefully for latent moose cud. "Yup.
Got up at home, stripped the bed, boiled the sheets. Steam-cleaned the carpets. Next I peeled off the wallpaper, and sanded the walls smooth."

"My goodness." The paint on Prill had dried, but it hadn't cured so it
came off with a brush. She stood patiently submitting to the process; for a
breed with such a ferocious reputation, this particular Doberman pinscher
was a milquetoast.

"So then," I guessed, "you eventually decided to earn some money with
your compulsion?"

"Yup. Figured I might's well make use of it. Got hired on by the help
agency. But it didn't turn out like I expected at all."

She peered into one of Monday's ears, found a white glob, and removed
it. "See, you can sell cleanliness," she added ruefully, "but you can't sell
craziness. And at this point I might as well call a spade a spade."

She patted Monday and released her. "Because craziness," she finished bluntly, "is what I've got."

Right. And among other things, that meant one lecture from me wasn't going to turn it off like a faucet. Even if she stayed I would still have to keep her away from Wade, away from Sam's belongings, and especially away from my father.

But a few more weeks of Bella's services, assuming I could prevent her turning back into the white tornado, would allow me to accomplish some other tasks that had been getting short shrift for quite a while around here.

The unpainted shutters, for instance, and the porch steps. That window screen, too. Also every doorknob in the house had come loose somehow over the winter; soon someone would go into a room and not be able to get out again except by bashing the door down.

Then there was the aforementioned yard work. I could've let it go, but in Eastport people tend to jump to colorful conclusions from bits of evidence like unmowed lawns and unweeded gardens.

Such as for instance that you've begun brewing amphetamines down in the cellar where the coal bin was, back in the days when your house had a coal bin. And being a woman with enough baggage to load a freight car—

When I moved here to Eastport I'd brought a troublesome ex-husband, a son with a substance abuse history and a habit of romancing the local girls, and a bankroll that everyone assumed had been assembled by my being a drug dealer—

I didn't need any more colorful conclusions. What I needed was a housekeeper who wasn't a crazy woman, at least for the rest of the day while I decided what to do about her.

So I kept probing. "Was there something particular that set you off?" I asked.

She glanced sideways at me. "Maybe," she replied guardedly. "I always was neat-like. More so when I'm upset."

Well, there was a start. "Did anything happen that day or maybe the day before, that you found especially distressing?"

But with this I'd gone too far. "You ain't going to let up, are you? You're going to keep poking and prying!"

Oh, what the hell. I put the steel back into my voice.

"Yes. Because I'll tell *you* something, Bella, you're on the edge, here. My only choices are to let you go or try to find out what's bothering you. Otherwise you'll never stop being such a...such a pestilence of cleanliness."

She nodded, but the look on her face said her mind was elsewhere. "That's right," she agreed in tones of unhappy preoccupation. "I'm a pestilence even to myself. At home, it's all I can do to dirty up a dish long enough to eat off it."

At her expression a new thought struck me. "You know, don't you? You *know* what the problem is. You just don't know what to do about it."

Whereupon she gave up, reaching into her purse. "Yes," she sighed. "It's this. And more like it."

With a show of reluctance she withdrew a piece of yellow lined notebook paper, thrusting it at me.

"I have," she confessed, "been getting death threats."

When I first came to Maine, I thought old houses were ones whose air-conditioning systems hadn't been built right in along with the sauna, whirlpool bath, and indoor swimming pool. Then I discovered Eastport, where the houses were so old that even the plumbing and heating systems hadn't originally been built in, and in some cases weren't securely established now.

And to make a long story short, one day when I was feeling psychotically optimistic I bought one of these houses, moved into it with my teenage son, Sam, and woke up the next morning having traded a gold mine of a career on Wall Street for a life in which just getting a nail hammered in straight was a major triumph.

In those first days I used to confront a balky window sash with the same miserable sinking sensation that Job must've felt, facing his trials. The only tools I'd ever used were the software programs designed to predict which foreign nation's currency unit might trump which other one's on any given day, so I could earn a penny per unit by trading a gazillion of them.

Patching a leaky two-hundred-year-old roof was a very different story, especially in December in Maine. I couldn't do it via computer; in fact just getting to the leak at all involved going up onto the roof, which at the time was coated with a sheet of ice.

Which is how I learned the two-step Maine method of patching a roof leak in the winter: (1) put a bucket under it and (2) wait until spring.

The next thing I learned was that heating an old Maine house costs the equivalent of the national budget of Peru, this being where I ended up wishing I'd moved that first January while the windows shook with the force of the gale blowing in around them.

You couldn't set milk out on the kitchen table unless you wanted it iced, and after a couple of frightening experiences I started putting a little antifreeze in the toilet tanks. Sam and I began wearing socks to sleep in, and by February we had added hats, mufflers, and gloves; we flipped coins over who would get to have the dog on our bed—at the time we only had one— and a couple of mornings I had to thaw the ice out of my eyelashes before I could open my eyes.

Finally one day when I was trying to write another check to the fuel oil company, to run the furnace which was so inefficient I might as well have been burning bales of hundred-dollar bills, the ink froze in my pen. In response I threw the pen across the room, wrapped myself in all the clothing I owned that I was not already wearing, and staggered down to Wadsworth's Hardware Store on Water Street to ask about buying a woodstove for the kitchen.

I figured that if we had one, Sam and I could just move into the kitchen, which was where we were spending most of our time anyway because (a) the rest of the house was too cold, (b) if you ran the oven constantly you might just keep frost from forming on the surfaces of your clothes, and (c) we cooked a lot because it was taking so many calories to maintain our body heat.

So I did ask. Whereupon the canny fellows at the hardware store sized me up in a glance, realized immediately that if they sold me a woodstove I would burn the house down with it, and decided to take pity on me.

"Here," one of them told me gently, "is what you need."

It was an absolutely gigantic roll of plastic sheeting, as thick as canvas, grayish colored, and so ugly you had to narrow your eyes just to look straight at it, and at first I thought the fellow meant I was supposed to wrap myself in it.

By that point it was an idea I'd have gone along with, I was so cold. But I didn't think I could get Sam to cooperate; for one thing, he had to go to school. And the task of sealing the dog up for the winter was beyond my capacity.

So I waited, hoping for further enlightenment. On the store shelves were many other products for winter insulation, but I had no idea how to use any of them, either.

While I stood there, a snowplow went by outside the big plate glass window. I could only see the operator's head over the drift he had piled up. Customers came in, stomped the snow off their boots, uttered a few syllables in a Maine accent so broad I could barely understand it, and were sent via equally few syllables to the proper aisle of the store.

The snowplow went by again. This time I could only see the top of the operator's bright orange hat. But at last one of the hardware store fellows returned.

"Havin' a bit o' trouble decidin', are we?" he asked me with a smile. His name tag read "Tim" and he pronounced the end of his question the Maine way: *ah we?*

"Yes," I replied gratefully. I gestured at plastic sheeting that came in so many sizes besides the roll, the packets of items confusingly labeled furring strips although I didn't see any fur, and tubes full of what appeared to be electrical cord, but why would you want ninety miles of it, and why was it so thin?

"I don't know what any of this stuff is, or what to do with the plastic," I admitted.

"You cover your windows with it," he replied. "It stops drafts. Or anyway, it slows 'em down some."

"Oh," I said, my heart sinking as I took in the truth:

I would be cutting big pieces from the rolled material, a challenge in itself. Also the tops of my windows were eight feet off the floor, so mounting the pieces would have to be done while standing on stilts. But if I didn't find some way to do it they'd be thawing me out with a hair dryer soon.

Tim hadn't been ignoring me, just giving me some space; for a newcomer to Maine it was sometimes a bit difficult to tell the difference.

"Look," he said finally. "How about I come over after work and show you how to do one of these? It's kind of a pain but it's not impossible once you get the hang of it."

Back in Manhattan any stranger who showed up at your door with a roll of plastic wanted to wrap your dead body in it. Later he would put you in the same landfill where he'd stashed the victims he'd murdered before you.

But if anyone in Eastport wanted to kill me, all they had to do was not help me now. I began telling Tim where I lived.

"I know," he said as he rang up the plastic and the ninety-mile heat cord, which turned out to be for wrapping around water pipes. Mine, I gathered, had not yet frozen solid only because I was new here, and was experiencing a sort of beginner's luck.

It wasn't, Tim suggested darkly, the kind of luck I could expect to last for long.

"You're the lady who bought the big old white house on Key Street," he went on. "From New York. Got a boy? Dog, too. Seems I heard you were in some sort of money business, back in the city."

I must have stared. In response his eyes twinkled. "Not a lot going on around here in the winter," he observed. "So we tend to get all the good out of any amusement that arrives."

The amusement being me. Humbly I took my change, and later Tim delivered my purchases and plowed my driveway. I stood by the window watching his Jeep's headlights move to and fro, feeling for the first time as if I were not completely alone here.

When he came in he accepted coffee and ten dollars; I got the idea that by offering the money I'd passed a small test. The plow blade was attached to the Jeep to generate cash, and knowing this without having to be told drew a nod of approval from him.

"I brought along a few other things I thought you needed," he told me, spreading them out on the kitchen table: a clawhammer, a pair of pliers, two screwdrivers—one Phillips head, one flat—a small pipe wrench, and a roll of silicone tape.

"With these, you're set for any emergency you can handle. Anything more, you'll need an electrician or a plumber. Later," he added, eyeing me closely, "I have an idea that might change."

And while I filled the hall shelves with the new tools this kindhearted semistranger had collected for me, he finally revealed the most important thing about putting plastic on your windows.

Which is *don't cut it first*. This will be your impulse, to cut a piece of plastic that seems to be of a size you can handle instead of having to maneuver the whole heavy awkward roll while simultaneously keeping your balance on a stepladder.

But put the plastic up first, pressing it to the sticky surface of the double-sided tape you have already affixed to the window trim and letting the roll fall to the floor. Spread the sheeting out at the top of the window, then at the sides, and finally at the bottom, smoothing it as you go.

Only when the plastic is fastened all the way around should you cut it, using a straight edge butted against the window trim for a guide. And presto, one whole window is covered with draft-busting plastic so hideous that the decorating police will come to your house and arrest you if they ever get word of it.

"Thank you," I told Tim sincerely when he was done with his demonstration, still not understanding quite why he had come over at all. Though he'd taken the plow money, he'd refused to be paid for his window-covering instruction.

" 'S all right," he replied. His hat had big furry ear flaps, accessories I had so far resisted. But as he pulled them over his ears I realized my notion of fashion was going to take a beating over the winter, too.

"Stuff some thick insulating material into all the fireplace and stovepipe openings," he instructed me as he departed. "In this old house, half your heat is probably goin' up them flues."

There was a wedding ring on his finger or I might've thrown him to the floor and ravished him right then and there.

"Stop up all the electrical outlets you're not using, the keyholes, mail slot and so on. I can't sell you a woodstove until you get somebody in to inspect your chimneys," he concluded kindly.

Later I learned that he belonged to the volunteer fire department, so I suppose there was self-interest in the woodstove advice Tim offered. And it didn't hurt that he'd sold me a lot of hardware products, the first but far from the last I would buy; soon whenever he saw me coming he would slide the cash drawer open and closed a few times just to make sure it was working smoothly.

But fire prevention wasn't the main reason for his visit, or planned profit, either. And although I didn't get it then, eventually I began to comprehend why he'd helped me on that frigid winter night.

He'd done it because he could. Because what goes around comes around. And in Eastport it can come with the devastating accuracy of a heat-seeking missile.

We grease the wheels of human kindness when we can, here; otherwise they might seize up on us some time when we can least afford it.

All of which brings me back to the unhappy woman sitting at my kitchen table that bright June morning a couple of days before we found Jim Diamond on the brink of death.

I wasn't sure helping Bella would turn the avenging angel of household hygiene back into an ordinary cleaning woman.

Also she was in possession of something I've always found to be a serious pain: that is, a series of apparent death threats.

None of which made me want to keep her in my employ, and I still wasn't sure I would. But something told me clearly that if I abandoned her now without even trying to find out a little more about her problem, the heat-seeking missile of "What goes around, comes around" might wind up targeting me.

Which in the end it turned out to anyway, and so did the frighteningly intelligent attentions of a bloody murderer.

Chapter 4

D eath threats," I repeated unhappily to Bella, peering at the note. "There are *more* like this?"

She nodded. "Started a month or so ago. I find 'em in my house, which is scary enough, 'cause how do they get in there? I keep it locked when I'm out. My daughter Kris lives there, too, but I don't think she wants to kill me."

Tears welled in her big eyes. "Besides, if she did want to I don't see why she'd bother to say so first. And why waste energy on notes? That'd be her attitude."

"She sounds charming," I said.

Bella glanced wryly at me. "Kris's got a temper just as much as her dad had. But she's all right."

"Are you bothering anyone? Quarreling with a neighbor, your dog barking, are you trying to get money from someone? That is," I added at her insulted look, "money someone owes you?"

She shook her head. "I don't like fighting, I've got no dog, and nobody owes me money. I just go along trying to live."

"And you do think the notes are serious?" I asked.

She frowned in reply, pointing at the yellow notepaper.

"Lookit the way the letters are pressed in, like someone was grittin' their teeth," she said. "And the hateful words."

I looked the note over again. "You know, I have to agree."

It was written in blue ballpoint, the letters gouged into the cheap paper. Interestingly, it included no misspellings and featured big words, including a favorite of mine: *exsanguinate*.

Right away I wondered why the term had been chosen instead of the simpler *bleed to death*. Was it to intimidate Bella with the sender's intelligence? Or did the sender use large words as a habit, not realizing how they would stand out?

"It does look unpleasant," I agreed, trying to think of all the big-word specialists I knew around here. But the only one I could come up with was my ex-husband Victor, and he wouldn't be threatening Bella. Victor is such a snob, he barely believes in the existence of people like Bella.

That is, unless they happen to be his patients, in which case he monitors them every waking minute and even talks about them in his sleep. He is, as I may have indicated elsewhere, a complicated guy.

"Have you told the police?" I asked Bella.

She nodded. "The chief came to my house." Eastport's Chief of Police Bob Arnold, she meant. "He set officers to watch, and the notes stopped. But when they quit watching, the threats just started right up again."

I came to a decision. "Bella, I'd like to talk to Bob Arnold myself about this. May I keep this note a while?"

"All right," she agreed reluctantly. "But please don't tell anyone else. It's already getting around town that I'm losing my marbles. And..." Her voice thickened with tears. "And they can't think that. I have to work. Somehow I have to have a job, and if people start thinking I'm off my rocker..."

"I'll keep it as confidential as I can," I promised. "But right now you *have* a job, and there's plenty to do. The kitchen floor, for instance."

She brightened instantly. "It's bad," she opined. "Very bad."

It was worse than that. But before I could give her specific instructions on how she might even begin repairing the damage—for once I thought her cleanliness mania might have met its match—someone knocked on the back door.

It turned out to be a pleasant-looking lady in her late sixties, wearing a light straw hat, a flowered dress, and white low-heeled shoes. Her short steel-gray hair curved neatly from beneath the hat in a becoming pageboy style.

"Yes?" I asked a little puzzledly through the screen door.

"The local Red Cross is having a blood drive," she informed me with a smile. "This is to tell you when and where it will be held, and to encourage you to give blood."

Thanking her, I took the pamphlet and donor card she offered and she went away.

"Hmph," Bella said when I came back into the kitchen. "Guess they don't bother canvassing the poor side of town. But I ain't so hard up I can't spare a pint of blood for a sick person. You never know, I might need one someday myself."

And there it was again, the "Do unto others" ethic, as if the universe thought I needed more reminding. I hurried out to try catching the lady to get another set of donor literature. But when I reached the sidewalk and looked both ways, she had vanished.

Supervising Bella, repairing that window screen, watching for the moose, and figuring out and fixing something to eat for dinner took up the rest of my day. But the following morning I set out to investigate Bella's problem a little further.

The Eastport Police Department was located in the old bank building on Water Street, one door down from the public library and one door up from La Sardina, our only Mexican bar and restaurant. Bob Arnold joked that it was the perfect spot for a cop shop; guys could get ideas for new crimes in the library, then soak up the courage to carry them out right nearby in the bar.

Not that Eastport's few active lowlifes spent much time in the library. And anyway Bob usually grabbed them and took their car keys right after last call, when they'd drunk enough to get reckless but before they could get into serious trouble. Because Bob knew his regulars and the felonious schemes they tended to come up with, and his First Commandment of law enforcement was Thou Shalt Prevent It.

"Pleasant day," Bob commented now, standing on the steps of the bank building with his thumbs hooked in his utility belt.

I climbed the concrete steps to stand with him, beside the old bank vault alarm still installed in the building's brickwork. His squad car was angle-parked a few feet away, radio sputtering intermittently. Between its eruptions of static I reported on my conversation with Bella.

Bob's round pink face creased in a grin. "Ayuh. Heard about you winnin' her at the church fair. Ladies at the sewing circle are takin' bets, I understand, on how long she'll last."

Working for me, he meant. "She's a strange one, that Bella," he added.

Which was one of the lines of speculation I wanted a stop put to. If I ended up needing to fire Bella, I at least wanted her to be able to go to work for someone else.

"If her behavior's unusual, it's only because someone's been threatening her life," I retorted. Bob wasn't taking the threat notes very seriously, it seemed to me.

I pulled out the one Bella had given me, but Bob had already begun shaking his head.

"Jake, first of all, these aren't threats. They're more like lists, wouldn't

you say? Even so," he went on, "I set two men on her house at night, sat
'em there whenever they weren't out on a call, kept 'em there two whole
weeks."

He made a face that communicated perfectly how useless this had been.
"And I *told* 'em, keep their traps shut."

So word didn't spread that Bella's house was being watched, he meant;
so the supposed perpetrator wouldn't get tipped to it and take a break from
his activities.

Which apparently he had anyway. According to Bella, the notes had
stopped while the officers were there.

"Nothing at all?" I asked. "No prowlers, no..."

"If a worm turned in the earth around that house, my guys had orders
to tell me about it. But it didn't."

Down in the boat basin, the schooner *Sylvina Beal* nosed away from the
breakwater, making her way between the dock and the mooring dolphin at
the entrance to the basin. Her vast scarlet sails filled, billowing like the
lungs of some great animal inhaling.

And then she *soared,* her long prow arrowing into the waves. Moments
later she broke free of the current, headed east toward the open water.

"Nice sight," Bob remarked. Wade said that if Bob ever saw an angel descending from heaven on a pearl-pink cloud, he would remark, "Nice
sight."

"She try her sob story on you, then, I guess?" he inquired, "when she
finished getting a rise out of me?"

"Yes," I admitted, wondering if after all I'd sized Bella up incorrectly.
"But Bob, she really does seem—"

"Yeah, yeah," he interrupted. "She's real convincing. She had those
deputies crying in their coffee, her story was so sad."

He turned to me. "But Jake, there's nothing to it. She has no enemies.
She has no money that anyone could be trying to get out of her. And as for
that house she lives in, the only ones'd be trying to get her out of that are
the mice an' squirrels. Oh, it's clean, all right," he added. "Spic an' span."

He'd heard, then, about the particular form Bella's distress was taking.

"But in every other way it's hardly fit to live in," he went on, "because it needs so much structural work. No view, either," he added before I could ask, "that anyone'd even want to get hold of just as a teardown, build something new."

It was a practice that had been going around like a virus here in the past few years, buying an old house with a great view of the water, then tearing it down and building a modern trophy-palace in its place.

"So you don't think the notes are serious?" I persisted.

He took his thumbs from the utility belt that supported his sidearm, radio, handcuffs, baton, and pepper spray. Except for the radio, the only time he ever handled the items was to put them on and put them away after his shift. But he always carried them; Wade said that when Bob was a kid he'd had a collection of four-leaf clovers and rabbits' feet.

"She's been gettin' em for weeks, and nothing's happened," he answered my question. "If they are threats. Like I said before, I still got my doubts about that."

I unfolded the one she'd given me and studied it again. "I see your point. They're not exactly messages, are they?"

"Somebody writes a threat, usually they say dear so-and-so, I'm gonna knock your block off," Bob agreed a little impatiently.

Bob liked straightforward crimes, which were mostly what he got around here. Break-and-enter, DUI, disorderly conduct; these, along with the occasional domestic dispute or downtown vandalism, are Eastport's idea of serious offenses.

" 'Mutilate, eviscerate, exsanguinate, decapitate,' " I read. " 'Amputate, mangle, chop.' "

I liked the plain finality of *chop*.

"Yeah," Bob said sarcastically, hearing it, too. "Somebody's a poet. Real what-you-call-it, a wordsmith."

But I sure wouldn't've liked it if I'd gotten the note, even if it was only a list of words with the threat merely implied.

By now the *Sylvina Beal*'s sails had diminished until the vessel was just a crimson dot on the dark blue water, beyond it the hills of New Brunswick rising in distant, hazy green mounds.

"Fourth of July in ten days," Bob said a little sadly. By this he meant what we all knew, that after the holiday the brief, intense Maine summer would seem to last only a heartbeat longer.

"Enjoy it while we can," he added, waving down the street toward the dock. There whole families gathered to cast lines into the water, hooking three or four mackerel at a time on their big mackerel jigs, parents helping kids drop their catch into buckets of water or throwing the fish back.

"Tell her we haven't dropped her, though," he told me. "Drive-by a couple times a shift; she calls, somebody'll be there."

But it was clear he didn't believe Bella was in any danger. Instead, his thoughts were already occupied by the thousands of people who would arrive in Eastport for the Fourth. He ran crowd control for the parade, helped with security for the port and for visiting dignitaries, and would be handling any problems created by this year's addition of a beer tent to the food kiosks.

Beer and crowds being, in his opinion, the two main obstacles to a small-town police chief's ability to sleep at night. But the event organizers had been insistent.

"She does have an ex-husband," Bob added as I started down the steps.

I turned back. "Bella? She does? Why didn't she mention him, I wonder?"

"Dunno. He's got a record, too."

Down on the dock a big black muscle car arrived rumblingly, looking disconcertingly like a crow among harmless sparrows. The invasion of out-of-towners had apparently already begun.

"No violent crimes against persons, though." Bob unhitched the radio and spoke into it. Near the dock a squad car extracted itself from a parking spot and began making its way casually out toward the fishing families.

"Bella's okay, Jake. Kind of person, you feel pretty sorry for her. Just never got the kind of helping hand a woman'd need, or a man either. So she's stayed sort of hardscrabble."

I listened as Bob went on, still watching the squad car.

"But she's got guts," he added. "Always managed to put food on her table one way or another. Worked at the fish hatchery when there was work there, tied Christmas wreaths in the fall. For a while she had a job at the plastics factory till that went bust."

It was a common story hereabouts, people piecing their lives together a step ahead of the bill collector. Sometimes a stroke of good luck or a kind deed made all the difference.

For Bella, it seemed neither of those things had happened. "You talk to him?" I asked Bob. "Her ex?"

"Ayuh. Took a ride, see him. He is not," Bob said, "what you might call an intellectual. Gave me the usual big mouthful of how it must've been some other guy."

The squad car pulled alongside the black muscle car, paused, then headed back toward the hot-dog stand at the entrance to the pier. Moments later the muscle car's driver seemed to decide that he had urgent business elsewhere, and departed the scene.

"But I checked on him," Bob said, "pretty well ruled him out. Big guy, never known him to be in a good mood. He doesn't even live here in Eastport anymore. Not since he got out of jail. Got himself a place down in Lubec."

Which is the next town along the coast to our south, at the mouth of the bay. It takes just ten minutes to get there by boat but nearly an hour by car.

"So he'd have to go to a lot of trouble to bother Bella. I mean, unless he's got a vessel," I said.

"Or if he hired one." Bob tucked his radio back on his belt, satisfied the squad car had prevented the muscle car's next likely tricks: a howl of engine, the shriek of spinning tires, and the smell of burning rubber as people scattered, the car accelerating between the peaceful fishing groups just to show that it could.

Because when it came to harassing ordinary citizens, Bob's Second Commandment was Thou Shalt Not Even Dream of It.

"Name's Jim," Bob said. "And from what I know of him he couldn't spell any of those words in the note. I also doubt he knows what many of 'em mean. He's not a verbal type of guy, either."

"Uh-huh." The muscle car came up the street toward us. Bob made a point of eyeballing it as it went by.

"So," he finished, "my sense is he's no poison pen artist. I think she'd have liked it, I found a way to lock him up again. But I didn't."

"Okay, then, thanks," I said, heading back down the concrete steps. But when I reached the sidewalk, Bob spoke once more.

"Jake. You found out who Sam's new girlfriend is, yet?"

A needle of worry jabbed my heart. My son Sam had been keeping the details of his romantic interest very close to the vest lately. "No, why?"

Bob shrugged, looking out over the water. The big fishing boat, *Quoddy Dam,* was loading up a party of tourists for a ride out to where the porpoises cavorted.

Thinking of Sam, I wished I were out there with them. The porpoises, I mean, diving down into the green, cold silence.

At last Bob replied. "You know how it is, in summer the kids have outdoor parties at night. Up in the woods behind the high school, or on the beach at Deep Cove if it's low tide."

He looked down the steps at me. "The next morning you find a cold bonfire and a lot of beer cans, and lately I've been hearing that a bunch of the kids are underage."

"I know," I said cautiously. "About the parties, I mean. It happens every year. But what's that got to do with Sam?"

Though I already feared I knew. Back in the bad old days, my son had supplemented an enormous drug habit with an equally sizable liquor intake. But when we moved here to Eastport he'd sworn off everything, suddenly and with little apparent difficulty.

That is, until the Christmas school break last winter when he drove home in a blizzard, coming in late when Wade and I were already asleep. The next morning Sam wasn't even out of bed yet when Bob arrived wanting to know why Sam's car was in a ditch over on Prince Street, half buried by a passing snowplow.

And Sam, horrifyingly, didn't remember.

After that it was AA meetings every day; counseling, too, for a while. Sam worked hard, I'll give him that much. But something had changed, and six months later he was still angry and oddly secretive.

Bob must have seen the fear in my face. "What do you want me to do, Jake?" he asked gently.

If he found Sam drinking at one of those parties, he meant. Because Bob wasn't only Eastport's police chief; he was also a family friend.

"Do you know something for sure?" I asked him. "Or who she is, even? The new girl?"

Bob shook his head. "Whoever she is, there's rumors the two of 'em have been at those parties. But I'd tell you if I had any actual facts."

A rush of relief went through me. Rumors weren't necessarily worth the paper Bella's threatening note had been written on.

"Okay," I said. "But if anything does come up for sure I'd appreciate it if you could tell me before you do anything about it."

"Yeah." He nodded, this being what he'd hoped to hear; that if there was bad news I wanted to know, that I wasn't just going to stick my head in the sand.

Or go down with the porpoises. Buried or drowned; the way it was between me and Sam lately I could choose from a whole range of colorful metaphors, each ending up with me not being able to breathe.

But this wasn't a problem I could solve by my usual method of crashing into it headfirst. So I left Bob surveying the town from his vantage point in front of the police station, put Sam back into the mental folder headed "Still Worried," and began wondering what else to do about something that maybe I *could* fix.

If I went home while Bella was still in a cleaning fit I was afraid she might pounce on me and scour the enamel off my teeth; her frenzy had diminished somewhat, but it had certainly not abated. And now that I had some dope on Jim Diamond, I figured I might as well match it with any I could get on Bella herself.

On Water Street, town workers were stringing red-white-and-blue banners from light poles while shopkeepers hung flags over freshly green-painted sidewalk benches and half-barrel planters of geraniums. Boys on skateboards whizzed around the big statue of the fisherman overlooking the tugboat mooring, amidst gulls swooping to squabble over fallen ice creams dropped by youngsters racing in and out of the soda fountain.

At the Eastport Art Center I paused to gaze at new offerings in the front window, oil paintings whose skewed perspectives and madcap hues captured the carnival feeling of Eastport in summer. But as if to say nothing was ever really that simple, the oils were flanked by large pottery masks whose smooth closed eyelids and enigmatic smiles implied they knew something I didn't.

As I stood there a voice came from behind me. "Hi, Jacobia."

It was Dinah Sanborne, dressed in black pedal-pushers, a big white linen shirt, and heeled sandals. She looked like a million bucks, and like exactly the piece of luck I'd been hoping for.

"Hi, Dinah. You're just the person I wanted to talk to."

In her mid-twenties, Dinah was part of the new, young crowd that had discovered Eastport over the past few years. Ambition, creativity, and more energy than a nuclear power plant were the characteristics the newcomers seemed to have in common.

"I wanted to ask you a little about Bella," I went on.

Dinah was the cofounder, with her partner Azenath Jones, of the home-help agency they'd called Gopher Baroque.

"Really?" she said, not sounding happy about the prospect. It was Gopher Baroque that had sent me Bella, as my prize from the church raffle.

"Come on," I said. "Walk with me a little."

Dinah's short, spiky dark hair had the New York look the bright young crowd here strove for: not too clean, not too dirty, not too deliberate. Effortless cool, as if you'd fallen out of bed quoting lines from Kerouac.

"Is there a problem?" she asked.

I stifled impatience. *Of course there's a problem,* I wanted to reply. *You sent me a head case for a housekeeper. Why wouldn't there be a problem, you dimwit?*

But Dinah wasn't a dimwit. Quite the opposite; she and Azenath were ferociously smart. They'd both seen that although in the winter Eastport had little market for housekeepers, in summer it did. Folks came to the island, many of them wealthy or what passed for it here, bringing parents, children, pets, and various hangers-on. Also, they entertained.

Which, I guessed, was why Gopher Baroque had sent Bella to me—not maliciously or carelessly, but as a last resort. They didn't want to fire her, knowing she needed the job and that they'd look like villains if they got rid of her, but on the flip side they also wouldn't inflict her on their more lucrative clients.

So I bit my tongue long enough to think of a mild reply, then delivered it. "She is," I told Dinah, "somewhat unusual."

Dinah absorbed this. A raffle prize that blew up like a stink bomb wouldn't be good Gopher Baroque publicity, either.

"That's partly why I want some background on her," I added.

She considered briefly. With her studiedly careless clothes and minimalist hairstyle, she looked as if she ought to be doing performance art in a chicly underfurnished but vastly overpriced warehouse space in the SoHo district of Manhattan.

There were lots of her there and only one of her here, however, another reason she and Azenath had chosen Eastport as their base of operations. Here the pair stood out. Especially Azenath, but that was another story.

"Let's get coffee," Dinah said finally.

But as we turned toward the Blue Moon coffee shop just down the street, a yellow convertible swung past the big granite post office building on the corner and pulled to the curb beside me.

A man leaned over the passenger seat, automatically giving Dinah the

once-over before looking at me. He had curly dark hair, green eyes, a determined jaw, and a master-of-the-universe manner that most women
found extremely attractive.

At first. His fingers tapped the steering wheel impatiently. "Jake," he announced in bossy tones, "we need to talk about Sam."

It was my ex-husband Victor, and what had just happened was a pretty
good summary of our history together. If another woman was present and
she had the equipment he looked for in a possible conquest—that is, if she
was younger and had a measurable blood pressure—Victor always gave her
the eye first.

Also, as far as I was concerned we'd needed to talk for about six months
now and we hadn't. I doubted there was any big urgency about it right this
minute.

"Right," I said. "Lunch at my house in an hour."

Victor didn't take well to my not dropping what I was doing to get in the
car. Instead he shot a look of strained patience at me and what he must
have thought was a seductive one at Dinah. She deflected it as coolly as if
she were made of porcelain.

" 'Bye, Victor," I told him sweetly, just as if I were not enjoying the hell
out of the sight of him and his yellow sports car getting blown off.

Then to the musical sound of twin carburetors rumbling away
grumpily, Dinah and I went into the coffee shop.

The Blue Moon was a haven of city sophistication plunked into an old
redbrick storefront on the edge of Passamaquoddy Bay. Going in, I always
felt I should be wearing a black leotard, carrying a book of poetry I'd written myself, and within shouting distance of my nineteenth birthday.

None of which I would ever be again, but never mind; the Blue Moon
was still a lot of fun. Inside, cool jazz floated from the speakers mounted
between old Village Vanguard posters on the exposed brick walls. Copies
of the *Times,* the *New York Observer,* and *Publishers Weekly* littered the tables,

many occupied at this hour by twenty- and thirty-somethings who looked as if they belonged in the East Village or San Francisco.

Dinah and I made our way past the counter stacked with thick white pottery mugs and baskets heaped with fresh pastry, then down the aisle between the red leatherette booths to the back of the room.

"Here okay?" she asked at a vacant window table, and I nodded assent. The air was a heady brew of warm aromas: chocolate, fresh-ground coffee beans, and smoke from imported cigarettes. Exotic liqueur bottles lined a mirrored shelf, but no one was drinking. The Blue Moon's owner had a liquor license only so people could smoke—at the time the state hadn't yet enacted a comprehensive no-smoking law—and the espresso machine hissed from five in the morning till after midnight.

"So," Dinah said when we'd settled and given our orders: a Fatal Chocolate Brownie and double mocha espresso for me—I doubted I'd get much eating done during lunch with Victor—and a French mineral water for Dinah.

She pulled a little gold case from her tiny black shoulder bag, and lit a Sobranie. "Oh, I'm sorry, do you mind?" she asked, after a drag on it.

I shook my head, mentally parsing the strategy of cigarettes but no chocolate, and coming up with *skinny*.

But I'd already ordered the brownie, and being me if I ever started smoking I'd be at three packs a day in no time. Mentally I scheduled a ten-mile walk to make up for half of the calories I was about to ingest, and returned to business.

"Bella," I said. "The housekeeper you sent. Due to my having won her like a heifer at a Four-H fair, I mean."

Dinah pursed her lips. There was a tiny white scar above her right nostril, just in the crevice; she'd been pierced, once.

"She's not working out?" she asked innocently.

I ate some brownie, sipped espresso. Together they went to my brain and detonated like an accident at the fireworks factory.

"Oh, of course she's not working out, for heaven's sake. Two other people already fired her on account of they think she's a whack job, she told me. So what did you think was going to happen this time—the miracle at Lourdes?"

Dinah's slender shoulders moved minutely, accepting this. "I'm so sorry, Jake. To tell you the truth, because it was you we hoped it would work out. Of course we knew there were risks to the idea, and we talked about whether or not we should try it."

I wasn't appeased. "You mean you both thought I might not notice a little more craziness, or that I might just not care?"

She hesitated, taking a tiny sip of mineral water. Then, "We sent Bella to you as her last chance," she confirmed.

Oh, great. "We'd heard you and Ellie White were quite good at sorting things out," she added. "Problems, that is."

"I see," I said evenly, when what I was really thinking was *ker-blooey!* Because a picture of Bella's predicament was coming clearer to me now, and it wasn't pretty.

According to Bob Arnold, Bella's peculiarities were well known. And Dinah's agency wasn't going to use her anymore, either, if she failed with me.

"So you thought Ellie and I might find out why she's off the rails, maybe even come up with a way to do something about it?"

Dinah nodded. "You two have done things like that before, in worse situations. And she's such a nice woman. We hated the idea of having to let her go." She put out the cigarette. "On the other hand, we can't keep sending her out the way she is, and if we fire her it's pretty certain no one else will..."

Yep, that swishing sound I'd been hearing was Bella's whole ability to support herself, circling the drain.

That is, unless I put a plug in it fast. On the sound system Sarah Vaughan started singing about a small hotel and how she wished she were there.

Right then I wished I were anywhere. Else, that is. And not together with anyone or anything, except maybe a double martini.

Instead I ate the last of my brownie. It tasted like dust, because it was one thing to think about having Bella around for one more day while I decided what to do about her. But it was quite another to commit to having her actually working in my own house for another—egad—three more whole weeks.

In three weeks, Bella would no doubt scrub the plaster off my walls. "But if it *didn't* work out, you'd send me someone else, right?"

For the first time, Dinah looked truly uncomfortable.

"Dinah?" I prompted her.

"Well." She swirled the ice in her glass, not looking at me. "The truth is, Jake, we don't have anyone else to send. We're booked up for the season."

"How nice for you," I said evenly, when what I was thinking was *oh, drat.*

"Yes," she responded, brightening. "At first we worried we might not have enough customers. But with all the summer visitors to Eastport this year..."

She glanced around. At nearly noon half the occupants of the tables were "people from away." Some wore khakis and rugby shirts and dock shoes from L.L. Bean. Others, like Dinah, looked as if they'd been transported here from somewhere intensely urban, with untanned or ethnic faces.

As a summer destination it seemed that while I wasn't paying attention, Eastport had arrived. "I see," I told Dinah unhappily. "So the bottom line is, if I fire Bella, you do, too. Even though there's so much demand?"

She nodded, reluctantly but firmly. "Azenath and I talked about it a lot. We think sending her out on another job would be just shooting ourselves in the foot. Word might get around that you can't depend on our people, that they might..."

"Alienate your spouse, infuriate your children, destroy your belongings, and drive you bonkers," I finished for her.

To give her credit, she did look sorry. But Dinah's spine was apparently made of space-age materials, designed not to bend.

Lunchtime arrived, as an avocado, tomato, and swiss cheese sandwich on nine-grain bread with alfalfa sprouts went by on a thick white plate.

Dinah blinked at the sandwich, fished the lime slice from her mineral water glass, and bit into it.

"We aren't sending Bella out again," she declared in tones of unmistakable finality, rising, "unless we feel she's got her head back on straight."

A vivid mental image of Bella's head spinning popped into my own, which wasn't exactly feeling so solidly anchored at the moment, either.

"It's your choice, of course, Jake, if you want to let her go. And we'll send you the prize in cash. Azenath and I decided that—"

"—together," I finished for her. When one of them spoke, the other one's hand probably moved as if it were manipulating a sock puppet, I thought only a little bitterly. "Okay, I understand."

Then I got up, too, because pretty soon my ex-husband would be at my house expecting something like one of those sandwiches. It didn't matter how spur-of-the-moment the invitation was; when Victor came for a meal he wanted something you could put a linen napkin alongside, plus the napkin itself.

"Dinah, one more question," I said as we got to the street. "Do you and Azenath know *why* Bella is behaving so erratically?"

She shook her head. "She *said* she was getting death threats. But we just don't believe it. And don't spread that around, all right?" she added anxiously.

That Gopher Baroque workers were in the habit of getting death threats, she meant. Bad PR, again, because if you hired one of them you most certainly didn't want the threats coming to *your* house.

"Anyway, we think there's something else going on with her. Azenath and I do, I mean," Dinah finished unnecessarily.

Just then down the street a large, colorfully dressed woman with long, dark hair stepped out of Wadsworth's Hardware Store, her arms wrapped around a lot of packages. The copper bracelets on her wrists glinted in the sun. It was Azenath Jones, whose smile as she glimpsed her friend Dinah could have lit up an airport.

I was about to tell Dinah that I'd seen one of the notes for myself, that it wasn't just Bella trying to provide herself with an excuse for her obsessive behavior, but Dinah cut me off.

"Otherwise all I know about her is, she's lived here all her life, she has a daughter I know absolutely nothing about, and she's so broke she just about got on her knees and begged for another chance to work for us," Dinah said. "So we sent her to you."

As she spoke, another familiar figure caught my eye. It was the lady who'd been at my house the day before, canvassing for the blood drive, her straw hat gleaming yellow in the sunshine.

Crossing Water Street just then, too, was our local bank manager Bill Imrie, young and blond and nattily dressed as usual in a white shirt, blue suit, and a red-striped tie.

His step was jaunty, but at the sight of the blood-drive lady he changed course abruptly and got back into his car, started it, and drove hurriedly away.

"Anyway," Dinah finished, "who could possibly want to kill Bella?"

That was starting to be my question also, and as I watched Bill zoom off it seemed my sanity might depend on my ability to answer it correctly.

Still, I'll admit I didn't yet understand the kind of trouble I was getting into.

It didn't even occur to me, for instance, that the penalty for a *wrong* answer could turn out to be my life.

Chapter 5

Back when we were married, my then-husband Victor Tiptree used to cheat on me with everything but the mannequins posed in department-store windows, and at the end there I was beginning to be suspicious of a couple of those. No blood pressure, of course, but they had the other attributes he liked in a woman: long legs, not a lot of opinions.

Lately, though, we'd come to a sort of accommodation. He didn't cheat on me, a situation I had arranged by divorcing him, and I didn't throttle him, an activity I avoided by keeping my hands a safe distance from his throat.

"There aren't any moose on Moose Island," he announced through a mouthful of deviled ham and hot baked beans on toast triangles.

We were sitting outside at the picnic table under the apple tree in my yard, because Bella was still inside and if he ate in there she might grab the fork out of his hand and wash it.

Up in the tree a nest full of baby robins cheeped vigorously. "How's your lunch?" I asked Victor.

With it he was having a tall glass of Moxie: an herb-based soft drink, popular in Maine, that resembles a cola in much the same way as, say, the H-bomb is like a firecracker.

"Fine." He forked up another mouthful. It was all I'd been able to put together on such short notice, and Victor maintained that this sort of food could destroy a discriminating palate in twenty minutes.

But he devoured it whenever he got the chance, mostly at my house. "Bella," I called through the kitchen window. With the newly repaired screen on it, she could hear me clearly. "Stop scrubbing."

She stopped instantly but her hands remained poised, her fingers clutching the scrub brush in a death grip. And to judge by what I'd seen of that previously cud-slimed kitchen, Victor was right: not only were there no moose on Moose Island, there were none anywhere in the world.

The place was so clean, he could have done surgery in it. No paint smears, either. I sent a prayer up to heaven that I would be allowed to keep Bella a while longer. If this went on, someday I might be able to come downstairs in the morning without getting hit by a wrecking ball of housework-based guilt.

"Bella," I called to her again, "will you please go home and get the rest of those notes? I want to look at all of them."

Ellie glanced up from the glider chair by the grape arbor where she was giving Lee a bottle of the stuff the pediatricians in Portland had prescribed. The feeding portion of the mommy program hadn't worked out at all the way that Ellie had hoped, but after a scary struggle when the baby was first born they'd finally found a formula she could thrive on.

Bella put the scrub brush down, looking as if she wanted to say something but didn't dare to.

Something like *oh thank you thank you thank you.*

Moments later she scuttled out to the garden and approached me cravenly, an attitude I didn't like at all; I thought if she tried kissing my hands I might have to get that scrub brush and smack her with it.

But she didn't. "All right," she said, a shy little quaver of hope coming into her voice. "I'll get the notes right now."

Whereupon I abandoned my plan of smacking her. No one had helped Bella in a long time, as far as I'd been able to learn. Wasn't it only natural that she might have trouble getting used to it?

"Bring them all," I repeated. "Try to put them in the order you received them. And come right back. We're going out later."

Aren't we? I added silently to Ellie, whose smile over the baby's head was all the answer I needed. During the day when the men were working on her house, she often brought the baby here.

But what the infant possessed in eating troubles she more than made up for with her sleeping abilities. So there were long hours in which Ellie—because I wouldn't let her do my household chores—felt underutilized.

Besides, like me, she was a snoop at heart.

Victor scraped the last baked bean from his plate and washed it down with a final swig of Moxie. "Do you," he asked hopefully, "happen to have any of that orange Bundt cake around here?"

He still hadn't told me what he wanted to talk about, but since we only really had one thing in common anymore I was afraid I knew.

And I wasn't looking forward to it. "Yes, and I'll give you some," I began.

His eyes brightened greedily. "If," I added, "you'll concede that I really saw a moose."

Whereupon Victor gave in at once. After all, he could always deny that he'd said it, later. My ex was good at denying.

"You cut me a slice of that cake," he declared, "and I'll cheerfully agree you saw little green men getting out of a flying saucer, right here in the yard."

Which only stiffened my growing determination to try solving Bella's problem, because if little green men landed in my yard they would need machetes just to hack their way to a place where they could ask to be taken to our leaders. I'd cut a few ragged paths to the picnic table and glider, but the rest of the place was fit only for a team of jungle explorers.

"Fine," I agreed, going in to cut him a slice of the cake. Meanwhile I hoped Bella really did know how to use a lawn mower, as she kept insisting.

On the other hand, she *had* figured out how to remove soaked-in paint from the kitchen floor. Contrary to her usual energetic cleaning methods, she'd taken a small wire brush, dipped it in hot, soapy water—because it was latex paint; if it had been oil, I suppose she'd have used turpentine— and rubbed the brush gently along the grain of the wood, removing the paint. Afterward she'd scrubbed the whole floor very thoroughly so the treated spots didn't stand out, then coated it with Mop & Glo.

And the result was brilliant. Noticing it as I put Victor's cake on a plate, it struck me that maybe I was underestimating Bella. Hapless she might be in the managing-the-ex-husband department; at coming up with a way of getting an unorthodox job done, however, she was clearly a shining star.

But I didn't have time to pursue this thought; when I got back outside, Ellie was putting the baby up over her shoulder.

"I think we'll have a nap," she announced, glancing meaningfully between Victor and me, and took Leonora inside.

Which left just me and my ex-husband, which was a bit like leaving just dynamite and a pack of matches. After a career as the brain surgeon you went to when all of the others had told you that (a) you should start making peace with your lifelong enemies and (b) those long wooden boxes were really quite comfortable, especially with the nice satin pillows they were putting in them nowadays, Victor had relocated to Eastport to be near Sam and, I believed, to scramble *my* brains whenever he got an opportunity.

Like now. "So, what's going on?" he mumbled through a bite of orange cake.

Ellie had made it, popping it perfectly out of the Bundt pan with a short, sharp rap that always precedes disaster when I try doing so. Also, when I made it that cake always came out as dense as concrete, but hers was so light that you had to hold it down on the plate with one hand just so you could put a fork into it with the other.

Overhead in the apple tree the mother robin arrived; the urgent cheeping grew frantic, then subsided. I will get through this peacefully, I told myself. "With Sam, you mean?"

But of course he meant Sam. It was why I'd let Victor come over here at all, because he'd finally shown some interest and I thought he should know the situation.

Whatever the situation was. "He's working on his school project," I told Victor. "Going out in the morning, coming home in the afternoon."

I took a deep breath. "But then he goes out again at night, I don't know where, and he won't tell me," I blurted miserably.

Victor stopped chewing. "Is he drinking?"

"I don't think so."

But Sam also wasn't meeting my gaze, saying words beyond the few very necessary ones, or smiling.

My bright, funny, exuberant Sam . . . he was never smiling.

Victor sighed heavily. "You know, you handled it all wrong," he began as if this were the most obvious thing in the world.

Which to him it was; I controlled myself with an effort. It had taken Victor six months to get up the nerve to have this conversation at all. Before now, he had offered me no suggestions and no support, just the slow head shake and silently judgmental gaze that always made me long to punch his lights out.

He scraped a few last crumbs off his plate as I struggled to keep my composure; despite my resolve, my head had begun pounding and a nasty little refrain kept repeating itself in my brain.

Just like always, just like . . . "What do you think I could have done better?" I demanded.

But he wasn't listening. "You never did know how to handle a crisis," he said placidly, licking his fork. "Even when he was a little kid, you used to—"

When Sam was a little kid he used to go for days, sometimes a few weeks, without seeing his father at all. Half the time it was because Victor was up to his elbows in somebody else's skull. And half the time . . .

Oh, never mind. It was the last straw, that's all. "Victor, put that fork down this minute. Before I stick it in your heart."

Suddenly I was gasping, feeling my own heart shriveling in anger. "What would *you* have done?" I demanded. "Tell Sam to find some other addiction? Like maybe women?"

Victor frowned, caught off guard by my unexpected attack. This was forbidden territory if we wanted to keep a peaceful coexistence going.

"You don't have to—" he began defensively.

"Yeah, I don't have to." My voice rasped in my throat. "But now I'm going to, because you know what, Victor? You didn't know what to do about Sam, either, so you stayed away. Because you were *scared*."

He blinked, his expression suddenly naked and defenseless. I was cutting way too close to the bone.

"You start out all intense because now that *you* want to, we've got to talk. Then you come over here," I hurtled on, "with your casual what's for lunch and what's going on."

"Jake, lower your voice," he said, glancing around uneasily.

I didn't. "All you really want is to let *me* know that it's all *my* fault. Which you make sure it is by never being around in the crunch."

After Sam broke down and confessed that he'd been drinking again, it was Wade who had walked me around the island, miles and miles in the snow, until my fear and panic dispersed enough so that I could even think. He'd taken the day off work to do it.

"Sure, you can criticize now," I went on before Victor could get a word in. "But when something's actually *happening*—"

Sam had stayed up in his room all the rest of that awful day and throughout the evening, so silent that I was frightened for him and walked right in on him when he wouldn't answer my knock, which I'd agreed I would *never* do....

"...*then* you've got a sick *patient*," I grated out. "Somebody *else* who needs your help, not your son, who is a member of your own goddamned *family*."

When Sam was born, Victor had been in the operating room doing a neurology procedure; in other words, surgery. Later I found out that it was elective surgery.

That he could have postponed it. Now he stared at me. "I'm very sorry you feel that way about it," he said stiffly, getting up.

Going into Sam's room that night, I'd found him facedown on his bed in the dark, weeping his poor heart out. And since then something irreplaceable seemed to have gone out of him. I desperately missed that constant little light of his that we'd both depended upon without even realizing it.

That I'd depended upon. And I still didn't have a clue what to do about it. "You'd better go, Victor," I said finally, all the fury abruptly drained from me.

Because in spite of everything, Victor didn't do things to be mean. He was what he was, broken in ways that were hard to get a handle on; he had his secret struggles just like anyone else.

"Yeah." He stared down at his shoes, jingling his car keys unhappily, as a memory popped into my head.

Soon after Victor and I met in New York, he took me to the Broadway production of *Dracula,* with its stark black-and-white costumes and Edward Gorey sets enlivened by small, throbbingly vivid shocks of red: a rose, a drop of bright blood.

Afterward Victor bought a red rose from a street vendor and gave it to me without a word. I remember it pricked my finger.

"Sorry," he said softly now.

"Okay," I said, tears stinging my eyes. *Just like always...* Some things never changed. "Me, too."

Then he left, brushing past Bella who was just returning, her eyes wide and her face stonily pale with some fresh shock as she strode through the tangled grass I hadn't had time to mow.

"What is it, Bella?" I asked tiredly.

In answer she thrust a handful of yellow notebook sheets at me, holding one back as if it alone were too terrible to reveal. "Here they are," she said, "just like you asked, only..."

"Only what?" Dully, I examined the notes. All were like the first one she'd showed me, lists of unpleasant words.

Bludgeon, gash, hack, lacerate.

Maybe they weren't direct predictions of violence, but you didn't think up lists like these if you were feeling cheerful. Or halfhearted, either. This kind of thing took work.

Ellie came back out and joined us. "Only what, Bella?" I prompted again, reaching out to take the final note from her and seeing at once that it was different.

Very different. Instead of a list of big-word terms that were threatening only by their definitions, this new one was a few sentences long, featuring complete sentences, capitalized letters, and actual punctuation.

Dear Bella, it read. *Very soon now you must depart. Gather your courage in both hands, confront your misdeeds, and prepare to be annihilated.*

It ended somewhat incongruously but I thought chillingly: *Yours sincerely, A Freind.*

Not "friend." And that was very odd. It was a simple word, yet quite often misspelled. But the note-writer was consistently spelling more complicated terms correctly.

Ellie and I looked at each other over Bella's head. She'd buried her face in her hands and was sobbing quietly.

"It was there when I got home," she whimpered when we'd taken her inside, made some coffee, dosed it heavily with sugar and brandy, and forced her to drink it.

"Because it's Friday," she added. "They always come on..." A hiccup escaped her. "Oh, pardon me," she said wretchedly.

Just then my father came in; I hadn't heard his truck pull into the driveway. Wearing a red flannel shirt, faded jeans, and ancient sneakers, he nodded a greeting and went down to the basement hastily, without pausing for conversation.

Seeing his stringy gray ponytail disappear through the cellar door reminded me that he'd already been at the sharp end of Bella's stick once. Evidently he didn't wish to repeat the experience.

I didn't want it repeated, either. But it was starting to look as if there might be only one way to prevent it, other of course than simply firing the housekeeper right this minute.

And I couldn't. I just couldn't bring myself to do it. There in my kitchen with a wad of tear-soaked tissues in her hands, she was too, too forlorn.

"Bella, I've spoken to Bob Arnold," I said.

She looked up. "I asked him who might threaten you, and he told me about your ex-husband," I added.

She sniffled. "And now I s'pose you'll want to know why I didn't say anything about him," she uttered in despair.

"Well, I did wonder about that," I said. "Don't you think he might be someone you should've mentioned?"

"No, I don't," she replied, with surprising vigor. "He ain't ever written a letter in his life, much less know any of those words. That's what the cops said, anyway," she added resentfully, "when they decided he wasn't doing it."

But Bob Arnold had only said it wasn't very likely that Jim was the culprit, not that he couldn't be. And despite her strong words, Bella didn't sound truly convinced, either, only resigned to the official conclusion.

"Look," I said, "what do you say I take a ride down there to Lubec and have a word with him."

She brightened. "Oh, Missus—I mean Jake, I'd be grateful. And he might tell you, too. Because, I mean, you aren't a cop. He wouldn't be scared that you'd get him in trouble."

Don't be so sure, I thought darkly, already planning what I might say to Jim Diamond as Ellie spoke up.

"You don't want that?" she asked Bella.

Bella shook her head. "Trouble makes more trouble. I only want it to *stop*. I want him," she finished bleakly, "to go away."

So, I realized, she did still believe her ex was behind the notes. Meanwhile all I wanted was a cleaning woman who didn't clean us right out of the house, while antagonizing my father out of it with equal efficiency. Or worse, one who ended up jobless and destitute with me feeling that maybe I could have prevented it.

"All right," I said. "You go on home, Bella. I think you've had enough exertion for one day."

She nodded obediently. "But you'll let me know?"

She meant if it wasn't Jim sending the threats. As she said this her face fell gloomily again at the notion that perhaps her ordeal wasn't over, after all. And as is so often the case, one unhappy thought led to another.

"Why," she asked with abrupt suspicion, "are you doing this for me?"

Her narrowed gaze went from me to Ellie and back. "You don't know me, not really. Why would you bother helping me?"

Surprised, I opened my mouth to assure her I had no ulterior motives, just my own selfish ones, mostly. But then I saw Ellie's face and stopped.

"Um, Jake?" Ellie said.

She was wearing her uh-oh look, an expression I usually only saw when I was (a) at the top rung of a ladder, and (b) about to be suddenly at the bottom rung.

"What?" I said quietly. Ellie's uh-oh look is infallible.

"Well," she said. "There is something you both should know."

Just then from her perch on the top of the refrigerator Cat Dancing pricked up her ears, uncrossing her eyes to the degree she was able to and looking expectant. At the same time both the dogs bounded in, wagging and grinning, and I heard my father's boot dragging hard across the cellar floor.

He was stubbing out a cigarette. It all meant someone was coming home; Wade, maybe, or Sam. "What?" I demanded of Ellie.

Footsteps came up the back porch steps. Two sets of them; one heavy and one lighter pair.

"Sam's new girlfriend," Ellie began. "I just found out about it on my way over here a little while ago," she added with an apologetic look at me. "I saw them together."

The girl's identity, I realized; Ellie knew it.

"Who—?" I began, but she just rushed on.

"But Victor was here then, so I decided to tell you later. And when she finds out about it, I'm afraid Bella might think..."

Oh, hell. Suddenly I got it. The back door opened as Ellie took a deep breath and was about to continue.

But she didn't have to. Because at that moment, all became clear.

Too clear. "Hi," my son Sam said in surprise, coming in with a girl who looked to be eighteen or so except around the eyes.

There, in her too-wise expression, she was twenty-five going on forty. "Hi," she said in tones mingling shyness and defiance.

Mostly defiance.

Wearing a T-shirt, jeans, and sneakers, Sam had curly dark hair, thick-lashed hazel eyes, and the agile look young men tend to get when they are comfortable around boats.

The young woman with him was neither pretty nor graceful-appearing in shorts, run-down-at-the-heels sandals, and a tank top so tight it seemed painted onto her slim torso. But under an expertly applied layer of makeup she did have a hard-bitten look of joie de vivre I thought boded ill for my peace of mind.

She also had a high, rounded forehead, slightly protuberant blue eyes, straight hair pulled back and fastened with an overly glittery big barrette,

and a short, stubby chin, which if it was not exactly receding was not exactly prominent, either.

In other words, if Bella Diamond was the *after* picture, this girl was the
before.

"You see, Jake, what I was trying to tell you was..." Ellie began.

"Mom, I want you to meet..." Sam started to say.

"Kris," Bella hissed furiously. "What on earth are you..."

Stepping up to me, the girl thrust out her hand. "I'm Bella's daughter,
Kris," she said. "Sam and I've been seeing each other a while. But I guess
you've figured that out by now."

Yeah, I thought, and probably the Romans figured out about the
Visigoths pretty quick, too. Kris smelled of cigarette smoke and the kind of
cheap hair-care products that are always heavily perfumed, and right away
I didn't like her cunning appearance, her sharp, sly glances around the
room as if mentally summing up the value of its contents.

Meanwhile Sam stood there looking as if someone had hit him with a
lead pipe. "Uh, we're going to go upstairs and listen to some music," he
said, angling his head a little dazedly at his companion.

Obviously he hadn't expected anyone to be here. Ellie and I went out
often, and Bella was so new he'd forgotten about her possible presence.

"Nice to meet you," Kris Diamond pronounced, taking Sam's hand pos-
sessively while her eyes glittered with triumph.

By contrast Sam's glance at her as the two of them left the room together
was meltingly sweet. Good heavens, he was in love; *poor Maggie,* I thought.

"Bella," I began urgently when their footsteps had gone on up the hall
stairs, "I swear to you I had no idea..."

"So," she said icily. "The rich lady's son and the housekeeper's daughter. Not the match you were hoping for, was it?"

"Bella, it's not what you think. I didn't even know..."

I put it together fast. Probably she thought I was trying to get her on my
side so when I made my move against the new romance between my son
and her daughter, she'd be with me.

And afterward I'd dump her. She chuckled without humor. "Sure, rich people are just *thrilled* when their kids marry the help."

That word again: *rich*. Which I wasn't, not in the grand scheme of things. But Bella didn't live in the grand scheme, did she?

She lived on a paycheck week to week when she could get one; to her, I was right up there with the Rockefellers.

"You're thinking what kind of daughter-in-law she's going to make," Bella continued, "and it ain't a good thought."

Well, no, Bella, it isn't. And I guess I felt defensive about this and a little guilty, too, about the money angle. So once again I opened my big mouth.

"Listen, Kris has nothing to do with it. Even if she breaks up with Sam tomorrow I'll still help you, I promise."

As I spoke, music blared abruptly from Sam's room upstairs, so possibly Bella didn't hear me. But I still felt held to what I'd said and not sorry about it.

Or anyway not very sorry. After all, how hard could it be to sort this out for her? The notes were nasty—but they *were* only notes. The volume on the music went down.

"And you," Bella added, "don't even know what she *is*, yet."

Which didn't sound promising. But Bella was right, as in the end she turned out to be about so many things. Despite my unhappy first impression, I *didn't* know what kind of a person Kris was.

Still, I had a feeling I was about to learn.

Half an hour later, after a trip to her house to talk to Wade and George, Ellie was on the phone to the list of contacts our husbands had supplied, to find out whether anyone was likely to have equipped our threat-note suspect with a weapon.

I might not have gotten anywhere with this line of inquiry. People around here are notoriously closemouthed about what they've got stashed in the glove boxes of their pickup trucks—or under the front seats of their cars, if they are really expecting trouble—and that was the kind of gun we were most concerned about.

But everyone liked Ellie and was glad to be able to tell her she was probably not about to have a bullet hole blown through her. Jim Diamond, they all reported, had no money, so he couldn't have bought a gun even if they'd have sold one to him, and none of them had given him one, either.

This didn't reassure me completely; it was the *probably* part I was still worried about.

Nevertheless, in a biggish nutshell that was how Ellie and I, the baby Leonora, my son's ex-girlfriend Maggie, and my father all went to Lubec on the bright June afternoon the day after the moose showed up. Our mission was to find out whether Jim Diamond was threatening his ex-wife Bella, and if so to make him stop.

But instead we found him dead, or so close to it as to make no difference. Which should have ended the matter, but didn't.

Not by a long shot.

Chapter 6

A week after we'd found Jim Diamond breathing his last, I finally decided to finish the shutter-painting job that the moose had interrupted. After all, winter would return any minute now and it would be too late to put them up.

Besides, if you want to be alone with your thoughts just announce that you're about to paint shutters and that you could use help. People will flee as if you'd declared you had plague germs and they were fun, really, so wouldn't they like a few?

Thus in complete privacy I got out the paint sprayer, which was designed to put paint onto a dozen shutters in a jiffy. Or so the ads for it optimistically proclaimed; the truth was a bit different. Up in the third-floor room I used for fix-up projects, I poured paint from the big can into the sprayer's receptacle.

Which was a challenge in itself; the paint ran down either one side of the can or both sides of the receptacle, but I got some in there eventually.

Next I screwed the paint-filled receptacle onto the sprayer body, noting that together the two parts of the apparatus weighed approximately a ton. Also, the job seemed to require at least one more hand than I possessed, a point not adequately covered in the instructions.

Smearing both hands heavily with paint didn't seem to be in the instructions either, but I hadn't needed them to tell me the job would take plenty of rags; for one thing I'd used this gadget before, and for another all my paint jobs take plenty of rags.

So after wiping off both hands, the sprayer receptacle, the front of my shirt, one leg of my jeans, and the side of my face, I picked the sprayer up again and turned to the final page of the instruction booklet.

By now, the only thing I didn't have paint on was a shutter. Also no matter how many times I used the sprayer, I never seemed to be able to liberate myself from the booklet, which in addition to a half page of English directions was also printed in pages of Italian, German, French, Arabic, Chinese, and what I suspected was Somali.

I flipped through the pages, pausing at *achtung!* which was precisely how I felt. But the next instruction seemed fairly simple: Aim, and pull the trigger.

By then it was what I was inclined to do, too, only with a pistol aimed at my head. Still, I'd gotten this far so I thought I might as well go through with the rest of it.

Okay, then. I looked around uncertainly to see what step of the preparations I'd left out. But I had stapled plastic sheeting to the walls, leaned the shutters against them, and put on the equipment required for the job: latex gloves (too late, but never mind), dust mask, safety glasses.

Last came hearing protection, heavy-duty plastic earmuffs to deaden the roar of the sprayer's compresser. When I pulled them on a cone of silence seemed to descend around my head, and paint sprayed from the gadget as I activated it.

Too bad the sprayer was aimed at my shoe, and we will omit the colorful string of curse words I emitted upon discovering this. But when I did get the thing pointed at a shutter and the trigger pulled, the device operated beautifully.

In fact it performed so well, I rashly decided to paint the backs of the shutters, too, working steadily under the bare hanging lightbulb with shadows gathering in the corners of the room and the uncurtained windows darkening toward night.

And while I worked, I thought about what had been wrong with Jim Diamond's apartment. The first problem, I realized as the paint sprayer roared distantly, boiled down to money.

He didn't have any; no job, and the very minimum of public assistance. Yet his home wasn't one room with a hot plate and the sort of shared bath that made cleanliness next to intolerable. It was a three-room flat with its own facilities, a phone—albeit not connected at the moment—and cable TV. Also that big boom box, equipped with CD player and speakers, was new, and the kind of thing that cost at least a couple of hundred dollars.

So where'd he been getting money?

There were a couple of other little details still bothering me, too. Such as no writing materials. No pens, no little pads of notepaper or even a pencil. How'd he been writing threats?

If he had been. And then there was the weapon. Jim's death had officially been deemed a homicide by the DA's office, and as predicted, the state cops had spoken to Ellie and me.

But not with any urgency. Like the Lubec cop, they'd seemed to think one of Jim's low-life pals had done him in.

I still wasn't so sure. According to Ellie, the thing on the stove had turned out to be a pork chop cooked to a lump. But he'd been cooking it in a cheap saucepan instead of the heavy skillet that someone had bonked him with.

To me it suggested the skillet hadn't been in the apartment when he began cooking, that instead someone had brought it to the scene and hit him with it. And that didn't conjure up the picture of two guys, a couple of six-

STICK 'EM UP

Before painting a newly sanded
surface, wipe it down with
a sticky rag called a tack cloth
to remove all dust.

packs, and a sudden quarrel. It suggested premeditation, but a skillet was an odd weapon if you were planning mayhem.

Speaking of which, there was another variety of it waiting for me downstairs, and even the loudest, most solitary fix-up project wouldn't postpone it forever. Much as I dreaded the idea, I'd decided I was going to have to talk with Sam about Maggie and Kris Diamond.

Not that he hadn't had unsuitable girlfriends before; to my sorrow, he took very strongly after Victor in this department. It wasn't the first time Maggie had suffered through one of Sam's brief, high-intensity infatuations with some other female.

And nobody thought it would be the last. But in the past he had always been open about them, praising to the skies the intellect of the marine biology student, the athleticism of the cross-country bicycle racer, or the beauty of the visiting landscape painter's daughter.

By contrast even now he wasn't talking about Kris at all. Nor did he seem to understand that this time, Maggie was at the end of her rope. She kept busy; in summer her child-care talents were hugely and profitably in demand, and I knew she was working on a project for the Eastport Historical Society, too.

But I was afraid that when Sam went to look for her as he always did eventually, she wouldn't be there. And I wasn't sure she should be; I thought his treatment of her was cruel. So when I went downstairs after cleaning the paint sprayer—

—this turned out to be nearly as big a job as painting with it; I swear the torpedo tubes in a nuclear submarine couldn't be as tricky to prepare for refiring—

I was ready to lay it out for him. After all, I intended to say, his dad's chronic Casanova act didn't mean *he* could...

"Hey, Mom, check this out," Sam said as I reached the front hall. He sat at the dining room table with his books and papers; sketches mostly, because they helped compensate for his dyslexia.

"Okay," I said, leaning over to see what he was so enthused about. This was perfect; I could engage my son in conversation, show that what *he* was interested in was also important to *me,* and...

"Pykrete," Sam pronounced, waving happily at his notebook as if he personally had just discovered the stuff.

Which was when I began having second thoughts. Opening up about the identity of his new girlfriend hadn't made him any more talkative about her, but it sure had improved his mood.

And lingering questions aside, by then I truly believed Jim Diamond's death had nearly ended my snooping activities; all I'd wanted was to stop Bella's hygiene hysteria and in that I'd succeeded.

There were just a few final doubts I wished to have settled. And Ellie and I had a plan to deal with one of them tonight. So was I really prepared to do battle on another front so soon?

Maybe. But . . . maybe not.

"What," I inquired with as much lively, I'm-your-mom-and-I-care-about-you interest as I could muster, "is pykrete?"

I was humoring him, but if I had to develop genuine interest in everything Sam got excited about I would be bedridden from the exertion.

"And what's so good about it?" I added.

"Pykrete is basically just ice, so it's cheap," he explained. "And it cuts easy. But it's also partly wood dust, so it doesn't melt. And it floats. Boy, oh boy, does it ever float."

"Wonderful," I enthused, still not quite getting it. But I did know he was happy about it. "And in practical terms . . . ?"

He nodded energetically. "That's it," he said. "*Practically.* Because I am working on my summer project, you know."

Yes, I did know. I just didn't know what it was, because he hadn't been talking to me very much lately. Also I was distracted by something I had not seen in a while: a smile on Sam's face.

"I'm re-creating a World War Two warship made entirely out of pykrete," he declared proudly.

In other words made out of ice laced with sawdust, a job he insisted on describing to me in all its fascinating (to him) and endless (to me) detail.

But it was the first thing he seemed truly happy about in a very long time. "Lord Mountbatten, Chief of Combined Operations for Winston Churchill during the war," he informed me brightly, "was the guy who introduced the stuff to Churchill."

I pictured a cartoon how-do-you-do scene: a block of dusty ice on one side, a large man with a cigar on the other.

"Mountbatten marched in there with a chunk of pykrete and dropped it into Churchill's bathtub," Sam went on.

I gathered it was a mark of Mountbatten's great courage that Churchill was taking a bath in the tub at the time.

"It's strong," Sam said, "and it doesn't melt. You can carve it. Don't you see, Mom? It's . . ."

He waved his hands at the complex drawing of a battleship in his notebook. "The war ended before they finished it up. But you could sail to *China* on this thing," he insisted.

"Uh, wait a minute. You mean you're building a real boat?"

He looked up, surprised. "Well, yeah. Not *full*-size, but . . . what'd you think I was doing, making another bathtub toy?"

Which was when it came over me again that he wasn't a kid anymore. If he decided to build an airplane, the next thing you knew he'd be doing a Lindbergh in it.

So despite my doubts, on the spur of the moment I decided he could take a man-size question, too. "Sam. Don't you think you're being a little tough on Maggie?"

His face instantly hardened. But if I'd backed off every time Sam's face hardened in our twenty years together, he'd have been the world's longest-living multiple-substance abuser by now.

Or he'd have been dead. "Maggie's a good friend, Sam," I reminded him quietly. "And she's stuck by you through a lot of things. Do you really think it's fair to just drop her flat the way you have?"

Considering the thin ice I'd just ventured out on, I could have used some pykrete myself. But as I waited for Sam's answer, a conversation from earlier in the day flew into my head.

"George says Sam asked him what it's like to be married," Ellie had told me. We'd stood in the yard raking up the piles of grass clippings that were left after Bella mowed it.

"Oh, God. What did George say?" I asked, the sudden reek of fear in my nostrils blocking the perfume of freshly cut lawn. As it turned out, Bella had really known how to run the mower.

"George told him that if you like working, worrying, and being tied down all the time," Ellie had replied, "it's as good a way to live as any."

Which was far from the way George really felt. "Tell him I owe him a strawberry-apricot pie," I'd responded gratefully.

And in fact I was baking it right now; I'd put it into the oven before I went up to the third floor.

But the pie's sweet fragrance contrasted with the sour look Sam now turned on me. "You're sure eager to get me back with Maggie, aren't you?" he accused. "Well, it's not going to work, Mom."

"Sam, I'm not—"

"Oh, yes, you are," he cut in hotly. "I know what you think of Kris and me. That she's not good enough for me because she's not well educated and she hasn't got any money."

"Sam, that's not true!" I exclaimed, taken aback.

But I couldn't very well tell him the real reasons I opposed the match so strongly. For instance, that the girl was two-faced and greedy: Over the past few days I'd noticed that Kris was so polite she made your teeth ache if she knew you were watching, but she turned over plates and examined the silverware to see if it was worth anything, when she thought you weren't.

Also she was so self-involved, she wore a locket with a curl of her own hair in it. I knew because Bella had told me about it, Bella not being a big member of her daughter's fan club, either.

This to me was the most ominous fact of all. "Look, Sam," I said. "It's not like I expect veto power over your girlfriends."

Although at the moment I'd have welcomed it. "But you have plans for yourself. Finishing school and being a boatbuilder...they're fine ambitions and you're doing so well. And Kris...well, she just doesn't seem to be going anywhere with her life."

His eyes flashed defiantly. "Yeah, because she's been here at home, sticking by her mom just in case her stepfather got mean again. Being supportive."

He gave that final word an unpleasant twist. "She could have gone to college; she's not dumb. She just didn't want to leave. And since she can't go, why spend a lot of time worrying about a career? To torture herself?"

"Well, she can go now," I pointed out angrily, stung by his implication that I hadn't been so supportive, myself. If I'd been any more supportive to that boy, I'd have been a trampoline.

"Jim's dead," I went on, "so Kris can resume her plans for getting a Ph.D. in astrophysics," I finished.

His face went blank. Oh, hell.

"Sam," I told him hastily. "I'm sorry. I didn't mean it, and I apologize to you and Kris both, very sincerely."

"Sure. Don't mention it." He stared down at his books.

"I just think you owe Maggie a little loyalty, too, that's all," I persisted. After all, he was already going to despise me forever, so what did I have to lose?

Also, I still had that big mouth. "Because even if things aren't working out romantically for the two of you, she still wants to go on being your friend. Isn't that worth something?"

Too late, I realized that this was yet another blunder. The "Can't we be friends" line was one Sam's father had used on me, and Sam knew it. And he didn't like it any better than I had.

"Maggie doesn't want to be friends," he shot back. "She wants us back together and she'll do anything to make it happen."

He slammed his notebook shut. "And you just like her because you think she'll keep me out of trouble."

This was what I got, I supposed, for having had a kind, funny, congenial sixteen-year-old: the twenty-year-old from hell. But his assessment did give me pause, being as it was so right on target. That wasn't the only reason I liked Maggie, but she was certainly the safe bet behavior-wise.

"She wants to be friends?" Sam repeated. "Fine. You be her friend. The two of you can have a great time worrying about me."

He got up. "Just don't rope me into it, because I'm telling you, Mom,

Maggie and I are done. Whether," he finished warningly, "you like it or not."

He swept up his books and papers, stalked toward the hall stairs, then paused uncertainly.

Seeing this, I knew that deep down he was as sorry about our fight as I was. After I divorced his father we'd had a rough few years, my son and I, but since then—until about six months ago, anyway—we'd been pals. Two against the world, and all that. And I missed it.

A lot. Probably he did, too, though you'd never have known it recently. Or I hoped he missed it.

The truth was, I was afraid to ask.

"By the way," he said, relenting a bit. "Have you seen my baseball caps? They were in my closet, but..."

Oh, brother. "No," I said hastily, "I haven't."

It was technically true. Wade had taken them to his house on Liberty Street to try repairing them where Sam wouldn't catch him at it. "Are you sure that's where you put them?" I asked.

Because I thought if I told Sam what had really happened to those caps, all hell would break loose.

"Maybe," he said uncertainly as he went on upstairs.

For a moment I stood pondering whether I ought to go up, too, and tell him the truth. Because how could I expect him to speak frankly to me if I wouldn't be honest with him? Thinking this I put my hand on the banister to follow him up.

But just then the timer went off on the pie.

And then the phone rang.

And after that, all hell really did break loose.

About two hours after the argument with Sam, Ellie and I pulled up in the Fiat to the rough-looking little house on Rye Street where Bella Diamond lived with Kris.

"You want to know, and I want to know. So let's just do this and then we *will* know," Ellie said persuasively.

It was Friday night, a week since Bella had gotten her most recent note, and she'd said they always arrived on Fridays. So if another threat *was* going to show up, it could come tonight.

"Anyway, what were you babbling about before?" Ellie asked. "*Who's* coming for a visit?"

I shut the Fiat's ignition off. This was a crackpot plan but it was our only one, so we were going through with it despite the phone call whose implications I was still reeling under.

"My dad's relatives," I said. "They've found out where he is and that he's not on the FBI most-wanted list anymore. They think now it's safe to come and get reacquainted with him."

My father ever being on the FBI list at all is a very long story whose major plot points include an explosion, my mother's death in it, and his supposed culpability in the event.

But when he'd showed up the previous autumn after an absence of about three decades, I'd learned—and eventually so did the Feds—that he'd never been the villain people believed he was.

That I, especially, had believed he was.

We got out of the car. Bella's house was dark; in the wake of Diamond's death—she'd taken the news stoically and there had been no services—she had gone to visit her aunt in mid-coast Maine.

"Lots," I added despairingly, "of relatives."

That was when I noticed the small plaster statue of a fisherman by the door on Bella's front porch. Like all such supposed clever hiding places, it practically screamed *there's a key underneath me!* So at least one thing was going well; this might be easier than I'd thought.

No one else was on the street as we approached the house. It had brown shingle-type asphalt siding, shutters at the small off-kilter windows, and a cracked front walk.

"Four sisters, three brothers, three nieces, and an elderly aunt," I told Ellie. "It was one of the sisters who called to say they were all coming for the Fourth."

We climbed the front steps, even shakier and more rotten than mine. The rusty cast-iron banister's bolts flopped loosely in their holes.

"Eunice," I said, still dazed by the implications of it all. "*My* aunt. I never even knew my father had brothers and sisters."

"You're sure Kris isn't home?" Ellie asked.

As we'd expected, the door was locked. It was a big solid Block lock, too, the kind you couldn't pop with a plastic strip, set into a newly reinforced door and frame. But that wasn't going to be a problem.

"Yup," I replied. "Kris told Sam her mom's aunt always gives her money when she visits."

I'd have given Kris money to stay there. "So now the house is empty," I concluded, "just the way we want it."

The question being, would it stay empty? Because there was still a chance it *hadn't* been Jim sending those nasty notes to Bella.

And I wanted to know for sure. An owl hooted in one of the trees dividing Bella's yard from the next one. I jumped about a foot.

"Guess I've gotten out of the housebreaking habit," I said.

Ellie's look at me in the darkness was unreadable. We had both decided to give up snooping when Leonora was born, agreeing that it was irresponsible now that Ellie was a mother. But it wasn't Jim's murder we were poking into now, just the notes.

Or so I hoped. "Here goes nothing," Ellie said, lifting the statue. And just as I'd thought, there was the door key. I swear all these key-hiding gadgets are created for the convenience of burglars; you have to be honest to be fooled by them. Moments later, we were inside, catching our breath and closing the door hastily behind us.

"Shine the flash around," I told Ellie, "but not at the windows."

It was just after ten, and from the lights in nearby houses I knew some of the neighbors were still up and liable to see us if we weren't careful. The flashlight's beam revealed a worn carpet, shabby pieces of furniture, a small TV. Everything was spotless. I examined a few library books on the floor by a chair.

Mystery novels, some romances, and a shiny new book about Princess Diana, this one by her butler's uncle's sister's greengrocer. There were a lot of crossword puzzle books, too, of the type you can buy on the newsstand, and a *TV Guide.*

"A dozen people? Are they nuts? Do they know what it's like here on the Fourth?" Ellie asked, returning to the subject of my father and his relatives.

And to the fact that in Eastport the Fourth of July is a weeklong, round-the-clock lollapalooza. Every lodging place in the county is booked solid for months in advance.

Which meant I couldn't send my newly discovered kin to a motel. I found my way to the kitchen. "Yes, yes, and they don't have a clue," I said.

The kitchen smelled powerfully of Ajax, fresh floor wax, and laundry detergent. "But to hear her talk about seeing my dad, you'd think it was a private audience with the Pope."

I still couldn't see much with just the flashlight. "And they can't come another time. I asked, but they've already bought nonrefundable plane tickets."

Oh, what the hell. I found a light switch and flipped it on. If the neighbors came, I'd tell them we were Bella's housekeepers.

Or something. "So what could I say?" I finished helplessly.

Ellie followed me into the kitchen, glanced around. Lying on the table was a Red Cross blood-drive brochure. Either Bella had found the Red Cross lady, or the lady had found her.

"So you told them they could come," Ellie said.

"Yep." I examined the kitchen some more. Something big was missing here, but I couldn't quite put my finger on what.

"Well, it was more like Eunice told me," I added. "But in the end..."

The floor slanted sharply in one corner. "Of course I did," I finished. "Big family reunion, all their hearts set on it?"

The back door was bolted and all the windows were locked. "All that time my dad was on the run," I told Ellie, "he couldn't visit them. The police were watching in case they got in touch with him, or vice versa. And according to Eunice they all knew that."

The rest of the house smelled of carpet shampoo, Windex, and lemon furniture polish. "But that's not the only reason," Ellie observed. "I mean, why you agreed to the visit."

"No," I admitted. "It's the idea of having relatives at all. People related to me by blood. It's blown me away a little."

"Well," Ellie said, "at least you know that." Ellie believed firmly that I had a rich, full interior life, most of which went unexplored by anyone and especially not by me.

Probably she was right. We went into the bedrooms, peering into the closets and opening dresser drawers.

"But let's not get mushy about the whole long-lost portion of the program, all right?" I added a little irritably. "It holds bad memories for me."

After the blast that killed my mother when I was a toddler and—so I'd believed—orphaned me, I'd been sent to her folks in remote southeast hill country, where it was an item of faith that my father was the devil himself.

And that I was his spawn. I'd been a young teenager when I fled those hard faces, climbed on a Greyhound headed for New York, and never looked back. But now here was a whole other set of kinfolk I'd never heard anything about; all I really knew was that I'd be damned if I was going to turn them away.

Dear heaven, though, a dozen of them, and over the Fourth!

"Let's get this search done with," I said. "I want to be out in the front parlor sitting quietly if anyone shows up."

I entered Kris's room with its bottles of dime-store makeup and hair products. The only thing faintly suggesting any serious interests was a letter from an admissions counselor at a beauty school in Portland, suggesting she come in for an interview.

This I thought was a good sign; a person could make a living as a beautician, even start a business and get something going.

A career, a life. But the letter was weeks old, stuffed under a bunch of teen fashion zines and a copy of *Rolling Stone,* and I saw nothing to make me think she'd done anything about it.

I glanced through more items: a set of fake fingernails, two miniature bottles of rum. Sam would have killed me for this. But Sam wasn't going to know.

And bottom line, I noted nothing strange anywhere in Bella's shabby-but-spotless house.

Just... something missing.

"So anyway, they're coming next week," I told Ellie when we met again in the cramped living room. There was a woodstove plugged into the fireplace flue and the night was chilly as they often are in Maine, even in summer.

I didn't want to leave live embers in the stove when we went out, though. I don't trust old chimneys even if Bella thought this one was safe enough. So we just sat there shivering.

"The whole dozen of them," I said, "and they're staying for ten days." We'd turned the lights back off, readying the house for the next stage of our mission.

Which consisted of waiting for someone who might not even show up. The darkness was claustrophobic, and my fingers itched for the matches and kindling by the woodstove. But I resisted.

"So listen, just to make sure we're both still on the same page," Ellie began, changing the subject. "Our theory is that if Kris isn't writing the notes, and Jim wasn't, either..."

"Then someone else was. Right."

"And if that person doesn't know Jim is dead, or doesn't care..."

"Uh-huh," I agreed. "Then whoever it is might just show up to drop off another communication tonight."

A sound from outside interrupted me. But when I peeked out the curtains (which smelled strongly of air freshener) I saw only a racoon shuffling away across the lawn.

"Anyway, Bella says she's quite sure Kris isn't leaving the messages. And from all those big words in them, I have to agree."

The raccoon knocked over a metal trash can somewhere down the street. "That girl," I finished unhappily, "is no Einstein."

By now it was nearly eleven. "Ellie, did you get the feeling that something was missing out in the kitchen?"

"Uh-huh." Her voice came out of the darkness at me. "I know what it was, too. Or I think I do."

"What . . . ?" A shadow moved on the curtains, startling me. But it was only a branch, sharply silhouetted by the streetlight.

Simultaneously the answer to my question came clear in my mind. What *wasn't* there . . . "A frying pan," I said.

I got up and moved with the aid of the flashlight back out to Bella's antiseptically clean kitchen. Over the stove was a row of hooks, and from the hooks hung a set of skillets.

Three of them, from smallest to large, all cast iron. Only the fourth, the very biggest one, was missing. I returned to the living room.

"Bella has a car," I said. A crossword puzzle book fell off the arm of the chair to the floor. "She could've gone to Lubec."

"Uh-huh," Ellie agreed. "And if Jim was threatening her, but she couldn't get the police to take the idea seriously . . ."

". . . she could have killed him," I finished Ellie's sentence. "I mean, if she was really afraid of him. But Bob Arnold said Jim didn't have any record of crimes against persons."

"It could be that was only because she never complained about him," Ellie countered. "He could have beaten her up every day of the week and twice on Sundays when they were married, but without a complaint the cops wouldn't even have known about it."

A thought out of left field struck me. "Sam says Jim Diamond was Kris's stepfather."

Unlike me, Ellie had grown up in Eastport. She was generally well supplied not only with the latest gossip, but also with the equivalent of its back issues.

"Yes. Bella and Jim got married before you moved here. Kris was eleven or so," she said. "I don't think she ever knew her real father. Bella changed Kris's last name."

"So if Jim did abuse Bella, Kris would have witnessed it. And she strikes me as the type who might do something about it if she thought something like that was starting to happen again."

"I suppose so," Ellie said doubtfully. "If *she* thought he was sending Bella the notes..."

"Then *she* could've flown off the handle and bonked him. But why would he?" I puzzled frustratedly. "Threaten Bella at all, I mean. He just got out of jail, we know harassment is a crime, and probably he did, too. So my question is, what *motive* could *he* have had for..."

"Especially if she was already giving him money," Ellie agreed. I'd already mentioned this point to her on the way over here, that Jim was getting money from somewhere if only to pay for that apartment.

"Because why would he threaten a person who was helping him financially?" Ellie went on rhetorically.

Another shadow moved on the curtains. "Yep. But we're not *sure* she was."

In fact at that point we weren't sure of anything; we were just tossing ideas around and both of us knew it. "What'd he go to jail for, anyway?" I asked.

"Check forging," Ellie replied promptly. "A lot of it."

"Huh. Do you know if he was working at the time?"

But I was willing to bet he was, even before Ellie confirmed it. Because back when I was a hotshot money professional instead of a struggling old-house fixer-upper, I'd turned a few scam artists upside down to shake the secrets out of them. And what I'd learned was that to be a successful check forger you don't just steal checks, sign your name to them, then go out and cash them.

That way spelled ruination. To run the scam correctly you needed business checks, plus a way to manipulate the business's accounts-payable operations. I explained it to Ellie.

"You mock up phony invoices to the business you work for, pretend to pay them, but write the checks to *yourself* instead."

Ideally you've also established an account with a bank where people don't know you well, so you can deposit the checks in your own name without a lot of pesky questions. Whereupon you're good to go until someone tumbles to your scheme.

And that could take a while. "But we already said Jim Diamond wasn't very smart," Ellie objected.

"You don't have to be smart, just nervy enough to do it." Because if you were smart, you'd realize your scam couldn't work forever. But check forgers never do.

Realize it, I mean. "Also, you need a cold heart. Someone's got to trust you, and you've got to betray that trust."

And speaking of banks... in a delayed reaction, the sight of that blood-drive literature on Bella's kitchen table popped a sudden memory of bank manager Bill Imrie into my head, doing an about-face in the middle of Water Street a week earlier.

At that point we hadn't even known that Jim Diamond was dead yet, but the fact that his ex-wife Bella was connected to my household must already have been pretty much common knowledge around town.

Hey, everything else about me was. At the time I'd figured maybe Bill just hated needles as much as I did. But...

"Ellie, was Bill Imrie in town back when Jim went on trial? And was Bill working at a bank?"

"Uh-huh. He'd been away in college, but by then he was back. He was a part-time teller at..."

She named a local financial institution.

"Fascinating," I commented, wondering if maybe it *wasn't* the Red Cross blood-drive lady Bill Imrie had been trying to avoid.

If instead maybe it was me.

Meanwhile Ellie was following another train of thought. "Bob Arnold could've been wrong about Jim," she said. "He might've had someone else write the notes, even deliver them for him."

She sat up straight. "Who knows, maybe Jim was the kind of guy who could come up with an accomplice if he needed one."

"Right, or..." But the rest of the thought eluded me, and by then I was only half listening anyway. I was watching that curtain again.

Another shadow shifted stealthily on it. This time the shadow wasn't branch-shaped. It was human-shaped, and as I gazed at it, it moved toward the front door.

Putting a finger to my lips I got up, crossed to the entry, and waited until I heard footsteps on the front porch.

Then I *yanked* the door open. "All right, now, dammit..."

A figure stood there, hands drawn up in startlement. "Stop right there!" I ordered.

Then I realized who it was. "Maggie?"

"Jake, what are *you* doing here?" The girl peered past me as Ellie switched a lamp on.

"I saw your car," Maggie managed breathlessly, still getting over the surprise of being confronted so suddenly. "I was driving by, and then I saw lights in here go on and off, so I–"

"Oh, for heaven's sake," I snapped, exasperated. "We were just waiting to see if someone..."

But then I stopped, because we'd been waiting here in case someone showed up at Bella's house, someone with no good reason to be here.

And someone had.

Maggie.

"I haven't been sleeping well," Maggie confessed a short while later. "So I've been going out and driving around."

Because of the recent breakup with Sam, she meant. Because her heart was broken.

I'd taken a few moments at Bella's to do some things around the house, on the steps, and under the windows. Then we'd gone to Ellie's place with Maggie following in her own car.

"Just driving and thinking," she went on now. "It's the only way I can calm myself down. Sometimes if I go far enough, I can even sleep afterward."

She sat in the rocker by the woodstove in Ellie's cozy, low-ceilinged kitchen while Ellie put the kettle on. It was just past midnight and George was already upstairs, asleep.

"You poor thing," I said, hearing the false note in my own voice. But Maggie was too upset to notice it.

"I'm sorry if I messed up whatever you were doing." She put a hand to her forehead. "Oh, I'm just making a fool of myself!"

Right, but was that all? Suddenly I wasn't so sure.

"I'm going to check the baby," Ellie said, with a transparent glance at me.

When she was gone I leaned toward Maggie. An air of safety seemed to envelop us, with the kettle beginning to simmer and a lamp burning low on a shelf in the corner of the room, its bright rag rugs and gingham curtains creating a familiar haven.

"Maggie, *are* you sure that's all you were doing? Just out driving?"

She hesitated, drawing her sweater around herself, seeming to take comfort in her surroundings.

Me, too. Bella's place was cleaner, I supposed. Since the baby arrived, Ellie's house had a slapdash air as if cared for by the cheerful warden of an unusually pleasant insane asylum.

But an operating room was clean also, and that didn't make it cozy. Ellie had a way of taking a tag-sale table, plunking a square of gingham and a green glass jug of wildflowers on it, and making it look like *House Beautiful.*

"Maggie," I persisted, "is there anything you need to . . . ?"

Tell me, I'd meant to finish. Such as that maybe Maggie was persecuting Kris Diamond, trying to get at her through Bella in some way I didn't yet understand.

That maybe that's what the threatening notes were all about, and it was Maggie we'd been waiting for in Bella's house.

But I didn't complete my question; her furious glance said she had already caught my drift and wasn't happy about it.

"Look, no one's going to hold your feelings against you," I said. "Whatever they are. But I need to know what's going on."

Maggie didn't like that, either. "Against *me?* That's a hot one."

She sat up straight, brushing her thick, dark braid back over her shoulder. "You know what kind of girl Kris is. I don't understand why you don't do something about *her.*"

Ellie came back with a sleepy-looking Leonora in her arms, and began fixing a bottle as Maggie got to her feet.

"I told you why I was there. I saw your car, I saw lights, I thought you might be in trouble so I came to find out. And that's all there was to it."

She sounded truthful. It was one of the things I loved about Maggie, that she was as transparent as a glass of springwater.

And as unlikely to be harmful. But now, as I listened to her, a whole host of unwelcome thoughts washed through my mind.

It would have been easy for her to learn that Bella and Kris were out of town, especially if this wasn't the first time she'd been watching their home. As for motive, if Bella were frightened enough to move away, Kris would probably go, too, since as far as I knew the girl had no other means of support.

So could that have been what the whole anonymous-threat deal was about? To scare Bella and Kris out of Eastport?

And then there was the matter of a car just like mine being spotted in Lubec. . . . But one thing at a time:

"Maggie," I asked her straight out, "was it you who sent Bella Diamond those threats?"

No one had told Maggie anything about them, that I knew of. But if she was behind them, then of course she would know what I meant. Waiting for her answer I watched her face for tiny changes that might mean she was composing a lie.

But she just gazed at me, her lips sorrowful and her usually ruddy cheeks pale with distress.

And didn't reply. "I'm sorry," she said instead. "I know I'm not taking things well. It's just that I know what she'll do to him, I know what she is, and–"

"What?" I broke in, unable to help myself. Because one thing I did believe was that this girl truly loved my son, even if love was screwing her up in a way I hated seeing.

Once again, she didn't give me a straight answer. "I'm not going to talk about it anymore," she said with sudden resolve. "What's the point? You'll just think I'm bad-mouthing Kris to get Sam back." She sighed ruefully. "And maybe I am. Maybe she'll be great for him, and I'm the one who needs her head examined."

The kettle shrieked, startling us all. Ellie got up, handing the baby to me as Maggie snatched her car keys from the table.

"Maggie, don't go. Have some tea with us. We'll talk it over and . . ."

I wanted to ask her about the notes again, and about my car, too. But she didn't let me.

"No. I've embarrassed myself enough." She shot a half-wary, half-apologetic look my way.

It was the wary part I didn't like, plus my sudden certainty that it *had* been my car in Lubec that day.

Not a tourist's car. Mine, because Maggie had driven it there the day Jim Diamond was murdered with a cast-iron skillet, a weapon that had almost certainly been taken from Bella's house.

"Anyway, I'm glad you two are all right," Maggie finished in subdued tones, and went out.

In the silence she left behind, Leonora stretched and settled herself in my arms, waving her tiny fists, her lips turned upward in a dreamy smile.

"So," I said after a moment.

"So," Ellie repeated vexedly. "And on top of everything else we don't know if someone showed up after we left. Someone who could be putting another note in that house right this minute and we might never find out."

"Oh, we'll find out," I said. "Bella will tell us. And unless I'm wrong we can find out how they got in, too."

I let Ellie take the baby, fished my own car keys out of my pocket. For our sleuthing errand Ellie had put on a navy jumper with a big pink rose embroidered on the bodice. Under it she wore a navy turtleneck, leggings, and moccasins with tassels, each tassel with a row of pink beads threaded onto it.

"Jake," she asked with a little smile, "what did you do?"

"Just took the ashes out of that woodstove of Bella's and spread some under each window," I replied innocently, "and on the front and back steps. If anyone did go in after we left, Bella's going to have a mess to clean up when she gets home. Maybe I'll even get to Bella *before* she cleans up, so I can tell her to preserve a footprint."

"Aren't you the sly one," Ellie commented appreciatively as she followed me outside.

In the driveway I paused. "But I'm starting to think there really might not be any more notes. Because it's just too coincidental, that skillet missing from Bella's." I voiced my worst thought. "Ellie, what if someone sent the notes to give Bella a good motive for killing Jim?"

"Sent the notes, stole the weapon, and used it on him. Then sat back to wait for Bella to be blamed. It could work, maybe..."

"In that case, no more notes will come. There's no need for them anymore. We've wasted our time at her house tonight."

Except for finding Maggie there. I didn't even want to think about that, much less mention it. But I had to.

"Maggie was in Lubec the same day Jim was attacked, too," I told Ellie. "She's not admitting it yet, but I'm sure of it." I went on to explain about the car.

"Oh, Jake," Ellie protested. "Surely there's some explanation. We both know her too well to think she could have..." She faltered.

"Clobbered Jim herself," I finished grimly. "And she's certainly got the least convincing motive of anyone, wouldn't you agree?"

"Yes. Killing Jim and framing Bella...well, it *might* get rid of Bella, if Bella really ended up being blamed," Ellie mused.

I couldn't believe we were even discussing it. "But getting Bella convicted of a crime wouldn't guarantee getting them *both* out of town."

"Right. If Kris got left here alone, it could drive her even further into Sam's arms than she *already* is," Ellie agreed.

"Exactly. She might even marry him, just as a meal ticket. And that would be the *opposite* of what Maggie wants."

"But Maggie might not have thought it all through that far," Ellie pointed out unhappily. "Still, I just can't believe...no, I *don't* believe it. She wouldn't, there *must* be some other..."

"I sure hope so." But at the moment I couldn't think of what it might be, and Maggie wasn't telling.

Ellie waited with the yard light on until I was in the car, before going inside. Glancing back, I saw the newly shingled roof of her house shining in the moonlight. The lamp in the kitchen went out and the one in the baby's room went on.

Then I drove home. At one in the morning the store windows along Water Street shone vacantly, not a soul around. At the fish pier the tugboats rode a high tide smooth as polished onyx. Down the bay, tiny lights twinkled on the bridge at Lubec.

Over it all hung a white, cold moon, as silent as the town. So silent that before I even turned onto Key Street up toward my house, I could already hear it: screaming.

Somebody was screaming.

As I crested the hill, the unmistakable strobing of a cop-car cherry beacon lit Key Street. It was pulled up in front of my house, the driver's door open and figures moving around it.

When I got nearer I saw who they were: Sam, Kris, and Bob Arnold. An icy little pulse of fear throbbed under my breastbone as the rest of me was already in Mom-mode: unnaturally calm in case I needed to remember how to get a bean out of a kid's nose, or how to tie a tourniquet. I pulled up and got out.

"...do that?" Sam was shouting at Kris. "You tell me! I just want to know how you could..."

Bob Arnold had stepped between them, but he wasn't having any luck shutting my son's mouth. Or Kris's, either.

"Don't be such a baby!" she snarled contemptuously. "Just a scared..."

"All right, now," Bob Arnold pronounced with authority. "I told you to cut it out."

Bob was ordinarily a calm, genial fellow. But he had a voice like a razor strop when he wanted one.

And he wanted one now. Sam stopped short and took a step back from the combat zone, which unfortunately was the middle of the street. The neighbors were watching from behind cracked shades or frankly between opened curtains.

"Yeah, tell him to keep his hands off me, too," Kris snapped when she saw Bob Arnold scolding Sam.

But this was a tactical mistake. Bob rounded on her. "You've had too much to drink, young lady. Go have a seat in the squad car."

She hesitated mulishly. "Go on," he repeated. "Considering what's happened in your family situation I *was* inclined to cut you some slack. Don't do anything to make me change my mind."

By now Wade was outside. "What's going on?" he asked with a stern glance at Sam, then approached Bob to find out the story.

"Mom," Sam said when he saw me bearing down on him. His hands spread in a bid for understanding.

Or mercy. Neither of which I was in the mood to grant. No resuscitation needed, apparently, but a good swift kick seemed fairly appropriate. "Mom, I was not drinking," he added hastily.

"Glad to hear it," I said, restraining myself. "So what is your excuse for fighting in the street? And what's that Kris said about keeping your hands off her? Sam, did you hit that girl?"

Never mind that I felt like slapping the fillings right out of *her* teeth, too. She wasn't my responsibility.

Sam was. He shook his head defensively. "She was hitting me so I pushed her away, that's all. I didn't—"

"Oh, great." Then another thought struck me. "What's Kris even doing here? I thought she was gone with Bella to . . ."

Sam's forehead furrowed. "You didn't know? They didn't go to the aunt's. They were all ready to, but . . ."

Just then Bob Arnold came over, Wade alongside him. Kris sat a few feet away in the squad car, the interior lights showing her bored, get-me-out-of-here expression, as if we were all just too annoying.

"Would somebody like to tell me what happened here?" I said.

Bob looked deeply unhappy, Sam was wearing the "someone else started it" look I'd last seen when he was seven years old, and Wade appeared ready to knock some heads together, preferably the ones belonging to the now-embattled young lovers.

Finally Bob spoke. "What I oughta do is yank 'em both in and slap on a misdemeanor apiece. But under the circumstances..."

"What circumstances?" I demanded. "Is it too much to ask that I be let in on what all of you seem to know?"

Wade put a hand on my shoulder. "Kris showed up here a little while after you left," he told me. "Very upset. I let her in, she wanted to see Sam, and they went out together."

"I know that much," I said impatiently. "I can see they must have..."

But then I realized: the threatening notes, Bella's erratic behavior, Jim's dead body. And the skillet...

That damned missing skillet. If I'd noticed it, the police investigators could, too. They'd have spoken with Bella, probably at her house, and noticed the empty space in her kitchen rack.

Only they wouldn't take an extra mental step and decide that Bella might have been framed. Why should they?

They'd just figure Bella had done it.

Bob confirmed my suspicions. "State cops have been keeping their investigation pretty much under wraps," he said.

Kris remained sitting in the squad car. Not protesting, not crying, not looking around to see if and when Bob Arnold might be coming to let her out. Just...sitting.

Her mother was sitting somewhere right now, too. And not somewhere good. All at once I felt an unwilling pang of sympathy for Kris Diamond, whether she deserved it or not.

"Putting the pieces together one by one," Bob went on, "the state boys were, asking questions nice and careful until they—"

"Bob," I broke in impatiently, "I know how careful they are. I'm a big fan of the meticulous investigation techniques used by the state police. But will you cut to the chase, please, and just tell me *what happened*?"

He pursed his lips briefly at me as if to say there was room in that squad car, and did I want it? But instead he went on.

"So they came up here, took Bella in for questioning in her ex's murder. And you know what that means," he added.

Yeah, I knew. It meant Bella was in deep and serious trouble, the kind she wouldn't have any idea how to deal with.

"But she isn't actually in custody? We can go get her when they're done with her?"

To my relief, he nodded. That meant they didn't have all they wanted yet. Not enough to arrest her and charge her.

They had just enough so that one little slip on her part could snap the trap shut. "All right," I said, coming to a decision.

I could worry later about what Bella might be saying and how to get her a lawyer if she needed one. "You go on inside," I told Sam in my best "I'm your mother and you'll do what I say" voice.

And to my astonishment, apparently it still worked. He swung around silently, stalked toward the house. The door slammed, and a moment later the light went on in his room upstairs.

I turned to Wade. From the look on his face I could tell he knew what I was going to say next, and didn't enjoy the prospect. Which was why what *he* said next took my breath away, as it always did when he stepped up to the plate so generously.

"Bob," he said. "About the girl." He angled his head at the squad car where Kris still sat.

"Yeah, I don't know what I should do about her," Bob agreed.

In the neighbors' windows the shades had quit twitching and most of the curtains were closed, as people figured out that all the excitement was probably over for the night.

I sure hoped so. Even with Wade being so good about it I was unsure how this was going to work out.

"I mean it's not like she's a kid or anything," Bob went on. "But I hate to just send her home alone."

"Listen," Wade said. "Why don't you just release Kris to us? She can stay here for the night and we'll go get Bella and bring her home, when the boys are done questioning her."

Bob looked as if he'd just been offered the grand prize in the Publishers Clearing House contest. "It'd be some nice to have her off my conscience," he said. "Though I doubt she'll make the sweetest guest, the mood she's in."

That was probably putting it mildly. The girl was a hellcat. But none of us felt easy about sending her home to an empty house. And it's like I said before. What goes around, comes around.

The trouble was, none of us had any idea that in this case it was going to come around so hard.

Chapter 7

Back in the house, the sight of the telephone reminded me again that Kris wasn't the only guest I would be dealing with in the near future.

In the past I'd listened with mild interest to stories of Eastporters whose relatives descended, bringing unusual sleeping habits, desires for hard-to-find brands of liquor, wish lists of scenic excursions requiring the map-reading skills of a jungle explorer, and the cheerful conviction that the hostess's kitchen was in fact a twenty-four-hour short-order grill.

But none of these tales had ever applied personally to me, so I decided to use Kris's presence as a sort of dress rehearsal. It didn't work out very well, though, since I wasn't rehearsing for the visit of a sullen five-year-old, and a tipsy one at that.

"You can wear these pajamas," I told Kris gently, handing her a pair of mine.

She snatched the set of flannels from my hand, wrinkled her nose at them, and flung them onto the guest room bed.

"Thanks," she said flatly, not meeting my gaze. "I have to go to the bathroom."

Yeah, I'll just bet you do, I thought uncharitably at her. But I pointed her in the right direction, at the same time offering a towel and washcloth.

"In case you want to clean up a little," I said with all the restraint I could muster when she looked impatiently at them.

"There's a new toothbrush in the cabinet over the sink," I added. She just smirked, took the pajamas, towel, and washcloth, and stomped down the hall.

"So I guess we're not up for any of that girlish heart-to-heart stuff tonight," I said aloud as she departed, but the only reply was the slam of the bathroom door.

While she was in there I turned one of the twin beds down and switched a lamp on, pulled the shades, and laid a quilt over the end of the bed in case she needed it.

Not that I expected her to appreciate that, either. But when she came back and saw it, she stopped short in the doorway.

I'd been working intermittently on the upstairs rooms over the previous winter, so it was the only guest room that had beds in it at the moment. The others lacked shades, chairs, dressers, and important sections of the walls and ceilings; they were, in a word, uninhabitable.

But this one, with its antique floral wallpaper, hooked rugs, and patchwork quilts spread prettily over the chenille bedspreads, resembled a room out of a happy, old-fashioned dream.

"You didn't have to do that," Kris said softly. "I can turn down my own blankets."

Still, she sounded like a child who was absolutely longing to be tucked in. "I know you can," I said after a moment. "Go to bed now. Is your head spinning? Are you going to be all right?"

"God, will you stop coddling me?" She climbed irritably into the bed and yanked the covers over herself. "I smoked some pot on the way home. It'll keep my stomach settled." She snapped the light out. But then, as I was about to pull the door closed, her voice came out of the darkness.

"Do you think my mother's going to be all right?"

I hesitated, wondering which she needed most: the truth, or a comforting lie?

In the end, though, I didn't give her either of those. For one thing, even I didn't know which was which.

"Wade or I will drive down to get her when she's finished," I told her. "We can talk in the morning about what's going to happen next."

I stepped back into the room. It smelled of forest from the blankets that had been in the cedar chest, and of sheets scented with lavender, and only the faintest sour whiff of alcohol.

So she'd used the toothbrush. "About everything that's going to happen," I added firmly, and left her to mull all the possible implications of that.

But she didn't mull for long because when I went back in a few minutes to check on her, she was already sound asleep with the quilt pulled snugly up around her shoulders and a tear glistening on her cheek.

The phone rang an hour later and it was Bob Arnold, to say that the state cops had called him as a courtesy. Bella was ready to come home.

"You want to go or should I?" Wade asked, looking up at me from the book he was reading: *Practical Shotgun Shell Reloading.*

"I'll go." It was three in the morning, neither of us had been able to sleep, and there was a ship due in port so he would be on the tugboat early tomorrow.

"You stay here," I added, angling my head at the ceiling, "in case the glitter twins up there decide to get frisky."

In his big chair by the fire with a plaid wool shawl on his broad shoulders, his stocking feet on a worn leather hassock, and the dogs at either side of him, Wade looked for a moment like a gentleman out of an English country hunting print.

"Jake, they're not children," he said gently. Meaning of course that if they got frisky it wouldn't be for the first time.

But I didn't care. I was still way too mad at them for the spectacle they'd made of themselves with their silly quarrel to want them to have any fun. Assuming I even wanted them to have any fun in the first place, which I didn't.

I still didn't know what they'd been fighting about; at their age it was probably little more than the equivalent of a playground spat, I thought unkindly. On the other hand, when I had Sam I'd been a lot younger than he was now, barely married long enough to wear my wedding ring to his christening.

"Well, try to keep them from swinging on the chandeliers, anyway," I replied, and went out.

The trip south to Machias went by in a flash: trees, fields, glittering water in the moonlight. Once a deer walked up to the edge of the road and gazed blankly at me, but I'd already passed him before he registered enough for me to do anything about him.

Like for instance not colliding with him. When I came out of the woods in East Machias the river had reached flood tide and a sea of cattails bristled on either side of the narrow bridge. Then after climbing the last long hill out of the river valley I was downshifting on the wide road into the village of Machias itself.

At the old redbrick courthouse I pulled into an empty spot in the parking lot. It was nearly dawn. The gray sky made cutouts of the trees and houses, and the daytime lights in the cell blocks of the county jail section of the building were coming on in a series of fluorescent blinks.

At the desk I stated my business to a bleary-looking night shift clerk, then waited on the wooden bench opposite the row of office doors. Moments later one of them opened and Bella came out looking ghastly, practically falling into my arms.

"Oh, thank you," she exhaled. "You can't imagine the things they're thinking about me. I answered all their questions, but it didn't seem to help any. They don't say it, but..."

Actually I could imagine. And I didn't like hearing that she had answered all their questions.

"Bella, shut up, okay? I mean it. You've talked enough for one night."

She drew back, affronted. But I just wanted to get her out of there before she could say anything else to dig the hole she was in even wider and deeper. And eventually she did come along with me, allowing herself to be put in the car and driven away.

"Bella, why didn't you tell me you'd been giving Jim money?" I asked when we'd crossed the Machias River again and were headed for home. If he didn't have another scam going, I thought it was the likely explanation. And if he had, he'd have had *more* money.

She jumped guiltily. Then she sighed. "I shouldn't have left it out. I know you were trying to help me."

Trees crowded the road on either side of us once more. Fifty yards off the pavement, you could be lost for hours or days.

"But I was ashamed for anyone to know I'd knuckled under to him. I thought if I gave him what he wanted, he'd stop bothering me. But," she added, "he didn't."

She sucked in a shuddery breath. "He just kept after me, and then the notes started and they could never catch him at it, and anyway they thought he couldn't have done it."

She turned, her face shadowy in the dashboard lights' glow. "Written," she clarified unnecessarily, "all those big words."

So she still believed Jim had been behind the threats. And she had probably told the police investigators so, too.

"They were fooled," she went on as we sped through the dawn, "and why ever shouldn't they be? It's no one's fault he was such a clever devil.

No one at all would've taken him any notice until he murdered me in my bed."

"Oh, now, wait a minute," I objected as we climbed through a series of winding curves. "Isn't that going a little far?"

As we rounded the last turn I had a clear look at a pileated woodpecker clinging to the side of a white pine. His huge crested head with its flash of bright red was like a danger flag.

"You may think so," Bella replied stiffly. "But I don't. I was the one married to him, after all."

To which I had no ready answer. Up until almost the day I divorced him, my friends thought Victor was the husband from the highest, most exalted level of heaven.

The few who weren't already sleeping with him, that is. We shot out onto a straightaway between a dairy farm and a paved lot where prefab houses sat on trailers, waiting to be delivered.

By now it was a little past five A.M. "What all else did you tell them, anyway?" I asked Bella. "The police, I mean."

Again she sighed wearily. "I told them what they asked. Why shouldn't I?" she added defiantly, "I've got nothing to hide."

Famous last words. "Did he threaten me," she said, "had I been there recently, could anyone say I'd been somewhere else at the time he was attacked. Whenever that was."

"And could anyone? Say you were elsewhere, that is?"

But she was right: It wouldn't be so easy coming up with an alibi for an attack whose timing was uncertain.

Bella just shook her head. "Except for when I was working at your house, I was alone."

As we crossed the causeway onto Moose Island, a heron sailed off toward the forested cliffs of the Shackford Head State Park.

"Bella, I hate to say this," I began as the bird's wingtips skimmed the water in the distance, "but you had a terrific motive to kill him. Having to give him money, thinking he was threatening you, that he might hurt you?"

She gazed morosely back out over the water on the causeway's other side. There a massive freighter idled waiting for clearance and for Wade to come and pilot her into port.

"Also," I said gently as we passed the long, flat expanse of Quoddy Airfield, "you *don't* seem to have any alibi. I mean, not even in a general way."

Her voice hardened. "That's right. Didn't know I was going to have to account for my time, did I? But I guess the worst part must have been the key. They looked very grim when I told them about that."

I glanced questioningly at her. "The one I had," Bella added, "to the door of Jim's apartment."

At this I just about drove off Water Street, down the dock, and right into Passamaquoddy Bay. "Bella, why in the world would you have a key to Jim's—"

"Home," she interrupted insistently. "I want to go home."

I'd been about to go the other direction, toward my house. There were more things I wanted to ask her, such as for instance whether they'd told her when she could expect to be in handcuffs.

And about that damned skillet; she hadn't mentioned it and I wondered if the police had. But she already had a death grip on the Fiat's door handle; I was pretty sure she'd just jump out if I didn't go where she said. So I followed her instruction.

"The key," I prodded. "Tell me about it, Bella. Now."

She sighed heavily. "When Jim got out of jail, he needed a place. He tried to move in with me, but I wouldn't let him."

We climbed Adams Street past the long uphill row of white frame houses, each with its neat square of green front lawn. "And no one would rent to him," she went on. "Because everyone knew where he'd been and what he was like."

A bully and a crook, recently released from jail. I could see why those might not be on a landlord's top ten list of desirable tenant characteristics. "So you vouched for him," I said as we pulled up in front of her house.

In daylight it looked even smaller and meaner than it had the night before. I thought about saying I'd been inside, decided not to.

Not yet. "And finally you found him a place in Lubec."

"I paid the deposit," she agreed in a monotone. "I told the landlord I'd be the responsible person on the lease. And I took a key, because if he skipped out–Jim, I mean–I promised I'd clean the place. After he was gone."

I shut off the Fiat's ignition. In the brightening light of summer morning on the island, the silence was pristine, the scent of beach roses floating sweetly in the still, clear air.

"So," Bella finished, "that's why I had a key. Making sure he had a place and a little money was the only way I could think of to make him stop coming around wanting something all the time. Which it didn't, anyway," she concluded miserably. "But thank you for coming to get me and–"

"I'm coming in with you. No, don't argue with me."

We got out of the car, Bella still insisting she didn't need anyone to accompany her inside.

"Humor me," I said, brushing off her protests. "And watch it. Looks like there's a patch of something on your doorstep."

It was the ashes I'd left there, undisturbed. Ignoring her curious glance at me I waited until she'd unlocked the door, then followed her in.

Here too the light of day was unkind. It showed worn carpets, old curtains faded from many washings, everything cheap but neat and orderly, and clean as a whistle.

Bella looked around disconsolately. "I'll have to make some kind of arrangements for Kris," she murmured. "I don't know what, but she can't be trusted living alone if they do really decide to . . ."

Her voice trailed off as she wandered into the kitchen.

There were no ashes on the rug. Nothing in the living room had changed from the way it had been when Ellie and I were here eight hours earlier. I picked up a book I hadn't examined before, noting that it was poetry.

"Do you have relatives she could stay with? Your aunt?"

A line from the first poem jumped out at me, assuring me that if I faced the void confidently, useful thoughts would ensue.

Yeah, sure they will, I replied mentally as I put the book down. Silence in the kitchen; I decided to wait until Bella had calmed down a little more before asking her about the missing skillet. "Or maybe you have some friends who could take her, until—"

A breathy scream of fear interrupted me. I ran, noting as I did so that there were no ashy shoe marks printed in the hall or leading from the bedrooms. In the kitchen the floor was unsoiled, too. But Bella leaned on the kitchen table with one hand.

The other, pressed to her heart, clutched a sheet of yellow notebook paper. "Another note," she gasped, thrusting it at me.

I looked around again. No ashes anywhere. Someone had been in here, but somehow had managed to avoid leaving any trace.

Except for the note, its cruel words gouged harshly into the paper as before. It was as if someone had known about the trap I had laid, and evaded it to taunt me.

"Oh, Missus," Bella moaned, her harsh features twisted in fear. "What am I going to do?"

"Bella," I said, "did you ever have one of those days when everyone seems to be trying to get your goat, just to prove that they can do it?"

She nodded, her lower lip trembling and her work-reddened hands in a palsy.

"Well," I said, "the good news is, I think two can play at that game. And as of this minute, I'm going to."

Maybe it was being tired, or being worried about Sam, or wondering how I would cope with a dozen visiting relatives. Or maybe it was knowing that somebody was laughing, thinking they'd made a fool of me. But start-ing now I intended to find out what was going on:

Jim Diamond's murder, the suggestion of Bella's involvement, the threatening notes, Maggie's worrisome behavior, and anything Kris might know about all or any of it, too...

In short, the whole intensely annoying mess. I was going to put a stop to it and never mind that so far, I had no idea how.

Something would come to me.

"So someone was there between the time we left and the time you brought Bella home," Ellie said thoughtfully.

I'd swung by to pick her up on my way back from Bella's, and we'd stopped to pick some of the wild strawberries ripening in the fields at the south end of the island overlooking the bay.

Gulls cried distantly in the wake of a small fishing boat. "Seems so," I said, popping one of the tiny fruits into my mouth. The baby was asleep on the backseat of the Fiat.

"And that means there's more going on than meets the eye. A sneaky in-truder who knew enough to avoid your trap..."

"*Nothing's* meeting my eye," I pointed out as another berry burst tartly on my tongue, its taste mingling with the fruity aroma of the lupine bloom-ing in tall purple spikes all around us.

"Nothing useful anyway," I added.

Ellie wore a yellow smock, a red T-shirt, yellow leggings, and green clogs over a pair of argyle socks. The effect was of an explosion at the Institute for Primary Colors.

And it was almost more good cheer than I could take under the circum-stances. I got up, feeling my knees creak with fatigue.

"You know, we said we weren't going to snoop in murders anymore," I reminded Ellie as we drove back toward downtown. "Now that you've got the baby..."

Out past the channel markers under a cloudless sky, the Deer Island ferry chugged through the swirling currents of the Old Sow whirlpool. "Are you firing me?" Ellie asked lightly.

"Of course not. But with Bella under suspicion, this could get a little hairier than we expected, that's all."

What I wanted was to give her a graceful out, if that's what *she* wanted. And I thought she might; before Leonora was born she had sounded pretty firm about it. But her answer surprised me.

"So let's just snoop in the notes," she replied, her tone disingenuous.

Hearing it while the ferry was on the whirlpool reminded me of the time I'd told Sam not to go out on the water. Later I'd learned that he'd made it to Campobello during one of the biggest storms that autumn. And when I confronted him about it he said he hadn't *been* on the water; he'd been on a *boat*.

But before I could draw any of the obvious parallels, Ellie stopped me.

"I know," she conceded, once again reading my mind. "This *is* all more complicated than we expected. But Jake, before Lee came I was full of ideas about how I would change when I was a mom. Everything was going to be different."

On Water Street, merchants swept doorways and climbed onto stepladders to water hanging baskets of petunias. In the pale morning light, a man tossed bundles of newspapers from a truck onto the sidewalk.

"Now that she's here, though, I'm not so sure that I should change," Ellie went on. "Because what if it just makes her think there are things *she* can't do, too?"

"You mean, when she's a mother?"

"No," she answered seriously. "Just because she's a girl."

I turned the corner onto Key Street. A trio of volunteers was painting and glazing the sashes of the big old redbrick public library's antique windows.

Ellie went on, "I mean, I don't want to get too overly..."

She paused, searching for the word.

"Militant?" I offered. We'd touched on this topic before.

"Right. Too militant. And I'm not going to wade into things foolishly, either. Especially not dangerous things. But George reminded me of something last night after you left, and it's got me thinking."

"About Jim Diamond?" At the top of the hill my own house came into view. *Porch steps, shutters, window screens, doorknobs,* I thought automatically.

And guest rooms. "No," Ellie replied. "About Bella. She has two brothers. George knew them in school, but I didn't."

"So? What've Bella's brothers got to do with anything?" I pulled into the driveway. Wade's truck wasn't there because he was on the freighter, or headed there. Sam's car was gone, too.

"Nothing directly," Ellie said as she unfastened Leonora from her car seat and lifted her. "But the brothers both went to college. One lives in a suburb outside Seattle now; he works for Microsoft. Other one's in Belgium, does something in gemstones."

"Ellie, I still don't see what that has to do with..."

Inside, pairs of clean cereal bowls, juice glasses, and coffee cups stood on the drainboard. Apparently Kris and Sam had breakfasted together.

"Guess they made up their quarrel," Ellie observed.

Sure, I thought, *why let a little screaming match out in the street get in the way of True Love?*

Monday and Prill trotted in to say good morning while Cat Dancing scowled cross-eyed from atop the refrigerator. Meanwhile I went on noticing transparent efforts to get on my good side.

There was coffee in the carafe and a note on the table from Sam: He'd fed the animals and taken the dogs out. The counter had been wiped, the floor swept, and the bread and cereal put away.

Still, I wasn't placated. When he knew I was mad at him Sam always went on super-fine behavior; after the boat-in-the-storm incident he'd made his bed, cleared the dinner table, and taken the trash out every day for two whole weeks.

After which he'd forgotten all about it, this being another way in which he resembled his father. "Wait here a minute," I told Ellie, and went upstairs.

The air smelled of shaving cream, mouthwash, and the faint steamy aroma of showers having been taken recently; not together, I hoped, but I wouldn't have been surprised. Drops of moisture ran on the bathroom mirror and damp towels crammed the hamper.

Sam's room was empty. So was Kris's.

Which was a relief. I wanted to talk with her about drinking in front of Sam; after all, somebody had to and he clearly wasn't going to do it.

But right now at least I didn't have to see her pinched face confronting me smugly while she explained to me that her behavior—and Sam's, she surely believed—was none of my business.

Then I saw the note written in what looked like eyeliner pencil, lying on her bed. *Thank You,* it said. She'd stripped the bed, too, and bundled up the linen, placing it on the floor.

The message and her unexpected delicacy about the sheets weren't what struck me most, though. That dubious honor was reserved for the material she'd written her message on.

It was a small, nondescript sheet of yellow notebook paper, just like the one Bella had found a little earlier on her kitchen table. On the other side was a short shopping list: nail polish remover, cuticle cream, breath mints.

I carried it downstairs where Ellie took one glance at it and absorbed the possible implications in a visible mental gulp.

"My, this looks familiar," she said. But as usual her next reaction was pure common sense. "The writing isn't the same as on Bella's note, though. And anyone can get this kind of paper."

"The writing on Bella's note could have been disguised," I pointed out.

"By Kris? Just because it's the same kind of notepaper? But I don't see why she might..."

"Try to scare Bella? Or worse, implicate her? Me either," I said. A sigh escaped me. "And you're right, it probably doesn't mean anything. So go on, finish your story."

Whereupon Ellie did, but there wasn't much more. The gist of it was simply that Bella's two brothers had both gone away to college and made lives for themselves, but she hadn't.

And now she was barely supporting herself. "Maybe she just didn't have the smarts for more school," I suggested.

But Ellie shook her head. Bella, she pointed out, had brains enough to survive here in Eastport, where just figuring out how to make a living—with or without a college education—could be a task as challenging as translating the Rosetta Stone.

"It wasn't about smarts. The *boys* went to school. The *girl* stayed home. It was what girls did and sometimes still do, that's all," Ellie said flatly.

I still didn't understand what she was getting at. "Even," she added, "me."

Which was when I got it, finally. "And what goes around comes around?" I asked.

Of course; the phrase was becoming my theme song. Or mantra. Whatever. "Even on to the next generation, sometimes?"

"Yes," Ellie replied. "Because think about it, Jake: After high school no one said a word to me about going to college. My dad needed me at home to help with my mother, and that was that."

Ellie's mother, whom I had known, had been a manipulative bitch. There is simply no other way to describe her. But her dad had helped things get bad at the end, there, too.

"So I stayed," she said. "Not that I'm sorry now. But if I'd been a boy..."

"It wouldn't have occurred to anyone to think you ought to," I finished for her. "Much less criticize you, as people certainly would have if you'd gone away."

"Exactly. It didn't occur to *me* to do anything else, see?"

Of course I did. The idea of options hadn't occurred to me, either. It was why I'd run away all those years ago, because running was the only choice I'd thought I had.

"So I did what was expected of me," Ellie continued. "More to the point, what I expected of myself. And if you think that it doesn't happen that way anymore, just look around."

Right. At the way Maggie kept waiting for Sam, for instance, putting up with whatever he dished out.

"I can't let it be that way again," Ellie said, looking down at Leonora. "I won't take foolish risks. Like I said before she was born, doing that would be a sin."

She brushed the baby's fine hair back tenderly. "And maybe we won't find out who's writing Bella those notes, or get her out of the trouble she's in. Right now I'm sorry to say it doesn't look as if we will. But we can still try, Jake."

At Ellie's touch Leonora woke and began squirming, waving her tiny fists enthusiastically at the great big world.

"And think about something else for a minute," Ellie added. "What if money wasn't *all* Bella gave Jim?"

I'd filled Ellie in on the things Bella had said on the way home, but now I must have looked confused.

"I mean," she explained, "Jim comes out of jail with nothing. He starts wanting money from Bella, money she doesn't really have. Anything else he needs, she might have to buy. Right?"

"Oh," I said, the light dawning. "And that would cost more money, wouldn't it? So Bella takes care of whatever she can some other way. By, for instance, giving him things of hers?"

"Exactly," Ellie said. "So maybe the skillet *was* Bella's at one time, but..."

When Victor moved up here I'd given him a coffeepot and a whole set of steak knives. Of course, giving him the knives was at least partly to keep myself from using one on him.

But the principle was the same. As for the small pan Jim *had* been cooking in, maybe he simply hadn't felt like dirtying a big skillet for one little pork chop.

"So the skillet could have been there all along," I said slowly. "In his place."

"Instead of someone else getting it somehow and using it on him, maybe to frame *her*," Ellie agreed.

"But in that case why hasn't *she* mentioned it?"

"Well, does she even know what the weapon was?" Ellie asked reasonably. "You're assuming the police told her, but they might not have. Even she would know enough to ask for a lawyer if they pushed her too hard."

By for instance accusing her of owning the murder weapon. Ellie was right; the police might not have wanted to tighten the screws so much.

"She has no money, so she's probably not going anywhere," I said. "They can afford to take their time."

"In fact," Ellie said, "last night's interview could've been meant just to throw a scare into her. To see what she'd do or say."

"Could be," I agreed again. Damn, why hadn't I asked Bella about the missing frying pan?

Although I knew the answer to that. When I'd left her, Bella had been cleaning up wood ashes, weeping intermittently, and muttering to herself. I couldn't have gotten the time of day out of her.

"What we need," I said, "is more information."

"Right," Ellie agreed. "And meanwhile, *I've* decided I can't let my own example be the biggest obstacle in this kid's life."

Leonora blinked slowly up at her mother. "Because for that," Ellie finished in determined tones, "you really do go to hell."

She hefted her daughter affectionately. "So come on, kid," she said. "We've still got most of the morning left and it's time for our walk. Let's get out there, maybe even capture an evildoer or two before they're all gone."

I got up also, infected by her optimism. It wasn't the worst way I could think of to avoid going to hell.

But I'd probably have argued more with her if I'd known how soon we were going to be in purgatory. Also, I was seduced by her belief that our snooping would be relatively risk-free.

Looking back on it now, though, all I can say is...

Not.

Chapter 8

After Ellie left, I headed upstairs to despair some more over my upcoming holiday company. On the third floor I stowed away all the painting gear, since if you couldn't sleep on it or bathe in it, it would be of no use when the relatives descended.

Next I visited the two unfinished second-floor rooms where I was going to have to lodge most of the visitors in some sort of comfort. This might've even been possible if they were willing to sleep on mattresses on the floor.

And if the rooms had floors. Too bad that in a burst of old-house-beautiful ambition I'd taken a crowbar to the linoleum that someone had cemented to those floors, a hundred years ago.

I'd hoped to find hardwood under the linoleum; instead I'd discovered water stains and sawdust. At one time there'd been a leak: as a result, the joists were so rotten that only the linoleum had kept the furniture from falling through to the room below.

Now I sadly regarded the exposed floor joists, so hideously in need of reinforcement that a person trying to sleep in here would have to hang from the ceiling light fixture like a bat. Just then Wade came in and found me gazing at the mess.

"You're home early," I said in surprise.

He shrugged. "Boat's got a paperwork problem." Since the World Trade Center disaster, security at the port had tightened. "Take 'em a few hours, get it straightened out. You poor thing," he added, massaging my shoulders gently. "You're sure they've got to stay here?"

It seemed that as he was coming home from the tugboat pier, he'd met Ellie on the street and she'd given him a heads-up about the long-lost-relatives problem.

"There won't be anywhere vacant," I said hopelessly. "By now even a spot at the campground has a waiting list a mile long."

He rested his chin atop my head, surveying the mess. Bare lath dribbled out crumbs of old plaster from the walls; most of it had fallen and I'd torn down a lot of the rest. Same with the ceiling, a cracked horror when I began trying to put it back up; in the end I'd cried uncle on that, too, because each time I got one section fastened securely, another came loose.

Winter, I'd decided optimistically. I would work on it next winter. But now . . .

"You told your dad yet?" Wade asked.

"No. He hasn't been here yet today."

The extent of the problem crashed over me. "Oh, Wade. What should I do? I can't put his folks in the yard in tents," I wailed.

For one thing, Eastport weather is tricky even in summer. It could be eighty degrees on the Fourth, or fifty and foggy. Also I still had no idea what my father's reaction would be.

He hadn't gotten in touch with them, once it was safe to. So maybe he didn't want to see them. Maybe he would *hate* the idea of their visit.

Wade's hands stopped moving on my shoulders, but I was too preoccupied to really notice. "I've got to find a way to feed them, amuse them, and oh, dear heaven, what about bathing arrangements?"

Why, with all these bedrooms, had no one ever thought about putting in even one more bath? We got along on a routine of politeness and staggered schedules, but that wouldn't work for a dozen guests.

"I'll have to farm them out," I said resignedly. "If worse comes to worst, Bob Arnold can put men in bunk beds in the holding cells at the police station."

With any luck they would be cheerful types and think it was an adventure. Otherwise—

"I might have a better solution," Wade said thoughtfully.

But I wasn't really listening. "Although I still don't know what to do about food. Bella can cook but she'll almost certainly be behind bars by then, and it'll be like feeding an army."

Dinah from the home-help agency had already said they were all booked up. So I wouldn't be able to hire anybody at this late date to assist in the kitchen.

"I will," I groaned, "just have to try." But try what?

Wade patted my shoulders comfortingly. "Look, you handle the food part and leave the roof-over-their-heads part of it to me, all right? And," he added firmly, "the bathrooms part."

"Wade, you're in the middle of roof work at George and Ellie's. You don't have time to do guest room repairs, too."

Besides, Wade's idea of company was a bunch of his buddies at his remote lakeside camp: watching a ball game on a battery-powered TV, eating pizzas from an enormous stack of them, burning the cardboard cartons in the woodstove, and traipsing outside to answer the call of nature. I wasn't sure what he'd do for houseguests but it wouldn't be ironed linen sheets, I knew that much.

"Go downstairs, now," he said with a mischievous smile. "I'm going to take care of it. All the comforts of home. Really, Jake, I will."

And when I still hesitated, he added: "By the way, Bella's here. When I left she was getting ready to scrub the pattern right off the kitchen countertops."

Oh, good heavens, at least I'd thought I was safe from her for the day. Instead I hurried down just in time to keep her from pouring a jug of bleach into the kitchen sink to disinfect it. Apparently her overnight experiences had reactivated her cleaning hysteria with a vengeance.

"Bella, put that down," I commanded her, wondering in annoyance why she couldn't have developed a carpentry obsession instead.

On the other hand, now was my chance. "When we were in your house earlier, I noticed there's a skillet missing. A big cast-iron skillet, from the set of them hanging over your stove. What happened to it?"

"Never had that one," she replied, still standing at the sink. "Bought the others separately, couldn't afford the largest one."

Simple answer. Plausible, too; those things are expensive. But it set off all my coincidence alarms again.

Big skillet at Jim's house, none at hers, and she says she never had one. I wondered if it was true and I meant to question her more closely. But when she turned to me I saw she was crying, which in her position I supposed I might have been doing also.

"Never mind," I told her. I could cross-examine her later. For now I meant to ask her instead to go upstairs, empty the bathroom hamper, and strip the rest of the beds. It would probably make her feel better and she could use some of that bleach, I thought uncharitably, on Kris's linens.

Before I could speak, though, there was a knock on the back door, and it was that pesky Red Cross lady again, wanting to come in. And you have to watch out in Eastport about giving people the cold shoulder; the next time you meet them they might be sitting across from you at a church supper.

So I curbed my impatience even though I was so tired, I felt as if I'd donated several gallons of blood already that morning.

"They've sent us out again," the woman said apologetically, "to visit anyone who indicated any receptiveness the first time."

Her hair looked fresh from the beauty parlor and her makeup was lovely, candy pink lipstick and creamy-looking face powder. A whiff of 4711 cologne drifted from her as I let her inside.

"Hello," she greeted Bella pleasantly. Her nails were done, and as before she was perfectly dressed: white blouse, tailored slacks, navy cardigan. "What they'd like to know is whether *you* know anyone *else* who might be interested in donating," she told me.

Seeing her reminded me again of noticing her on Water Street just as bank manager Bill Imrie had begun crossing the street toward her. At which point, he had abruptly reversed course.

Now it occurred to me that I really ought to talk with Bill about Bella's problem, first because the details of Diamond's check forging were probably known to him; it was just the kind of thing bank people would gossip about.

And second, because I wanted to rule out the notion that had struck me about it later: that his quick about-face *wasn't* from a desire to keep a Red Cross blood donation needle out of his arm.

That instead he'd wanted to avoid *me*.

It was unlikely, but probably it *was* something I could learn for sure, which would be a nice change from the way everything else had been going, lately. So I left the Red Cross lady telling Bella why she should persuade her friends to become a pint low right along with her, and went into the telephone alcove.

Sunlight slanted in through the wavery old panes of the dining room windows, glinting on the freshly polished andirons in the fireplace. Bella would have climbed right up the chimney to scrub the flue if I hadn't stopped her. And the room did look as lovely in the daytime as it did by candlelight, except where she'd taken some of the finish off the hearth tiles while rubbing them with kitchen cleanser. I reached for the phone; the bank was open on Saturdays until noon.

"Hello, Bill?" I began when after a minute or so the bank's canned "on-hold" music ceased and he came on the line.

"Good morning, Jacobia." Cordial enough, though in his voice I was certain I heard an undercurrent of something.

He was busy, probably. So I got right to the point. "Bill, a question has come up over here and I thought you could probably answer it for me pretty efficiently."

"Right." His tone didn't soften one iota. "So what can I do for you?"

Huh. Bill was a crispy critter this morning. But there could still be a lot of reasons. . . .

"Well, I'm trying to help Bella Diamond out of a pickle. You know her ex-husband has, um, passed away very suddenly."

Which I thought was a reasonably acceptable polite code for *bashed on the noggin fatally.*

"Yeah, I heard. What's your question?"

I sat up straighter. Bill wasn't busy. Bill was ticked off.

"I need to know details of the crime he was convicted of a few years ago, that he went to prison for."

Silence on the phone. "The check forging he got caught at," I persisted. "Probably it's got nothing to do with his death, but just for completeness, I thought . . ."

"Why are you asking me?" Now he sounded irritated.

Irritated, and a little scared. Which was when I decided he *had* changed direction to avoid me, the other day in the street.

It still made no sense. But when I was a money pro, people used to acquire whole new identities to avoid me, and transfer those identities to new addresses on other continents, after they had defrauded clients of mine and were trying—with no success whatsoever, I might add—to get away with their shenanigans.

So I knew that tone of voice.

"Bill, I don't expect you to be able to give me a chapter-and-verse. But I figured you're probably familiar with it in general terms, so you might know how Jim Diamond did it, and who else was involved."

There was another vast silence on the phone. Out in the kitchen the Red Cross lady went on telling Bella how to explain the details of blood donation to her friends, with special emphasis on the no-pain part of the deal.

Sure, that's what *they* say. My arm tingled just imagining it as I sat there with silence coming out of the telephone.

The silence went on. Still, I figured maybe Imrie wanted to think before he spoke. Being a bank manager did involve a certain amount of conversational prudence.

That, anyway, was the charitable explanation. But eventually it dawned on me: He wasn't going to say anything at all, because the silence wasn't Bill Imrie thinking about what to say.

It was a dead phone line.

Apparently at my question about Jim Diamond's past crime, the prudent local bank manager had taken an extremely imprudent action.

He'd hung up on me.

Eastport's branch office of the National Bank of Lewiston was located in a new cedar-and-glass building down by the water, on the spot where a sardine-canning factory used to be. I pulled into the parking area next to where the old foundation had been made into a garden of hardy shrubs, their loam still studded with glassy cinders from the canning factory's coal furnace.

Inside the bank I shot a look at Bill Imrie, who was at one of the teller's windows. Once I had his attention I strode into his office and closed the door firmly behind me.

The office featured pale textured wallpaper and bland art, as if it had come in a kit labeled "Contents: one office." I sat in the client chair, doubting I'd have to wait long; the look I'd given Imrie could've melted those cinders out in the yard.

Moments later he entered, trying to appear unflustered. "You know," I said mildly, "I'm not accustomed to being hung up on."

"Jacobia," he began, "we must've gotten disconnected. I was trying to call you back, and—"

"Shut up, Bill," I interrupted pleasantly. But the effect wasn't pleasant. I hadn't meant it to be.

"Seeing as you've been silly enough to let me know you have something to hide in the Jim Diamond situation..."

He bridled, precisely as a person ought to when unjustly accused. But Bill was a young man, maybe only twenty-five or so, with thick curly blond hair and eyes that had not yet learned to hide what was going on behind them.

"Oh, cut it out," I told him. "You're not fooling anyone. I used to eat guys like you for breakfast."

A mournful look came onto his face. "Look, I panicked," he admitted. "That's why I hung up. You surprised me, and I didn't know what to say."

He took a deep, unhappy breath. "Because the thing is, it hasn't come up for a long time, all that business with Diamond, and I'd thought finally that..."

That it had all gone away, whatever it was that he wanted so badly not to talk about. I almost felt sorry for the poor guy. But not so sorry that I quit fishing around pretty aggressively.

"Want to tell me?" I asked. "I can keep a secret. Or I could start talking your part in the Jim Diamond business around town, get the gossip mill started up again. Just," I added sweetly, "the little that I know already."

Which was nothing. But *Bill* didn't know that. He took the hook so fast I thought I might lose a finger.

"All right, all right," he agreed at once. "But you've got to promise to keep me out of it, whatever's going on now. And I'm not talking about it here, either," he added.

I frowned inquiringly at him. Bill explained. "I know you found Jim's body, and by now so does everyone else in Eastport. And a lot of them are bank customers."

"And you think just from my being here they'd think you were involved? Isn't that kind of a stretch?"

"Maybe. But maybe not."

Interesting. "I'll be leaving at noon," he went on.

I indicated that lunchtime would work. "You know where my place is?" he asked. "Kendall's Head Road, a mile out on the left?"

I knew, but I let him elaborate while I went on sizing him up: broad shoulders, evenly carved features, a crooked grin with just the right amount of boyish mischief in it.

That is, I'd noticed the grin on other occasions. He wasn't wearing it now. And from the level of his discomfort it occurred to me that maybe Bill Imrie was about to offer some eye-opening revelation about the recently deceased Jim Diamond, perhaps something that violated the banker's code of conversational prudence.

But instead it turned out to be about himself.

Kendall's Head Road climbed precipitously from Route 190 onto the bluffs overlooking Passamaquoddy Bay. On the water side, summer places perched on stilts over the hillside, while older dwellings occupied the gentler-sloped side of the curving road.

A mile from the turnoff I pulled onto a paved drive leading down into a little valley. A neat white farmhouse with a long glassed-in porch and a row of sharply gabled windows sat at the end of the drive, which opened into a macadam parking area in front of a well-kept small red barn.

A pair of goats stood placidly cropping the grass in the fenced yard adjacent to the garage; as I got out of the car, Bill Imrie was filling their water trough with a garden hose.

"Hey," he said resignedly at the sight of me. "I'll be done in a minute. Go on inside if you want. Make yourself at home."

In the bright glassed-in porch he'd started tomato plants in cardboard milk cartons and geranium cuttings in Styrofoam cups of rich black dirt, ready to be planted outdoors. Through the side windows I could see a strawberry bed with the straw mulch pulled back from it, and a row of raspberry canes.

Nice place. Taking his advice about making myself at home to heart, I went on into a neat, bright kitchen, opening the fridge to discover that Bill followed a healthy low-fat diet. Then I had a brief, moderately instructive tour of the rest of the house.

The two upstairs bedrooms were pleasant but unrevealing. In the bathroom, however, I found a short white terry bathrobe on a hook behind the door, and a few makeup items in the small wicker basket on the commode.

So Bill had a girlfriend. From the window I spotted him on his way in and hurried back downstairs. By the time I reached the porch again he was pulling rubber shoe-covers off his wing-tips and dusting his hands together.

"Bill," I said sincerely, "this is all very lovely."

I waved at the freshly mowed green lawn, apple trees whose pruning looked to be right out of an arborist's textbook, and the garden plot, newly tilled and ready for those tomato plants.

"Do you do it all alone?" I asked.

"Yeah. This was my folks' home. They passed away some time ago." But not long enough ago for grief to have eased entirely, I saw from his pained expression.

"I'm sorry, I didn't know," I said into an awkward silence.

He managed a smile. "It's okay. I should probably sell the place. Just can't seem to get my mind around doing it, though. So I guess I'll wait for prices to go up, maybe get some out-of-town millionaire to take it off my hands someday."

He tried for a laugh, missed by a mile. "Come on in, Jacobia."

I followed him through another door into an old-fashioned farmhouse parlor. White curtains were tied back from sparkling windows, hooked rugs were spread on the wide-plank pine floors, and two maple rockers were pulled like a pair of old friends up to the enameled woodstove.

It was like a polished shrine to a bygone way of living, but with a startlingly luxurious element. The upstairs furniture had been ordinary stuff, but every piece here had been handbuilt out of what looked like rock maple, designed with an artist's eye by some kind of furniture genius, and created by a real craftsman.

"Bill?" I said, looking around. "Did you do this?"

It hadn't been bought anywhere around here, of that I was certain. You couldn't buy things like this at all, in fact, or even dream about them, unless you happened to be that millionaire Bill had been talking about.

He looked genuinely pleased for the first time. "No. My dad. He drove a truck for the town, plowed snow in the winter, fixed roads. All that kind of thing. But in his off time..."

He waved simply at the astonishing items of furniture. Owls' heads were carved into the knobs of the rockers' arms, feather by feather. Tables stood on legs made to look like fresh birch bark, down to the tiniest knot-hole.

"He liked working with wood," Bill said, setting two cups of coffee on a tray before us.

Uh-huh. And the Wright brothers had liked tinkering around with airplanes.

"I'll show you the sawmill later if you want," he went on. "I still use it pretty much the way my dad did, cutting hardwood for furniture makers, instrument builders, and so on."

He swallowed some coffee. "Hobby of mine. But now I think we'd better get down to business." He raised the subject as if it were medicine and he knew he had to take it.

"All right, look," I said, "I'm not trying to jam you up in any way. I just thought you might know what Jim did, that got him sent to jail for check forgery. I mean, *exactly* what he did."

Bill laughed, not happily. "And you came to me because...?"

On a hunch, because you avoided me, I thought.

But I didn't want to say that. Let him go on thinking maybe I knew more than I did. That way he might be less likely to lie.

"Well, the phony checks had to get cashed somehow," I evaded, "and no bank would do that if they *knew* the checks were forged."

A little breeze stirred the curtains, fresh with the smell of newly tilled earth. "Which means," I added, "that Jim figured out a way to fool the bank."

The coffee was excellent. "So I thought it might be a sort of case history," I continued. "Something bank employees get taught now, I mean, to keep it from ever happening again."

A lock of blond hair fell onto Bill's forehead as he stared down at his hands. Except for his sadder-but-wiser expression, he didn't look much older than Sam.

"Which was why," I finished, "I thought you might remember, even though at the time I know you were only a ..."

And that was when it hit me. From the look now on Imrie's face he might as well have been a hundred; despite his youth, I was looking at a man who had eaten the fruit of knowledge and found it bitter.

Very bitter. I took a wild guess. "It was *you*, wasn't it? Ellie said you were a young bank teller back then. So you'd have been perfect. Diamond ran some sort of a scam on you, didn't he?"

Imrie nodded miserably. "Give the little lady a great big hand. Yeah, it was me."

No wonder he'd reacted as if I'd tossed him a hot potato. But it still didn't explain why he'd avoided me so determinedly on the street the other day.

"Not that it was so hard for you to figure out," he went on. "Cops didn't have any trouble either, at the time. Looked around for the biggest dope in the world, and came up with me."

"But you were never charged with anything?"

He shook his head, looking almost relieved now that the cat was out of the moneybag. "No. Diamond finally came clean. Told the cops I didn't know anything, I was just the patsy he used to get checks deposited into his account. Because they were good checks on the face of it, and I didn't question anything else."

"What kind were they?" A car went by on the road outside, its engine sound dwindling as it rounded the curve. Then there was only the bright summer silence again.

"Diamond had a job at a combination lumberyard and building supply outfit in Machias," Imrie said. "He was using the lumberyard's checks, forging the signatures, and fiddling the accounts somehow to cover the amounts of the stolen ones."

Just as I'd thought. Bill's mouth twisted sourly as if tasting the memory. "Later I was too busy trying to clear my name to care much just what he'd been doing to the accounts. I just know that he fixed it so he could write checks to himself and deposit them."

Which would mean that Diamond had access to the lumberyard's computers. I wondered how he'd gotten it.

But for now, I wanted the rest of Imrie's side of the story. "You were always the teller. He waited, I mean, until he saw you at one of the windows. Figured out your schedule, probably?"

Imrie nodded. "Sure. And what did I know? Maybe people who knew him better would've questioned the situation."

Sorrow clouded his expression. "Someone with more experience might have wondered why he was getting paid so well. But I was just a kid; I'd come home that year from college to take care of my dad. Mom was gone by then."

Something odd there. But Imrie was on a conversational roll and I didn't want to say anything to stop it. "So Diamond cleared you. Didn't he have to admit his own guilt, in order to do that?"

"Yeah. It surprised me, too. I don't know, maybe they made some kind of a deal with him." Puzzlement wrinkled his forehead. "Not that it helped much. They'd already started investigating me. Word got around."

Pain replaced the confusion. He wasn't used to talking about this and now that he had, old feelings were surfacing.

"Like I said, in his younger days my dad had been kind of an unofficial big shot in town," Bill told me. "Fixture down at the firehouse, big on the town council and all. You know."

I did. Wade was like that now, and so was George. And once you had that kind of standing in Eastport, it would be a crushing blow to lose it.

If for instance your golden-boy son was accused of being a thief. "Was your father," I inquired gently, "very ill at the time?"

A nod. "I still think that's what finished him off, having it going around that I was a crook. You don't get that kind of dirt clean with a single washing, if you know what I mean."

"You seem to have come out of it okay now," I offered. But his answering glance was sharp.

"Sure. Unless I tried to get bank work anywhere else. Know how seriously anyone would take me outside of Washington County?"

I did. Here at least there was hope of being given another chance. Anywhere else, though, he'd get an impersonal background check. After that, he might as well be wearing a burglar's mask and carrying a swag bag.

It was time to go. "Listen, Bill, I didn't know about this. I mean, I didn't pick you to ask thinking I'd be able to get some information just by rubbing your nose in..."

Oops, not a nice way to put it. But he merely waved it off. "That's okay. Tell you the truth, when I heard Diamond was dead I wanted to talk to someone about it all anyway. I just didn't know it was going to be you."

He shook his head ruefully. "Brought it all back up for me, if you know what I mean."

Sure, like a recurring sore. I still felt sorry for him. Just not enough to believe him, or anyway not completely.

"But if you could just not spread it around, the whole sad story I've had to live down once already..." he added.

Walking out, he gave me that smile again, too old and far too world-weary. "It's taken me a while to earn back people's confidence, I mean with their money and all."

"I can imagine." In Maine, the trust people tended to have in institutions—even federally insured ones—would've left room in your average thimble.

We got to my car. "Given the choice between you and stuffing their cash in a mattress..."

"Yeah. For a while, most picked the mattress." His laugh this time sounded sincere. Hearing it, the goats trotted to the fence, nudging each other and uttering goat greetings.

"But they've gotten over it and maybe someday," Bill added, "I will, too."

His voice hardened. "I'm not going to talk about this again, though. Say what you want, to whoever you want, but I've told you what I know, now, and far as I'm concerned the whole subject is closed."

I opened the car door. "I understand. But Bill, there's one other thing. On Water Street the other day? You were about to cross but you changed your mind. How come?"

He turned slowly. "What? I don't...oh."

He made a pretense of thinking. Then his face cleared elaborately. "Now I remember. I'd left my wallet in the office, in my desk drawer."

He mimed patting his pocket, finding the wallet missing. "So I had to go back and get it," he finished glibly.

"I see. Well, that explains it, then," I said, getting into the car.

Sure it did. As I drove away, the bright blond-headed young banker was reaching in through the fence, scratching one of those pleasant-looking billy goats on its bony forehead.

They at least appeared to have perfect confidence in him.

Too bad I still didn't.

"Why didn't I ever hear about Bill Imrie and the checks?" I asked Ellie half an hour later.

When I got back to my house, she'd returned from her walk and the

Red Cross lady was just leaving. To Ellie, her spiel covered the amount of blood needed to make one unit of plasma, used for burn victim treatment.

"So you can see why we want *every possible local donor,*" she added with a meaningful sideways look at me.

I had not yet signed my donor card. "But I am considering it carefully," I assured her as I closed the door.

"That woman," I told Ellie afterward, "is relentless."

"I guess you have to be," Ellie agreed. "Especially because some people are such chickens about it."

She of course had signed her card immediately. Now she was making our lunch: cream cheese, black olive, and pepper sprout sandwiches on seven-grain bagels. Pouring us each a glass of iced Moxie she sat down across from me.

"Probably the reason you never heard about Bill's troubles is that whoever did know about them kept their mouths shut out of respect for his father," she said.

She bit into her sandwich. "I didn't even know, myself."

Which was saying something; Ellie's nerve endings seemed to pluck local information out of the air.

"But Bill thinks . . ."

"Sure he does. That everyone knows. Because he's so sensitive about it. But Pops Imrie was part of the old guard in Eastport. Family went way back. Bill was the town's fair-haired boy. Literally," she added, "not just because of that blond head."

She drank some Moxie. "Smart, great athlete, went to college and did real well there. He could do no wrong."

I bit into my sandwich, all parts of which were designed to flood well-being back into my physiology, the olives especially. And some of the Moxie herbs do seem to have medicinal properties.

"So when he came back . . . ?" I prompted.

She nodded, chewing. "Like I said before, staying home to take care of the old folks is something a girl might be expected to do without a second thought. But when a son does it..."

She swallowed, sipped. "Well, you'd have thought Bill Imrie had redeemed us all of original sin or something, the way people praised him."

"So even an imaginary blot on his reputation would have hurt him in his own eyes. And he's right that in the bank industry anywhere else, it might still hurt him for real."

I thought a moment. "So Bill probably wasn't happy with Jim Diamond," I said. "But he didn't express any anger toward him. It was more like he was mad at himself."

Despite olives and Moxie, fatigue was still trying to shut my brain down; I wanted to put my head on the table and snore.

Ellie looked at me, then started a pot of coffee. "Bill finished a degree at the community college and the bank kept him on, obviously. And whatever guilt-by-association there really was has faded, too. So maybe he figures least said, soonest mended."

"Maybe. Or it could be he likes another old saying better. I mean the one about revenge being a dish best served cold."

"Hmm. And served silently? Being as from his point of view, Jim Diamond wrecked his life?"

"Correct. Get Bella all worked up over threatening notes *she* thinks came from Jim, then kill Jim, and bingo, Bella looks good for it while Bill stays conveniently out of the picture."

Monday padded over and asked politely for an olive, accepted it delicately, and chewed it with many strange wrinklings of her furry black Labrador face.

"I don't trust him," I told Ellie. "There's still something he wasn't saying to me."

Noticing that Monday had gotten a treat, Prill the Doberman eyed me hopefully, so then of course I had to give her one, too, even though she didn't like olives and spat hers out swiftly.

I picked it up, fed it to Monday. "Where is Bella, anyway?"

"She finished upstairs, then went down to the cellar to help your father get ready to flush the radiators," Ellie replied.

"Oh." I'd seen his truck in the driveway, but figured the sounds down there were just the normal clanking and thunking of the plumbing, complaining about the indignity of actually having water running through it.

"I think she'd be happier if he let her clean them out with a brush, but in the end she accepted his argument that the brush would have to be about ten miles long," Ellie added.

Radiator maintenance was a task my father had taken on, and I had to admit the old cast-iron behemoths gave more heat after a century's worth of sediment had been forced from their clean-out valves. But the job had to be done in summer: if one of them should explode under an onslaught of pressurized water during the winter, it would sit atop an iceberg until spring.

"She's not scowling and shooing him around with a whisk broom anymore?"

Ellie shook her head. "First thing he did when he got here today was mix up some secret chemical for her, that takes the dirt off old windows. And since then she's his number-one fan."

Old etched-on dirt eats right into the panes, leaving a film no commercial cleaner can remove, and I could imagine the key to Bella's heart being made of sparkling window glass. Dissolving her antagonism that way was typical of him, too. It takes an old warrior, my father had told me once, to understand peace.

I hoped he'd remember that when I finally managed to tell him who was coming to visit.

"Anyway," I said, "I think Bill Imrie deserves some further attention. The way he keeps his folks' old place up, that's kind of weird, too. It's like a shrine. And I don't like his story about why he avoided me the other day, either."

I finished my Moxie. "And now I've got to go try to track Maggie down and have *that* conversation," I added, not looking forward to it one bit.

Because I still felt certain that Maggie couldn't have killed Jim Diamond. But that didn't mean I was going to let her look me in the face and lie.

Ellie started rinsing our plates. "Speaking of unwelcome, Victor was here while you were gone." She drank the last of her own Moxie so she could wash the glass.

"Darn, what did he want?" My ex-husband regularly came up with requests that could've put two Quaker meetinghouses on the brink of a nuclear exchange.

"Invitation to dinner tonight. I told him he could come. I hope that was okay?" She poured us both some coffee and got two oatmeal lace cookies out of the jar.

"Is that all? Sure, I guess so. But how come he wants to?"

I didn't mind that Ellie had gone ahead and given Victor the invitation. She knew it was easier to reject his more outrageous requests—such as for instance would I agree to having my head psychometrically modeled for a medical paper he was writing, a measuring process that would've meant first shaving off all my hair—if you'd already agreed to several simpler ones recently.

"Um, because he knew Sam asked Kris to come," Ellie replied.

Which pricked my ears up. "And? I'm getting from your tone that there's more to this story?"

In the maid's room the baby woke from her nap and let out a stunning wail to inform us that she was ready now to rejoin the day's activities, with emphasis on the word *now*.

"Well, actually, yes there is," Ellie replied. "But listen to all of it before you react, Jake. It's not a bad idea."

Victor with an idea, in my experience, was a lot like Hitler having atomic weapons, a good way to deliver them, and a map of Washington, D.C.

"Victor wanted to know if he could bring Maggie with him," Ellie told me. "And after I heard him out I told him that was all right, too."

Bored, hungry, and probably needing a diaper change, Leonora the

Magnificent emitted another howl that could have cleaned all those antique hot-water radiators out all by itself.

I wanted to howl, too. "Why in the world did you..."

"Jake, it's about Kris. Victor has met her."

He hadn't, before. "Really," I said, pausing to consider the possible implications.

Because Victor was a hound. On one of our early dates, one of the first things he asked me was whether or not I happened to own a G-string and tassels. Which I suppose should have raised my suspicions, but I'd thought it was a joke.

And it was on me.

"Victor hates her," Ellie said. "He despises that girl."

"But...why?" After all, Kris was female and had a pulse. And for all her flaws she had a spark of vitality, as well, one that to my mind only made her more dangerous.

"Well, apparently Sam and Kris ran into Victor downtown this morning, and Victor says the first thing Kris asked when she met him was what he did for a living."

"Oh," I breathed comprehendingly. So he wasn't planning to put the moves on her. "And Victor told her..."

"Yes." Ellie looked quietly pleased, the way she always does when she's plotting something. "He said when she found out he's a doctor, she was so happy she nearly swallowed her tongue."

It was just the sort of unpleasant image Victor would come up with, but in this case I thought it was appropriate.

"Money," I said. "Victor thinks Kris is only after Sam for Victor's..."

It was what I believed, too, even though it was absurd. Most of the time when I was married to him, we paid off Victor's school loans. Then for a little while when we did have money, we spent it just as fast, having Sam and living in an Upper East Side building so expensive we might as well have built the place ourselves out of bricks of platinum.

"So Victor smells a gold digger," I said. "Fascinating."

After our divorce I moved to Eastport and put most of my money into my old house, and soon thereafter Victor moved here and put what remained of his earning power down the drain by trading a career as a brain surgeon for one as a small-town physician.

As a result the idea of anyone in our family being wealthy was hilarious. But like her mother, Kris had different standards of wealth. Also she wouldn't understand that if you wanted to get rich nowadays, you didn't go into medicine at all.

To her, Victor probably looked like King Midas and Sam like the heir apparent. And Victor had spotted it.

"So he wants us all to have dinner together. You know, just a kind of happy-family get-together with you, me, Wade, George, Sam, and Kris. And Maggie," Ellie added, "because he thinks that way, by comparing us all together, Sam will be able to see Kris's true colors and come to his own conclusions."

Leonora's yelling was getting louder, and so was the clanking from downstairs. But even through the din I could still parse out the malevolent brilliance of the plan. Because you had to give Victor one thing: In the evil-genius department, he was a star.

"Sam would never break up with Kris just because I say it's what he should do," I mused aloud.

"And you know Maggie, she wouldn't make a face if she had a bad oyster in her mouth," Ellie agreed.

"Not usually," I said doubtfully as a picture of Maggie rose in my mind: unhappy, and laboring under the weight of a secret.

Ellie read my expression. "Listen, why don't you take Maggie aside tonight, explain to her exactly what's been going on, and *then* ask her again about the car being in Lubec?"

"Huh. It's an idea. Because if I take her into my confidence, she might . . ."

"Precisely. She might return the favor. Heck, it's worth a try, isn't it?

And for what it's worth, next time I need a sitter I'm still going to hire her."

The baby's cries had subsided momentarily to whimpers, but a second onslaught was due any moment.

"I agree," I said. "I mean, anyone can do anything if they get pushed hard enough, but I just don't think..."

"Me either," Ellie said. "Also, I don't see how it could hurt to wait until *after* Victor's plan has a chance of working, before you ask her about it all again."

She had a point. Maggie was lovely and always so gracious and easy to be around, I knew that even in her current mood you could put her at a dinner table with Victor and not have to worry over what might happen.

Or at a table with Kris. "Next to her, Kris is going to look like something out of a fun-house mirror," I admitted.

Of course Sam already knew the differences between the two girls. But actually seeing them together could be something else again. "Especially," I added, "if I clue Maggie in to the plan."

"Victor said he would," Ellie replied. "Clue her in."

"And he knows what to do?" I asked. "You don't think he'll forget himself and start charming Kris's socks off just because she is young and female?"

Socks being the least of what Victor could charm off when he got going. "He knows," Ellie assured me confidently.

Just then a funny sound came from the kitchen radiator. It had always been the most troublesome one. My father had mentioned he thought it had something stuck in its outflow tract.

Right, like maybe a grenade. Suddenly that radiator began rattling and trembling as if it were on a launch pad, waiting to take off.

Seeing this, a horrid premonition struck me. "Ellie, help me get these dogs out of here."

Cat Dancing sank her claws into my forearms when I grabbed her; we made it into the maid's room to snatch up the baby just as the radiator's takeoff sounds modulated to something more like a volcanic eruption.

I shoved both the dogs outside; Ellie ran with Lee. "Shut it off!" my father shouted. "Turn the valve—"

Cat Dancing let go and scrambled away from me. Her tail had vanished hastily around the newel post of the hall stairs when...

"Off!" my father shouted again.

...the radiator exploded.

Owing to the fact that my old house had been turned into a plumber's paradise by the radiator explosion, we barbecued that night out on the beach.

It was low tide at Gleason's Cove, the air sweetly briny after the long warm day, and the dogs galloped happily away across the expanse of stony beach, play-fighting over sticks of driftwood and crunching up tasty sea-urchin shells when they found them.

Soon after we got there Kris Diamond arrived in fine form, wearing a tiny pair of shorts, heeled sandals that positively begged for a broken ankle, and a halter top she'd apparently made out of a couple of shiny black Band-Aids.

"Nice," Victor commented sourly, noticing that Sam couldn't take his eyes off the girl. "See the hard little muscles in her arms? Later she'll turn him upside down, shake the cash out of his pockets."

My father had stayed home to supervise the plumbers, who said they thought they could create something that wouldn't spew water everywhere by midnight or so. And Bella, whom I'd at first thought of inviting to come along, had insisted on staying there, too, in case there were messes to be cleaned up.

"When she gets done with that boy," Victor went on bitterly, "there'll be nothing left but a pile of fingernail clippings and a few bone fragments."

For once Victor and I were in complete accord. I pulled a bottle of Sea Dog ale out of the cooler for him, then opened one for myself. "May I have one of those fruit sodas?" Maggie asked, coming up behind us.

I handed her one. With her dark, wavy hair loose, dressed in a white scoop-necked T-shirt, tan cargo shorts, and a little red kerchief tied at her throat, she looked scrumptious.

But not scrumptious enough. Sam slung his arm playfully over Kris's bare shoulders, pulling her off balance.

"Sam!" she shrieked in mock protest. The sandals weren't all that made her sway; it seemed to me she'd already had a few beers before she got here.

"Sa—*am*!" Victor mimicked her under his breath.

"Don't," I warned him quietly. "If you make her into your victim, Sam is only going to want to defend her."

"I'd like to make her a victim, all right," he retorted darkly. "What the hell's the matter with that boy?"

He was trying to help, so I decided now wasn't the time to remind him of the womanizing example he'd so helpfully provided over the years. In the war between men and women, his strategy for most of his life had been the equivalent of taking scalps.

Meanwhile, Wade and George had just about finished cooking the steaks. "...guy's got a real nice old Harper's Ferry rifle he wants restored," Wade was saying as I approached the grill. "He lives right near Limestone, so he took me over and showed it to me the last time we were up there. Lots of work, thing's been in someone's basement..."

George said something I couldn't quite hear, ending in the word "...expensive?"

"Nah," Wade replied. "We worked out a deal."

Wade didn't talk very much about the gunsmithing bargains he arranged with people, but I had no doubt the deal he'd made was in the other guy's favor. For one thing, he never missed a chance to put a little something into the system just in case.

Or anyway that's what I thought the whole Harper's Ferry rifle thing was about. "Hey," I said as he and George looked up at me, their barbecue tools in hand. "You guys just about ready?"

They were. With the steaks we had steamed corn on the cob, baked potatoes with sour cream and freshly minced chives from Ellie's garden, and strawberry shortcake on her miracle biscuits, so high that you have to break them into morsels before spooning the berries onto them.

With fresh whipped cream, naturally. And by the time we got to the dessert the evening was getting chilly, a thin fog creeping in at us from across the water, so hot coffee from the thermoses was welcome, too, as we pulled our chairs nearer to the driftwood bonfire Ellie and I had built.

Out on the bay the red and green running lights of fishing boats glowed in the dusk, the vessels' black silhouettes on the invisibly turning tide. A foghorn sounded, followed by the lonesome clanking of a channel bell, as the stars came out.

I moved to the chair next to where Maggie sat, and felt her stiffen at my approach.

"Don't," she warned tonelessly before I could say anything. On the beach, Sam and Kris were tossing a glow-in-the-dark Frisbee, the dogs racing between them.

In the firelight Maggie's face was as smooth and uncommunicative as one of those pottery masks down at the Art Center.

So I skipped the part about confiding in her; it wasn't going to work. "Maggie, I know you took my car to Lubec. You parked right across from

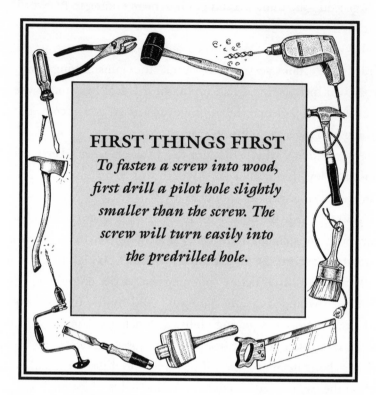

FIRST THINGS FIRST

To fasten a screw into wood, first drill a pilot hole slightly smaller than the screw. The screw will turn easily into the predrilled hole.

Jim Diamond's place, the cop said so, the day before we found Jim. And I want to know why."

She turned to me in the fire's orange glow. "Are they asking you about it? The police?"

"No. But Maggie..."

"Then let it go." She sounded close to tears. "I didn't have anything to do with it, Jacobia. You believe that, don't you?"

The fire's reflection on the incoming tide crept nearer. "I believe you, Maggie. But I still need to know what happened."

"No, you don't." She stared straight ahead to where Kris and Sam played. "I was out for a ride. I went to get an ice cream at that place with the umbrellas over the tables, remember it?"

I remembered. And it could have been true. But she was too upset for that to be all there was to the story.

Besides, the first time around she'd denied being there at all. And she still sounded guilty and miserable.

"Maggie—" I began again.

"Look, either you trust me or you don't. I don't know any more about what happened to that man than you do," she declared. She got to her feet. "And if you *don't* trust me, then tell the police I was there. Let them ask me about it."

So there it was: Put up or shut up.

"No," I said, after a moment. "I'm not going to do that. But Maggie—"

You can trust me, too, I was about to say. *Whatever's wrong, I'll try to help you.* But before I could, she walked away from me, and Wade came and took her place.

The moon began rising, a huge fiery orange orb from behind the distant hills of New Brunswick.

"Nice picnic," he observed serenely after a while.

"Mmm," I agreed. "I guess. But Sam was supposed to see the obvious difference between Maggie and Kris at this little affair. And instead I don't think he even noticed that Maggie is here."

I glanced back toward the picnic table. Near it, George was giving Leonora a bottle while Ellie put items back in the hamper and Victor stood by supervising.

Just then Sam and Kris came back from the darkness on the beach. "Give me a break, it's not like I'm driving," I heard Kris say as she reached into the cooler for another beer.

Sam mumbled something in reply. Maggie was there, too, and said something I didn't hear.

But Kris did, and she didn't like it, flying off the handle at once. "What do you mean, where was I?" she demanded. "You think I had something to do with what happened to my stepfather?"

"I didn't say that. I just asked where you were that day, is all." Maggie spoke clearly, putting a little steel in her tone. This only fueled Kris's anger further.

"You know," Kris said shrilly, "you're pathetic, the way you keep hanging around like anyone wants you anymore."

She'd been drinking all evening, waving it obviously under Sam's nose in a way that made me furious, though he hadn't seemed bothered by it, sticking to sodas.

"Kris," he began uncomfortably. "Forget it."

She turned on him. "Oh, sure! Big help you are. Your big fat friend here can just about accuse me of murder and that's okay."

Maggie wasn't fat. But she wasn't thin, and of course Kris would attack her at a vulnerable spot.

"All right, now," Victor stepped in, seeing Maggie flinch. "That's enough of—"

Whirling, stumbling until Sam caught her, Kris laughed in his face. "Shut up. I've seen you watching me, you old letch."

Of course he'd been watching her; we all had, Victor perhaps a little more than the rest, but hey, she'd bought that trip. Hadn't she been putting herself on display all evening?

"If you must know, I was with Sam all that day," she snarled. "He's my *alibi*." She put a nasty twist on the word. "I could tell you what we were doing, too," she added even more unpleasantly in my direction, "but you wouldn't like it."

Yeah, I'll bet I wouldn't. Wade tightened his arm around my shoulder, sensing with perfect accuracy my strong desire to slap the taste right out of the girl's mouth.

"But you wanted him gone," Maggie said evenly. "He was the reason why you're still living with your mother, instead of pursuing a career in..."

She paused in pretended thought. "Let's see, now, what was it? Nursing? Social work? No, wait, it was hair. Yeah, that's it, the deep science of beauty technology."

Kris lunged for her but once again Sam caught her. "Hey," he tried soothing the enraged girl, "don't give them any more ammunition."

She struggled with him, then caught sight of us staring at her. With a pathetic attempt at regaining her dignity, she straightened and spoke.

"You think I killed Jim? That's what you think?" She laughed harshly, looking around at us in the firelight.

"After what happened to him over those forged checks, you think *I'd* commit crimes? Oh, please, give me a little credit."

Sure. Two cents' worth. And she'd already used it up.

"It's ridiculous anyone even suspecting my mom, much less me." Then the beer hit her again and the laugh dissolved into a sob.

"But you know, I'll bet she really did it," she contradicted herself, her words slurring. "I bet he scared her so bad she went to pieces and—"

"Kris," Sam said helplessly, "come on. Cut it out, you don't have to—"

"What?" she snapped at him. "I don't have to what? Defend my own *mother?*"

Which wasn't exactly what she was doing. Instead, she'd been stating the obvious, that Bella had a very good reason to want Jim dead. I wondered suddenly if Kris was really as drunk as she looked. Sam drew her closer to him protectively as her shoulders sagged.

If it was a drunk act, it was beautifully done. But of course she'd had practice at the real thing.

"You're right," she mumbled. "I don't have to do anything. I don't have to lie, either. I'm glad Jim's dead. If Mom did it, more power to her. For once she stood up for herself."

She sniffled loudly. "But it's not my fault they're both born losers, is it?" she demanded of all of us. "It's just not my fault, so can we talk about something else now? Please?"

She sounded like a victimized little girl. And to some degree, she probably was. But just listening to her, my bullshit detectors zoomed into the red zone, and my suspicions didn't diminish a bit as Sam led her out of the firelight toward his car.

She was giggling again, holding the car keys teasingly away from him. I saw them glinting, got up, and started toward the pair to grab the keys.

Sam got to them first. "No!" Kris objected petulantly as he snatched them. But she made no further protest as he got her into the car, then drove away without a further word to any of us.

"That went well," Ellie observed dryly into the silence when they were gone.

"Girl's a few buckets short of a barrelful," George said.

"I do not," Victor repeated exasperatedly, "understand what Sam sees in her."

But Maggie, who had watched their taillights dwindle into the darkness, had a more insightful comment.

"I do," she told us. "I understand. Kris is fun. Or anyway she makes him think so."

Victor looked at her as if the word came from some obscure foreign language.

"Fun," she pronounced carefully for him again. "Laughs. The feeling you have when you're doing something only for enjoyment?"

Maggie shook her head, knowing a lost cause when she saw it, and appealed to the rest of us. "Like when they were on the beach throwing the Frisbee and she kept missing it, not being able to throw it straight to him?"

I hadn't seen it, but Maggie had been keeping a sharper eye. "So he would have to put his arms around her and show her how," the girl went on, sarcasm creeping into her voice again.

As she spoke the memory of Kris's bare arms came back to me. As Victor had first noted, she did have those hard little arm muscles.

"I've seen Kris throw a Frisbee before," Maggie said. "With other people at the park. And believe me, she didn't need anyone to show her. When she wants to, that girl could take your head off with a Frisbee."

Or with a big cast-iron skillet? The question rose unbidden to my mind.

"She likes parties and music," Maggie said bitterly. "Staying out all night, taking wild dares, going too fast in cars. And she really likes drinking."

Sam liked those things, too. It was how he'd gotten into so much trouble over the winter, letting himself think he could hang out with people who were doing them, just not doing them himself.

"That's why Sam likes her," Maggie repeated. "Maybe tonight she was kind of a drag. But even her bad behavior . . . well."

She paused, deciding how to put it. "If you think you're bad yourself, it's nice to know there's someone even worse."

"Okay," I interrupted. The fire was nearly out, and George was loading the cookout stuff in his truck bed. "I get the idea."

None of it sounded like fun to me. But Victor wasn't done with the subject. "How'd you find that out?" he wanted to know.

Wade was loading the dogs into the sturdy wire cages he had bolted into his truck bed for them. But even he stopped to listen to Maggie's reply.

"He told me," she said simply. "I finally went and asked him what the big attraction was, and that's what he said. That Kris was a lot of fun, and I . . ."

Her face crumpled. "And that I wasn't."

Her words hung in the silence by the dark moving water, with the moon staring pitilessly down like a cold, unblinking eye.

"Maggie, I'm so sorry," I said finally, moving to put my arm around her. But she wasn't having any.

"No!" she said, stepping away from me. "Just don't, okay?" She managed a smile. "I'm fine. I came here tonight because Dr. Tiptree wanted me to, but I knew it wouldn't change anything."

"What did you say to Sam?" I asked. "I mean after he . . ."

Thinking, *the selfish little son of a bitch.*

She shook her head ruefully. "I told him I was done being his emotional punching bag, and I didn't want to know any more of his secrets," she replied. "Or hers, either."

"Come on," Victor told her. "I'll drive you home."

Maggie nodded and let herself be guided to his car. To me it was just one more familiar, not-to-be-trusted thing about Victor, that he could seem so strongly to be the person you should turn to when you needed someone.

But at the moment I was profoundly grateful for it.

Victor's car rumbled into my driveway a little later as I was helping Wade get the dogs in, moving in tired silence to lift Monday down off the tailgate while Prill allowed Wade to assist her, his arms gathering her long legs as if they were a bouquet.

"Hey," Victor said, his car door slamming.

"I'll get 'em," Wade said, taking Monday's leash from me.

I went to meet Victor. "What is it? I thought you were going home after you dropped Maggie off."

"I was. But Maggie told me something on the way back and I thought you ought to know. The fight Kris and Sam had the other night in front of the house? Maggie told me what it was about."

"And?" I was staggering with fatigue.

"They were at a party. She was drinking, he wasn't."

I'd known that much.

"Kris started teasing Sam. Saying he was a Goody Two-shoes, tied to his mother's apron strings, that kind of stuff."

That was also little beyond what I'd already suspected. Kris was a disaster waiting to happen, and the fact that Sam's eyes had not been opened to her tonight discouraged me immensely.

"Maggie knew this?"

Victor nodded. "Sam told her. It's what she meant about not wanting to hear any more of his secrets."

"So what's the punch line?"

"At the party he stuck to Coca-Cola," Victor said. "But Kris was pretty loaded. And she grabbed Sam and kissed him."

I frowned, puzzled. "I don't see what's so bad about—"

"Right, but she had a mouthful of bourbon at the time. And when she kissed him, she spit it into *his* mouth."

I just stared at him, my heart thudding suddenly. "What did Sam do?"

"Spit it out again. That's what the whole fight was about, her trying to sabotage his sobriety. Although of course she claimed it was a joke, she didn't mean anything by it, et cetera."

Sure. All the things you tell someone you're trying to hurt, when you don't want them to know just how vicious you are.

Or you haven't figured it out yet, yourself.

"I gather it wasn't the first time it's happened," Victor went on. "Maggie says Kris has done it before."

"She's known that, too?" I felt outraged. "Why didn't she tell one of us sooner?"

Victor shrugged. "You know how it is. She probably felt that if she told on him, he'd hate her for it. Which he would."

Frustration seized me, that this was all so difficult and it didn't seem I could do anything about it.

"Victor, what's this all about? Sam was doing so well. Even after his slip last winter, he was upset for a while. But he just got right back on the horse, and—"

"Maybe he's still upset. Maybe it's just hitting him, Jake, that he's going to be riding that horse his whole life."

He studied me. "That it wasn't just a kid thing, something he'd grow out of. Something he could control. Maybe what's really bothering Sam is that he knows last winter could happen again."

And that's Victor. He can go along for months as brainlessly as one of those department-store mannequins, then come up with an insight as brilliant as a meteor streaking on the night sky.

Exhaustion hit me, making me sway. I'd been up for thirty-six hours. "Victor, I have to go lie down now."

"Yeah. Okay." He walked back to his car, turned as if to say something else. But I was too tired to hear it.

Inside our house, Wade took one look at me and knew enough to leave me alone. Bella had gone home by then; my father, too. And Sam was still out.

Ignoring the wreckage of radiator repair work littering the kitchen, I went upstairs where I took a shower, collapsed into the bed whose covers Wade had already turned down, and slept like the dead.

Not until early morning did I wake again, sitting up with a start, my heart hammering as if I were still out in the moonlit driveway listening to Victor. But it wasn't my ex-husband I was hearing in my head.

It was Maggie, taunting Kris with her supposed career plans. Sam could have told Maggie about the beauty school idea. But there was another way she could have learned about it, too. She could've seen the letter Kris got from the school, some time when she was alone in Bella's house.

Thinking this I got up quietly so as not to wake Wade, and looked into Sam's room. He was there, snoring softly, one tanned arm hanging down over the side of his bed.

Hating myself for it, I sniffed the air for stale alcohol and detected none. Finally I checked my robe pocket for the magic wand that would make everything okay for him.

I'd have given anything for that magic wand. But I'd lost it around the time his father and I began fighting like a couple of wildcats, and I'd never found it again.

Down in the kitchen I put coffee on, then took the dogs out and fed them, picking my way between pipe wrenches, hacksaws, crowbars, and the other heavy tools the plumbers had used to get the remnants of exploded radiator apart from the rest of the system.

By the time the coffee was finished I'd pulled a warm sweat suit from a hook in the hall closet and put it on, along with a pair of thick socks from the backpack I kept stocked in there.

I gathered a collection of items from the tool shelf and slipped my feet into the insulated sneakers Wade had given me on my last birthday, because even though it was June and the sun was rising, the thermometer said it was only 52 outside.

Out in the yard, I found Ellie already at the picnic table with her own coffee. It was George's morning to have the baby, a privilege he guarded jealously, so she was alone.

"Hi," I said, not surprised. If the sky was light, Ellie was up. I sat across from her.

With me I'd brought latex gloves, wire brushes, a scouring pad, and a coffee can full of paint stripper in which I had been soaking the old hinges that belonged to the shutters.

Because if you're going to go to the trouble of drilling all new holes for them, they might as well look good. Spreading the things on the table, I repeated Victor's revelations of the night before, and what I'd been thinking since then.

"Oof." Ellie blew a breath out. "So Kris and Maggie both had reasons to get rid of Jim; Kris because if he were gone she could leave—she wouldn't have to stick around to try to keep an eye on Bella's safety—and Maggie because if he were gone Kris really might."

She thought a moment. "*And* Maggie thinks Kris is actually a danger to Sam, not just Maggie's rival."

"Correct," I said unhappily, fishing the first shutter hinge out of the coffee can with gloved fingers. The paint stripper had taken off the first few paint layers and softened the rest to the consistency of thick clay.

I applied the copper scouring pad to the hinge. It took most of the paint sludge off with a couple of swipes.

But not all of it. "And I can believe that Kris would stay, too, to support Bella, even though she's such a little..."

Numerous vulgar terms came to mind, but I didn't pronounce any of them. "Sam got between me and Victor a couple of times," I added quietly.

Ellie gazed sympathetically at me over the rim of her coffee mug. "Oh," she said softly, "that must have been..."

"Yeah. Not so good." I scrubbed the hinge with a wire brush. The screw holes were the worst part. "Sam didn't much like me back then, but he'd have fought tigers for me anyway, because I was his mother."

Three crows flapped into the yard to perch on the power line near my house, and began belting out a raucous early-morning concert.

Only a few more hinges to go. I dipped into the stripper and came up with another one. The crows cawed vigorously, as if each big black bird were trying to outdo the next.

"That still doesn't mean Kris did anything to Jim. Or that Maggie did either," Ellie mused thoughtfully.

Out in the street a garbage truck rumbled by. The crows all flapped off, leaving the power wire bouncing.

"And it certainly doesn't make sense that Maggie would have *planned* to do anything to him," Ellie went on reasonably. "For one thing, if that had been her intention, why go there in *your* very recognizable car when her own is so nondescript?"

"Maggie could have started out just going for a drive. Once she was on the road she could've made a spur-of-the-moment decision to talk to Jim, maybe to see if he could be persuaded into doing something about Kris."

"How would she know where he lived?" Ellie objected.

"I don't know. But she seemed to, when we were there. Don't you remember, she pointed up at the sign in the window? And then backtracked about it right afterward as if she didn't want us to know she knew."

"If she did it on the spur of the moment," Ellie said, "what about the notes?"

"I don't know that, either." The last bit of paint came off the final hinge. I put the wire brush down.

"The notes don't make sense, and neither does the skillet. I mean, if you meant to do something serious to someone, would you arm yourself with a frying pan?"

"Nope." Ellie screwed the cup back onto her thermos while I pulled off the latex gloves. Inside the house, both dogs danced welcomingly as if we'd been away for hours.

Ellie stopped in the hall, surveying the radiator wreckage. "Meanwhile, has Wade said what he's going to do to get the guest rooms ready in time for your relatives yet?"

"No. For all I know he's planning to line up Porta Potties on the sidewalk. But right now I can't worry about it."

Actually I could. It was running constantly in the back of my mind like an annoying tune you can't get out of your head. But I hadn't been able to think what I could do about that, either.

Ellie got ready to take the dogs out. I always had to chase them around to get them leashed up, but she had been walking them semiregularly, lately, so now she just jingled their collars together and they sat before her like furry angels.

"Look," I said when she'd gotten Monday neatly lined up on one side of her, and Prill on the other. "Don't say anything to Maggie about any of this, all right? Or to anyone else."

The dogs looked like a couple of bookends. If I'd tried to make them sit still that way, they'd have been doing somersaults.

"As it is now," I went on, "we feel like we're not getting anywhere. We probably don't *look* like we're doing very much, either, assuming anyone's paying attention."

Ellie nodded thoughtfully. "But that could be a good thing if it's making whoever's behind all this feel safe."

The dogs gazed adoringly at her. "If we keep a low profile, somebody might get careless, drop a little hint?" she added.

I looked out past her through the screen door. Long shafts of early-morning sunlight sparkled in the grass, and the air had a fresh, nothing-has-gone-wrong-yet smell, sweetly invigorating.

"And maybe it will be just the bit of information we need," I agreed with Ellie, not really believing it.

But I wasn't ready to give up. "So when you get back, how about if we keep trying to find out more about Jim Diamond?"

"Sure," she said enthusiastically. "After all, he's the dead guy, so maybe we should figure his death had something to do with *him.*"

She stepped outside, the dogs gamboling around her. "But we will be tactful, Ellie," I warned. "And careful. Because whoever we're after is on the far side already."

Of the line, I meant, between most of the population and the tiny, unpredictable fraction of it that has committed murder.

Chapter 10

The rest of the morning went reasonably well at first. Freighters can dock on Sunday as well as any other day so Wade headed off to work, and Sam left for a meet-and-greet with some marine engineers at the boat school—

I asked, but he couldn't remember whether or not he'd told Maggie about Kris's beauty school aspirations—

—and when they'd gone I hauled the shutters down from the third floor where my father had stashed them again, because I had a feeling we might soon be spreading sleeping bags up there.

But three flights of stairs separated the third floor from the cellar and I could only carry one heavy shutter at a time, so by the time I was done I'd had a workout.

Which was why when Bob Arnold came by a little while later he found me in the yard, collapsed on a lawn chair.

"Is Bella all right?" I asked, sitting up.

He nodded. "Ayuh. For now. If the state boys come after her again," he added darkly, "I doubt it'll be just for questions. Drove by her place twenty minutes ago and she was still there, though. You training for a triathlon? Or just getting ready for summer complaints like everyone else?"

By which he meant all the visitors the town would be getting, in...ye gods, only five days now. "Mine might be flopping on the third floor if Wade doesn't get his act together," I began.

But then I stopped, noticing Bob's expression. He hadn't come by to talk about possible deficiencies in my hospitality.

"Sam here?" he inquired.

"No, he's at the boat school this morning. Why? Do you want to talk to him?"

"Nope," Bob replied. "Just wondered."

In other words he *didn't* want Sam to be around when he said what he'd come to say; oh, great.

"Jake, why don't you come on downtown and have a coffee with me?" he asked. "I don't know why, but I always feel like I need a wingman when I go to the beatnik joint."

It was what Bob always called the Blue Moon. "You could wear a beret, start smoking French cigarettes," I teased as we rode in the squad car down Key Street. "Write some free verse, read it aloud on Friday nights."

"Yeah. If I think of anything that rhymes with handcuffs, I might try it," he said as we parked and got out.

He jingled the cuffs on his belt as he spoke, eyes alert for the routines he monitored, which consisted of people's usual locations, activities, and companions. It was the exceptions to the routines, Bob always said, that you had to watch out for.

"Nice day," he remarked.

On Water Street, a beer truck was backed up to the side entrance of the Waco Diner. Two shaven-headed guys were helping unload the cases, their tattooed arms bare in the sun.

Bob frowned at the sight. "Supposed to be three of them," he explained at my questioning glance. "I think I might take a ride to Bozzy Maxwell's later, ask his mom what he's up to instead of showing up for his job the way his probation officer told him."

Like I said, exceptions. They could get you killed, he claimed, even in a little island town like Eastport. I was still wondering what exception had him visiting my house, inviting me for coffee. And I already suspected I wasn't going to enjoy finding out.

Once we got inside the Blue Moon and had our mugs and a pair of sandwiches—it was close enough to lunchtime and the kitchen was featuring shaved Canadian maple ham with arugula and smoked Gouda—he got down to the business of telling me.

Or rather, he delivered it like a bolt out of the blue, the one thing I hadn't thought of even though it was in front of my nose.

"I need you to tell me Sam wasn't in Lubec the other day, driving your car. The day Jim Diamond got killed," he said.

I grabbed my coffee mug, washed down a bit of the arugula that had snagged in my throat. "Funny, I was going to ask you some questions today, too," I managed, vamping for time.

Of course it was Sam that people would think of, not Maggie. Sam was the boyfriend of a victim's estranged stepdaughter; in the absence of another suspect, all you'd need was a sprig of parsley to make him look like the blue-plate special.

And now if I asked Bob any of my own questions, such as for instance more about Jim Diamond's background, he'd know I was still very interested in Jim's murder. And he would wonder if it was because I was somehow trying to protect Sam.

Instead of Maggie, whom I didn't want getting into trouble, either. And I especially didn't want to put her there myself. "No," I replied, "he didn't have my car that day."

Bob watched me. "Seems like for a minute you weren't sure."

"I was just thinking. One day's like another when you're in a routine, you know."

Routine being what that Lubec cop had been in the habit of noticing, too. And a jazzy little Fiat ragtop wasn't part of it.

"But I'm sure he didn't," I said, not adding why.

He nodded slowly, savoring his half-decaf mocha java. Mine was good, also, or it had been until I stopped tasting it.

"Why'd you ask?" I didn't want to continue this conversation. But I didn't want to be ignorant of the reason behind it, either, in case it was something else I hadn't thought of.

Bob's look at me was unfooled. He knew there was more that I wasn't saying. He also knew there wasn't another car like mine in all of Washington County.

Meanwhile, as I sat there the whole thing fell together for me: the Lubec cop *had* put my car in his report. But a truly fine suspect was already in the state's crosshairs, so the local cop's report of the car's being there had been given the brush-off by the state investigators.

They didn't want their nice neat case screwed up. And the Lubec cop didn't like *that,* so he'd called Bob Arnold for a chat.

It was Bob who'd put two and two together and come up with Sam. And having done so, he'd decided to get proactive in trying to keep Sam out of a possible jackpot.

"Question arose, that's all," he replied mildly. "Glad to be able to put an answer to it."

And, his calm gaze added silently, *give you a heads-up.* Bob didn't think Sam had gone to Lubec and bonked Jim Diamond. But he did know the car had been there, even if he couldn't prove it.

Furthermore, he knew that if the fickle finger of legal fate got a reason to stop pointing at Bella—

—for instance if my snooping should happen to show that she *hadn't* killed Jim, but failed to replace her with a slam-dunk, no-doubt-about-it version of who *had*—

—then the question of who had been driving my car that day would come up again, this time a lot more seriously.

"So where are they on Bella, anyway?" I inquired. "Any idea of when the DA might decide to bring charges?"

Bob shrugged. "Whole case is circumstantial. No prints on the weapon, no one saw her there that day. But she told 'em about the notes, can't account for her time, and it turns out she had a key to Jim's place, too. None of that's looking good for her."

"Yeah, she told me about the key. So she could have had opportunity, and they know *she* thought he was threatening her. Do they know he was . . . ?"

I rubbed my thumb and fingers together in the "money" sign. "A serious drain on her finances? Yep, they do," Bob replied.

Oh, terrific. "But it doesn't make sense, if you were planning a murder, to bring along a frying pan for a weapon."

"Sure," Bob answered. "But how many murders've you ever heard of actually made sense when you laid it out cut-and-dried?"

Good point. Murder is a numbskull thing to do. Doesn't stop folks, though. "So they'll charge her pretty soon," I concluded.

"That's what I'm hearing. They'd like more evidence but they have a game plan, so I think they'll get what they want. Use some leverage, get her confession, end of story."

Leverage could only mean . . . "Kris? They'll go after Kris?" By now my mind was racing. Where *had* Sam been that day, anyway?

I didn't know. Bob nodded through a bite of sandwich.

"Yep," he said again. "Kris had access to the key and the weapon as much as Bella did, and you figure she couldn't have liked Jim. Guy's making a lot of trouble for them both."

He touched his lips with his paper napkin. "Not that Kris likes anyone much that I can tell, unless there's a way she's figured out that they can do something for her."

"Right," I said bleakly. "I've noticed that, too." I told Bob what Victor thought about Kris, that she was a gold digger.

"But Sam doesn't seem to have tumbled to it, and I'm afraid he never will." Or anyway not until it was too late. Besides, at the moment that felt like the least of my problems.

"Uh-huh. Wish I could help you there," Bob said. "But if it was illegal to fall for the wrong girl, half the male population would be behind bars." He ate the pickle off his plate. "Anyway, if Bella doesn't play ball they'll make noise about looking at Kris for it, and then that Bella will give in so fast it'd make your head spin, to keep her daughter out of hot water."

Yep, that's what I thought, also. Whereupon if I managed to show that she *hadn't* done it, I would just be moving a whole pack of trouble a lot closer to home.

And at that point, it would be too late for Maggie to help by revealing she'd had the car. By then, the police might decide she was only saying so to protect Sam . . . oh, what a tangled web.

"They'll do it before the Fourth," Bob added. "Afterward, the court'll be jammed up with stuff people were up to while they were celebrating. All this summer hilarity stretches the county's resources in the law enforcement department," he added wryly.

In other words, on top of everything else I was going to be deprived of Bella when I needed her most, just as I'd feared. It was a selfish way of looking at it, I knew.

On the other hand, Ellie and I were the only ones doing anything on her behalf, so I absolved myself. "So what'd you tell the Lubec cop?" I asked. "I mean, just out of curiosity."

"What he already knew. That right now Bella's officially only a person of interest," he replied swiftly, this being the point of the whole conversation in the first place.

"But if she lawyers up, or it gets to the point where they have to offer her a public defender," he went on—

Which it would; it was just a matter of time, now.

—"whoever's representing her is going to get the chance to put that car into play. Got to, to get any reasonable doubt. The car," Bob emphasized, "that looks just like yours, that the Lubec cop saw on the day of Jim's murder."

By which he meant that whatever I wasn't saying had better get cleared up fast, because things were about to get serious.

"Interesting music," Bob remarked, changing the subject.

He'd said what he needed to about Sam's vulnerability, his belief that my car had indeed been in Lubec the day Diamond was clobbered, and his own questions about what it was doing there.

Now the ball was in my court. "Yeah," I replied about the music. "I think I like it."

It was a group called Funkhouse on a private CD label out of Massachusetts, a trio of music school guys, not exactly tuneful but very listenable. Maggie had told me about them the last time she and I had been in here together.

Thinking of Maggie again made me feel even more anxious. This whole situation was developing so many traps, I was sure I'd put a foot wrong any minute.

And if I did, someone who didn't deserve it could end up in big trouble, maybe even my own son.

But that wasn't my only concern. "Bob, do I still need to be worrying about Sam and Kris? About the drinking parties and all?" By now the gatherings were the least of my concerns, but I still had to ask.

Angling his head at the speakers set near the Blue Moon's ceiling, he considered while his fingers tapped the complex beat of the music. "I don't know," he said finally. "There haven't been any more big blowouts like the other night."

"Thanks for that, by the way. Your restraint," I said.

I didn't add *and for this conversation, now*. He knew.

"Don't mention it. Way I look at it, official measures are the last resort when it comes to the kids, you know that."

He drank the last of his coffee. "So I guess the answer to your question is, maybe not right this minute. I just always hope a quiet period isn't the calm before the storm, is all."

"Yeah. Me, too." But I was afraid it was. Another thought struck me as we went out. "Say, there isn't some kind of charity scam going on around here lately, is there?"

He glanced over in surprise. "Not that I know of. Why, you got a complaint about something?"

"No. It's just that a lady who says she's with the Red Cross blood drive keeps showing up at my house, but I haven't heard of her being anywhere else. Or seen her, either, except once right here downtown."

In front of the Waco, three shaven-headed fellows instead of two were now tossing crates off a shellfish truck. Spotting them, Bob nodded to himself and crossed a task off his mental list.

"There's a blood drive, I know that much," he said. "Guys at the firehouse wanted me to sign up; I told 'em sure. Never know when I might be a quart low myself."

The flashback hit me hard as he said it: Bob wounded, down in the snow, nearly bleeding to death as he lay in my arms.

It had happened several years earlier, but it still felt painfully vivid. "Right," Bob said quietly, his somber look letting me know he recalled it as well as I did.

Although from an entirely different perspective. Still, I'd settled the blood drive question. "Bob..."

"What?" He turned, waiting patiently as I struggled with the impulse to tell him everything, even about Maggie.

But then the impulse passed, and as he watched it happen he nodded minutely again. He trusted me; also he thought he owed me. He believed I'd saved his life back then, which maybe I had.

Besides, from the legal point of view it was early days yet. Bella hadn't even been charged—

Bob wasn't saying so, but from his manner I thought he didn't believe she'd killed Jim Diamond, any more than I did—

—so he was cutting me some slack. Anyway, for all either of us knew an event might still happen that would change things for the better.

One did, too. Happen, that is.

But it didn't make things better.

In fact, looking back on it now I have to say that the *making it all worse* part of the program was only just beginning.

When I reached my own front yard I had a brief interchange with Bella, the details of which I barely bothered to process before sending her home. One thing the current confusion did seem to have improved was my ability to deal decisively with her; if I didn't, she would drive me all the way around the bend instead of only halfway around, as she'd done already.

Next, I noticed that my father's old truck was here. Inside the house I found that he'd cleared up all the plumber's mess and brought the shutters back upstairs again.

Also, he'd apparently decided to put the cleaned hinges onto them, or I assumed as much when I saw him out by the picnic table with a shutter in front of him. But as I joined him there and saw what he was really up to, all the pleasure I'd felt at the notion of for once *not* having to do it myself fled instantly.

"Dad, why are you...?"

The newly cleaned hinges were piled on a sheet of newspaper. But he wasn't doing anything with them. Instead he was filling up the screw holes in one of the shutters with plastic wood.

"Hate to tell you this," he said when he saw me. "But I had a whack at that hardware."

My heart sank. Each shutter took two hinges and, because I'd bought them secondhand, each already had six screw holes, three per hinge. And now as I watched, I remembered what I'd forgotten about the process of taking all of those hinges off, to ready the shutters for painting.

They'd been *loose,* the screws falling out of the holes. That meant the holes had to be filled with something the screws could bite into. And six screw holes times twenty-four shutters added up to . . .

Wordlessly I picked up another woodworker's syringe. He'd thinned the plastic wood with turpentine so it could be drawn up into the syringe's barrel and forced out through its nozzle.

"Got to be done," he said sympathetically.

Next came the drying time; the plastic wood had to harden. After that each hole needed drilling again, with a drill bit just a little smaller than the hinge screw that was destined for it.

Only then, and after several more hours of careful drill work, could the screws be reset without fear of their falling out again. Or worse, falling out after the shutters were rehung, so that in the next big storm they would fly right off the house.

As always, having my hands occupied with a physical task put my mind at ease. But not for long.

"Jake," he said, filling another screw hole. "I saw Sam an hour or so ago up in Calais."

It was the next town to our north, and it had a McDonald's, a Subway, and a Taco Bell. Sam and his buddies went there often.

"So?" I wiped up some stray plastic wood.

"He was at Kendall's jewelry store. I was there picking up your package," he reminded me.

Right; I'd ordered a brass plate for the front door, with my last name and Wade's engraved on it.

"He didn't see me," my dad went on. "He was buying a ring. Little chip diamond."

The words hit my heart like punches.

"I didn't know better," he said, "I'd think he really means to marry that girl."

Kris, he meant. "Oh, good lord."

Sidelong look from my dad. "You know," he pointed out, "you married Victor. Seems like you managed to end up all right."

"That was different. First of all, I only did it because there was nobody to stop me. And at the time Victor wasn't a big threat to my sobriety, only my sanity."

My father nodded. "Very true," he agreed in the tone he used when he meant he wasn't going to talk about it anymore, but that I should reexamine my assumptions about it.

My assumptions so far consisting of the certainty that, in the universe of romantic possibilities, Kris was a black hole and Sam was being sucked in, never to emerge.

And I didn't see how any rethinking on my part was going to change that. Meanwhile there was another topic on my mind, and now was my chance.

"Dad," I said after we had worked in silence a while longer. "Have you ever thought about getting back in touch with the home folks?"

The ones, I meant, who were planning to descend en masse in a little over twenty-four hours.

"Nope," he said tersely, squeezing another dose of plastic wood into yet another screw hole.

Deftly he removed the woodworker's syringe, wiped the excess with a red bandanna wrapped around the end of his index finger, and inspected the result.

"Pesky stuff," he commented. "Too thin and it won't dry, too thick and you can't get it all the way to the base of the hole."

"Right," I said. His laconic answer had taken me aback.

"The thing is," I began again, "I know it's been a long time since you've seen any of them. . . ."

Over thirty years, actually. Being a bomb builder for a crew of bank-robbing, social-justice-demanding anarchists wasn't the career path they'd have chosen for him, probably, though being an impoverished clan of hill folk they'd have surely held plenty of revolutionary opinions themselves.

For instance, that rich folk victimized the poor, that the legal system ran on infusions of cash, and that visitors from any branch of government whatsoever should be met with closed mouths, narrowed eyes, and loaded shotguns.

But they'd have drawn the line at bank robbery, and at the blast that destroyed a Manhattan town house, shattered windows for blocks around, and killed my mother.

For much of my life I'd believed that my father had done it, made some stupid mistake that had ruined all our lives; or worse, that it had been on purpose. When he'd shown up here in Eastport years later, sure I would reject him, he'd watched warily from a distance for a long time before approaching me.

He hadn't set the bomb off. In the end the FBI realized it, too, and quit spying on his relatives in case he got in touch with them. But now it seemed maybe he hadn't even wanted to.

And still didn't. "It could be a nice thing," I ventured, stirring drops of turpentine into the plastic wood.

"For all of you," I continued, adding a touch more turps.

The hard-and-fast rule of working with plastic wood is that the stuff dries hard and fast where you don't want it to, slowly where you do.

"I mean catching up on the news. Talking over," I persisted, hearing my own note of desperation, "the good old days."

My dad set the woodworker's syringe down on the picnic table and turned to me. "They think I killed your mother," he said.

At the look in his eyes I was struck silent.

"They *still* do," he insisted. "Everyone back there does, and there's no way I can ever prove to them that I didn't."

My dad hadn't only been the explosives genius of the bunch; he'd been the pacifist as well. Bombs were for distraction, not human destruction, he'd said. But one of his pals had disagreed and the blast had been to discredit my dad, or kill him.

That guy was in a witness protection program now. So no one would ever be prosecuted and my dad would never be officially cleared.

Still... "Look, I can see why maybe Mom's folks would blame you," I said.

The ones who'd taken me afterward, hating me because I looked like him. Talked like him, too: big ideas, sassy mouth. But they were all dead now, gone to glory right along with the snake handling and the speaking in tongues.

"Jake, I couldn't have taken you with me, you know. Me on the run with no address, always keeping out of sight..."

"I know," I said, regretting my remark about there being no one to stop me from marrying Victor. "Don't worry about it."

Half the time with my mom's folks I'd wanted to put my hand in the deadly snake cage just to get it over with. Victor was just another version of the snake cage, but that's a different story.

"The thing is," I began, gathering my courage.

Whereupon I was finally about to tell him that all the blood relatives either of us still had were coming to Eastport. And that although they hadn't mentioned the subject, it didn't sound to me as if they thought he'd murdered my mother.

But before I could, my father looked up and stopped what he was doing. Slowly, his gaze fixed on something behind me, he put down the woodworker's syringe full of plastic wood.

"Don't make any sudden moves," he said quietly. "Turn your head a little, to where I'm looking."

So I did, and then I saw it, too, in the forsythia bushes at the back of the yard.

Huge, unbelievable. It was magnificent.

It was the moose.

"**Did you know** a moose can roll its eyes in two different directions?" I demanded of Ellie. "Independently of each other?"

The moose had stood looking at my father and me while also watching a cat stalk a sparrow at the far end of the yard. It had a long horsey face, nostrils the size of grapefruits, and a pendulous lower lip that looked as if it might be about to speak.

Finally it had ambled away toward the woods behind Hillside Cemetery. Deer lived there, and foxes, and there were rumors of a lynx. So it would be a good place for a moose to hang out.

"I don't care that he was eating the forsythia," I enthused. "He can eat the whole yard, I'll buy more geraniums for him..."

I stopped. Ellie's look at me was patiently long-suffering. "What?" I demanded. "Why are you...?"

"You didn't tell him, did you? Your dad. You didn't tell him about the visit."

"I was on the verge of it. I was about to. But..."

"Right. Pretty convenient. Moose shows up, ends your whole conversation."

To hear her, you'd think I could summon wild animals into my presence anytime, like Dr. Doolittle.

"I am going to do it," I said. "I got started. But then—"

"Where's Bella?" Ellie interrupted, letting me off the hook. It was mid-afternoon and the kitchen was oddly peaceful.

"I sent her home after she showed up with a pressure washer. She said before she got started on inside housework she wanted to clean the dirt off the outside. She was insistent about it."

Manic, actually, was a better term for what Bella had been. It was a project I could have gone along with, except that on my old house the paint would have dissolved along with the dirt, and under that paint was two-hundred-year-old clear cedar siding that the power washer would have saturated with water.

"So I gave her the day off. It was the only way I could get rid of her. And after we saw the moose my dad went over to her place, too. He needed a break from the shutters, so he's helping her put some more locks on her doors. Ones," I added, "that don't have handy keys hidden on the porch."

Not that it would do any good. I was starting to think our mysterious note writer should switch to smuggling gold bricks out of the Federal Reserve Depository.

For one thing, it would get him—or her—out of my hair. "You load that cedar siding up with water and the house might as well be draped in damp newspaper," I went on. "It'll never really dry. You'll never get paint to stick to it again."

Which was not what most house painters said about the idea of pressure-washing old houses, but that was because most house painters weren't up for grinding it off with a grinder. The only useful wood/water combination I'd ever heard of was pykrete, the ice-and-sawdust mix Sam had told me about. Speaking of whom:

"Hi," he uttered crisply as he came in.

"Hi," Ellie and I both replied.

He went to the refrigerator, pulled out a chicken leg and a bottle of soda, and went up to his room with them.

"Hmm, I see we're doing really well in that department, too," Ellie commented.

"Yeah." I told her about the ring at Kendall's. "He's being a butt-head," I concluded.

Ellie didn't answer. "My dad thinks I'm worrying too much," I went on. "And I suppose you think I ought to leave him alone about it, too, don't you?" I accused, seeing the look on her face.

"I think maybe you've pushed him into a corner, is all."

From the Snugli carrier strapped to Ellie's body, Leonora opened her eyes and uttered a syllable of infant contentment. In her pink stretch-knit sleeper and little white booties she looked sweet as a lollipop.

"Just wait till *she* starts acting up," I fumed.

But then I was struck by a new insight: My dad was right. I'd turned out halfway decent despite ghastly early decisions. And in the end Sam's decisions might *not* be ghastly.

Hey, it *could* happen. But even if it didn't, probably I should quit trying to exert control I didn't have.

And couldn't get. "You know," I said slowly to Ellie, "maybe it's not Sam who's being the butt-head around here."

She was dressed in a pink sweater that matched the baby's sleeper. With it she wore a red turtleneck, chartreuse leggings, a gold-flecked hair ribbon, and the kind of gentle smile she often displayed when I showed signs of not being an idiot.

"How long have you known?" I asked. "That I've been..."

"Pounding your fists and stomping your feet and acting as if your son's behavior was all about you?"

I stared. That pretty much summed it up, all right.

She shrugged. "Couple of weeks."

"And how long were you planning to let me get away with it?"

Another shrug. "Until you got over it. I knew you would."

She put her hand on my arm. "I," Ellie pronounced with radiant simplicity, "have confidence in you."

They've got her picture in the dictionary, I hear, beside the word *friend*.

"Anyway," she said, "I think we should get back to work on the Jim Diamond thing, the way we planned."

Instantly my defenses snapped reflexively up again. "But Ellie, they're coming and my dad doesn't want to *see* them...and the guest rooms... and Sam's still hanging out with Kris, and—"

"You're waving your arms around," she observed placidly. "Put them down before you hurt yourself, Jake."

So I did, whereupon she explained to me what we were going to do for the rest of the afternoon. And I will admit her ideas were smarter than anything I could've come up with, given my state of mind.

But they also led to something more dangerous than either of us planned on encountering.

Lots more.

Chapter 11

Azenath Jones was a short, fortyish woman with long, wavy chestnut hair, an engaging smile, and a figure that went beyond plus-size.

Way beyond; Azenath was what Victor would have called a time bomb of avoirdupois, while getting out his blood pressure cuff. Still she carried her size with dignity and aplomb, even humor.

Her eyes, summing me up in a glance as I entered her office with Ellie, were a peculiar shade of light golden brown, and so intelligent I felt as if my bone marrow was being scanned.

"Hello, ladies," she welcomed us in her gravelly voice. For her work that day at the Gopher Baroque agency she wore a vast purple silk paisley caftan, black harem pants, gold sandals over fire-engine-red toenail polish, and masses of copper bracelets on both plump freckled wrists.

"Lovely child," she added, inspecting Leonora, but having paid this compliment she dismissed the infant instantly from her attention.

Babies clearly weren't high on Azenath's list of interests. "Now, what can I do for you?" she asked us.

The office was on the top floor of the Hixton Building, a newly rehabbed nineteenth-century structure overlooking the water. One wall was exposed brick, two were whitewashed barn boards, and the third was glass sliding doors leading onto a sunlit deck.

Azenath's desk was an old oak table whose rich finish was partly covered by a leather-bound green desk blotter. "Well, as you probably know, I spoke with Dinah," I began as we sat across from her.

Her businesslike expression softened. "Yes, she told me. I hope Bella hasn't given you any further—"

"No," I interjected hastily, "she hasn't."

The last thing I wanted was more trouble for Bella, whose whole future depended upon her remaining employable in Eastport.

Assuming, that is, that she stayed out of jail. "But we need to know what you learned about her before you hired her," Ellie told Azenath.

Because as Ellie had realized, working in people's houses was a tricky business. The clients and the employment agency had to trust the employee completely, and if that trust turned out to be undeserved everybody could lose big-time.

And Azenath hadn't just fallen off the pumpkin truck. "Some specific information you were looking for?" she asked, narrowing her eyes.

"The name of the firm Jim Diamond defrauded with his check scheme, for one thing," I put in.

We could have gotten it out of public records, or Bob Arnold might've remembered. We could have asked around town, too, or questioned Bella. But the former would take a trip to the Machias courthouse, while the latter would betray our ongoing interest.

And I wasn't kidding about keeping a low profile, even with Bella herself. Besides, as Ellie had pointed out, Azenath would know. She'd have dug up everything about Bella before sending her out to work under the auspices of Gopher Baroque.

"And anything else you can tell us about the whole case, for another," I finished. "Because..."

I searched my mind for a plausible reason. While I was doing so, Azenath came up with a real one.

"Bella's in trouble," she said simply. By now, word of the housekeeper's being a suspect would have gotten out.

"Yes," I admitted. No sense screwing around with Azenath. Besides, as Ellie had also realized, Azenath wouldn't gab to anyone else about Bella's problem *or* our interest in it. After all, Bella was still an employee of Gopher Baroque.

And like bank manager Bill Imrie, Azenath knew mud rubs off.

Unfortunately that meant she might not gab to us, either. In fact at first it didn't seem she would; instead she just went on gazing at us from behind that big desk.

So I gave her some incentive. "Bella's a good worker. I like her a lot. She's a little bit nuts and I enjoy that in a person."

For the first time Azenath's smile became warmly genuine, showing white teeth. Her office smelled faintly of patchouli oil.

"And?" she inquired. "I agree about Bella, by the way," she added.

"And if I can keep her out of trouble, I'll keep her on," I promised rashly. "It would mean an ongoing commission for Gopher Baroque and an ongoing success story for your business, too, a long-term local placement."

I'd remembered what Dinah had said about summer being their busy time. What they needed was business during the winter. By my promise I was volunteering to be the poster girl for that, *and* taking it on faith that once the current difficulties were over I wouldn't have to keep Bella in line with a whip and chair.

But I could worry about all that later. "So to *help* me keep her out of trouble, what I want in addition to what you learned is what you thought about it all," I finished.

"Who else," she deduced accurately, "was in on the scheme?"

Just then Dinah came in, dressed as if she'd just gotten off the subway in lower Manhattan: contrasting tank tops in black and turquoise, a gray zippered sweatshirt with a silver thread in the fabric, black jeans faded to the right shade of gray, and black high-top sneakers with little white ruffles poking out.

"Oh," she said to Azenath, nodding briefly at Ellie and me. "I didn't realize you had..."

The information in the glance that passed between them could have filled a book; *War and Peace,* maybe. At the end of it Dinah nodded, went into her own office, and closed the door behind her.

Which only confirmed my sense of the closeness between these two. If one got the hiccups the other drank backward out of a glass. I didn't know how they'd found each other; there seemed not the slightest hint of a romantic connection between them.

But I knew not everyone was capable of being that kind of friend, and respected Azenath for it. Moments later she confirmed another of my opinions about her, that she wouldn't hire the Archangel Gabriel without doing a background check.

Ten minutes after that, we had what we'd come for: more facts on what Jim Diamond had done to get sent to prison.

"And the name of the business?" I asked.

"That I don't know," Azenath said. "It was a mom-and-pop lumberyard and building supply business, now defunct, I know that much," she said, confirming what Bill Imrie had told me.

"The owner was ill when Jim Diamond went to work there," she added. "Likely that was how he managed to get his scheme going. The boss being half out of the picture already, I mean."

I agreed that it was a logical conclusion. An illness or family crisis made small businesses especially vulnerable to such things.

"Do you know what he did there? I mean what his job was?" Ellie asked.

Azenath nodded. "He was a salesman. And that's what puzzles me. If he'd worked on the office side, I could see how he got at the accounts, and even how he could steal blank checks. If the owner trusts you, you can steal a business blind before anything trips you up, assuming you have hands-on access to the books in the first place."

Again I agreed. "But a salesperson wouldn't have had that kind of access in the normal course of doing business."

"Correct," she responded a little patronizingly, as if I were a bright student. I wasn't used to being addressed that way.

But from Azenath it was all right. "So there's a pair of mysteries still unsolved," she added. "How he did it, got the checks he forged and fiddled the books to cover his tracks."

"It didn't come out in court?" I asked, surprised.

She shook her head. "Took a plea, saved the county the cost of a trial. Said enough to clear the bank teller the cops thought was in on it with him. But that was all. His lip was zipped, and he went off to jail without clearing it up."

Ellie spoke up. "And the other mystery?"

Azenath looked up as if the answer should be obvious. "Well, the money, of course. That's the other thing he wouldn't say."

She pushed herself up from behind her desk and crossed to the big windows. Out on the water a motor yacht idled, waiting for a signal from the harbormaster to come into the boat basin.

A thought struck me. "Where'd you get all this information?"

She turned. "I called the attorney the court had appointed to defend him at the time. I'd met this guy before, he knew I was on the up-and-up, and I told him I just wanted to be sure there was no lingering suspicion of Bella being in on it."

"But then he got chatting," I guessed, "and...?"

She chuckled throatily. "Yes. Amazing what people will tell you, isn't it? Not anything confidential or privileged, of course, but he did like the sound of his own voice."

From the other office I heard Dinah on the phone, telling someone they'd have to go on a waiting list.

"At that point," Azenath went on, "I could've asked for more details. But after he'd reassured me I didn't have to worry about Bella, I didn't need them."

Sure. Once her own concerns were handled, she wouldn't have cared who Jim Diamond drove out of business. She returned to her desk, tented her plump fingers atop it.

I took it as a signal that our time with her was nearly up. "So what's your theory about the money?"

She shrugged. "Once he'd deposited it, Diamond withdrew it in cash as soon as he could. I don't even know how much it was."

Over thirty thousand, though; that's what made it a felony. And if it drove the victims out of business, it could have been a lot more.

Azenath raised her large arms gracefully, let them fall with a jingle of copper bracelets and a swish of loose silk sleeves.

"It's doubtful he spent it. No new car, anything like that."

Right, and a guy like Jim wouldn't have had the forethought or know-how to stash it by some other method—in some offshore account, for instance. Also, the kind of weasel who swindled his employer generally went for flashy vehicles and department-store shopping sprees, anyway.

"So," Azenath inquired simply, "where is it now?"

In the light from the big windows her long wavy hair had an auburn glint, and she looked beautiful in the caftan. She didn't choose clothes to minimize her size, and I liked her for that, too.

"What an interesting question," I said, smiling.

Thinking, *Yes. Follow the money.*

"I thought you'd enjoy it," she said. "Possibly someone else knows the answer, but not I. And now that you've picked my brain clean of every morsel it contains," she added suggestively.

"You have work to do. Of course." Ellie and I got up.

"So the business is going well," I remarked to Azenath as she walked with us to the door.

Against the backdrop of the windows she was a large, dark figure, almost menacing, and the patchouli oil was suddenly overpowering. Then she stepped toward me, her face came into the light, and the perfume unaccountably faded.

"Yes. Dinah and I are pleased with the way things are going so far."

Which I thought must be an understatement. Dinah's phone had rung with inquiries several times during our visit; it seemed to me these two women had come up with a license to print money.

"Good luck on your inquiry," she added pleasantly.

"Thanks. And Azenath, if you could just..."

Nodding, she made a lip-zipping gesture. "Confidential, of course. Who knows, Dinah or I could need your help some day."

She put out her hand to touch Leonora's smooth cheek with a red-tipped finger. "Sweet little thing," she murmured.

Then the phone rang again and before Ellie and I had even gotten out of the office, I felt sure Azenath had forgotten us.

"The nerve!" Ellie said indignantly when we had gotten down to the street. "She didn't even ask Leonora's name!"

"I'm pretty sure Azenath calls all babies 'it,'" I replied. "But don't take it personally. She's just all business, is all."

"I guess," Ellie grumbled, then pounced on the thing Azenath had suggested without ever quite saying it.

"An accomplice. Not Bella, but Azenath still thinks there must have been someone else in on Jim's fraud scheme," she declared.

"Right. Someone who helped Jim *and* who might still have some of the money." It would have been a very good reason for Diamond not to want to talk about it: to preserve the stash.

And more recently, it could provide a motive for murder. "What we need now is someone who was there at the time. Someone with an idea of who Jim's accomplice might have been."

Ellie frowned. "At the business he defrauded? But how are we going to find someone like that? From the sound of it, the place has been gone since he went to jail. We'd need a time machine to go back and..."

Brilliant as usual. "A time machine," I repeated. "Yes, it's just what we need."

And fortunately, I was pretty sure we had one.

It was only a short walk back up Key Street to my house, but during it I thought we might as well have been in a time machine already. Men from the VFW were painting the outside of the band shell on the library lawn; in it, high school students practiced for the Fourth of July concert, tooting out "Yankee Doodle."

"...needles in haystacks," Ellie fretted.

Meanwhile the ladies from the Historical Society draped the lawn's picket fence in patriotic tricolored bunting, chatting about the strawberry shortcake social scheduled for the holiday.

"...moved away, or gone to work on freighters, or up to the woods to work for the lumber companies," Ellie went on.

She meant the ex-employees of the lumber-and-building-supply company Jim Diamond had driven out of business.

But I was only half listening. All the summer scene needed was about twelve thousand happy visitors here to witness the parade and band concert, cheer the traditional Eastport Fourth of July competitions—

—the greasy-pole walk (out over the cold salt water), the codfish relay race (with the codfish gripped in your teeth), and the blueberry pie-eating contest (nice change from the codfish) were my personal favorites—

—and finally to see fireworks being shot from a barge out in Passamaquoddy Bay, on the last evening.

And from the number of RVs, camper trucks, and other tourist vehicles streaming into town already, it seemed we would have at least twelve thousand visitors before the festivities even began.

Bang! A cherry bomb went off behind the Motel East, and then what sounded like an M-80. A smoke puff floated up as a bunch of middle-school-age boys ran laughing from the scene.

"Bob Arnold," Ellie observed, "will have his hands full."

"Good," I said. "All the easier for us to snoop without him noticing." Or anyone else either, I hoped.

"But I still don't see..."

Then I revealed my plan. "Oh," she breathed comprehendingly. "You're right, Jake, that'll work."

At my house we greeted the dogs, put the baby down for her nap, and then rooted through the phone alcove until we found the time machine I'd been talking about: an area telephone book from when I'd first moved here, seven years earlier.

"Don't you ever throw these away?" Ellie asked.

There were seven of them stacked in the alcove, including the current one. "I try."

I shuffled through to find the earliest one. "But I feel so guilty putting them in the trash and I can't seem to get them to the collection place. So they pile up."

Fortunately, phone books stack neatly; otherwise Bella would have made short work of them on her first day here. I opened the old and the new one to the same yellow pages listings.

There were only a few lumber-and-supply outfits in Washington County, so identifying the one that had vanished from the listings was easy. Let's see, Pinkham's was still there; so were EBS and Guptill's. But wait, here was one that hadn't survived... "Duckworth's Building and Hardware," I read. "Machias."

"Really." She peered over my shoulder. "In *that* case..."

"What?" I demanded impatiently.

"I remember Duckworth's. My dad used to take me there. It was on a side street," she recalled. "There were barns, a lumber warehouse, a couple of equipment sheds, the main store, and..."

A mental light went on as I imagined it. "A house," I said. "Is that it? Did the owners live there?"

She nodded slowly. "Right on the premises. And maybe—"

Maybe they still did.

The noonish brilliance of a Maine summer afternoon gives you the idea that you have more time than you really do. But as Ellie and I passed the turnoff to Lubec with the sun still high, I felt something like evening closing in even though the sky remained bright.

"Want me to drop you off somewhere?" I asked casually. "The park, or maybe the library?"

Fed, changed, and played with until she began nodding again, Leonora slept peacefully, strapped into the car seat behind us.

Ellie thought about my offer. "I guess not," she said. "If I change my mind, though..."

Her hesitation meant she too felt gun-shy about this visit. Unfortunately, there is a one-to-one relationship between you getting closer to a killer, and the killer getting closer to you. So possibly some precautions were in order.

"Okay, look," I said. "First we have to find out if anyone from the family even still lives there. After that only one of us has to get in. Probably the other one should wait, and set a—"

"Time limit," Ellie finished my thought. "Wait outside for a set period, then—"

"Knock on the door, try to find out what's cooking. Use your judgment, but if things don't seem right to you—"

"Right. Go to plan B."

Which could be anything from calling the cops to driving the car through the door, depending on the situation. Zipping through the wilderness stretch between Whiting and Machias, I relaxed a hairsbreadth behind the wheel.

We had to make allowances for Leonora: her presence with us today, and the fact of her existence generally. And since having Ellie stay outside the Duckworth house might also help ensure *my* continued existence, I thought our plan would work out well for everyone concerned.

Because after all, neither of us could tell yet what I might find there; last time, it had been a corpse.

"Turn here," Ellie said after we had crossed the Machias River twice: once on the causeway where the old railroad station stood like a wooden ghost, again at the bridge over Bad Little Falls with the water rushing and tumbling beneath us.

I followed her direction onto a narrow, curving side street that climbed along the riverbank. Here, sea captains' mansions with turrets topped by ornate cast-iron widows' walks hulked as if peering down on us, their fan-lighted front doors flanked by rows of mailboxes for the apartments the houses had been cut into.

After that came smaller homes, their exteriors covered with aluminum siding. Finally the street narrowed, pavement dissolving to gravel as a set of farm buildings loomed ahead.

DUCKWORTH'S, read the faded black lettering on the red barn. Behind a chain-link fence stood sheds, utility buildings, stacks of wooden pallets, and an old forklift parked by a loading dock.

I shut off the car. The whole place was as still as a held breath. Leonora stirred, smiling and waving her arms as Ellie leaned back to unbuckle her and bring her up front.

Then Ellie turned to me. "Go get 'em," she said.

So I did, although still a little doubtfully. The house at least looked harmless enough, a pleasant two-story Victorian with white siding, black shutters, and a wide, sunny front porch with a pair of wicker rockers on it.

Pink geraniums bloomed between white eyelet curtains at the windows, and an old Irish setter scrambled up to meet me as I climbed the iron-railed front steps.

"Hey, boy," I said, leaning down to smooth his silky ears with one hand, pressing the doorbell with the other.

Not until I heard footsteps did I realize I hadn't planned what to say. "Hi, you don't know me but I'm here to root around in your painful past" didn't seem quite appropriate.

And the alternative–that I was an Eastport busybody looking to find out who really bonked Jim Diamond with a skillet–wasn't what Emily Post would have recommended, either.

But my lack of preparation turned out not to matter, since when the door opened and I saw who lived here, the unexpectedness of it forced every other thought from my head.

"Why, hello," said the gray-haired, beautifully groomed lady who greeted me. "What a pleasant surprise."

It was the Red Cross volunteer who'd been in Eastport asking for blood. "I'm Lydia Duckworth," she said kindly, stepping aside to let me in.

"Do excuse the mess, I'm working at home today. Would you like a cup of tea? And your friend," she added, peering through the front window, "perhaps she'd like to come in, too?"

The mess consisted of a neat stack of papers on the rug by an armchair, a fountain pen atop the stack, and a lamp angled to illuminate the wheeled writing table pushed away from the chair.

"Thanks, but she wanted to walk a bit. To settle the baby," I improvised, hoping Ellie's next actions would confirm me in this.

They did. From between the drawn curtains I saw her get out of the car with Leonora in her arms, strolling under the trees away from the house to where the road became a grassy track.

Distantly, a kettle whistled. "As you like," Mrs. Duckworth replied cheerfully. "Now, I'll just be a moment."

While she was gone I looked around the immaculate parlor with its groupings of African violets blooming moistly on doilies near the windows. Hummel figurines in a display hutch faced gold-framed photos, several of which were of Lydia Duckworth and a man of about her own age, early sixties or so.

In each successive photograph the man had lost weight, his face in the final one gauntly knowing and his eyes huge and dark. *The owner was ill,* Azenath Jones had said.

"Now, what can I do for you?" Lydia Duckworth inquired when she had returned to pour the tea.

Crunch time; what should I say? Over in the corner the Irish setter sank into his bed, smiled gamely at us, then snored.

"Come, come, don't be shy," Lydia Duckworth urged quietly. "I gather you haven't come all this way just to sign up to give blood." She poured for both of us. "And whatever it is, you needn't worry about shocking my feelings. I assume that it must be something about Jim Diamond's having been murdered?"

She glanced at the shelf full of photographs, her pale gaze lingering on the ones of her husband before returning to me.

"I know your reputation, you see," she added gently. "And that of your friend. When you first moved to Maine you might have counted on anonymity for your inquiries."

She smiled a little mischievously. "But not anymore."

I sipped tea to cover my confusion; so much for a low profile. "Why don't you tell me what it is you want to ask, and I will answer if I can," Mrs. Duckworth suggested.

Her eyes had gone steely behind the gold-rimmed half-glasses as she looked at her husband's picture.

"I'd like to know, too," she said. Her tone was no longer quite so gentle. "Who Jim's helper was back then, I mean. Although I can't say I'm sorry he's dead, even if it means he can't tell us."

She looked up. "Forgive me if I'm jumping to conclusions. But surely it makes sense that his accomplice might've had a hand in his murder."

She was a quick study. But then, she'd had a lot of time to think about it.

Still, I wasn't ready to confide in her yet. I waved at the papers she'd been working on, the Red Cross logo visible on them.

"It's a long drive from Machias to volunteer in Eastport," I remarked.

"It is," she agreed immediately. "But my husband had so many blood transfusions during his illness, and they had no spots open for volunteers any nearer by. I keep busy with my charity work," she added. "I find it keeps me from becoming bitter."

Because what you put out there comes back to you, or so she probably hoped. A clock ticked hollowly somewhere in the house.

I thought about how quiet it would be in my own house if Wade and Sam were not living in it, and decided suddenly to tell her what I'd come here to learn instead of angling for it.

"It's about my housekeeper," I said. "I think you know her?"

She nodded, listening carefully without interrupting until I finished. What she said then surprised me.

But like I said, she was a quick study. "When I first became a Red Cross volunteer they told us that when you go into people's houses, you go at your peril."

She glanced out to where Ellie sat with Leonora on the grass under a maple tree across from the barn.

"Bring along a friend, have the friend wait outside for you, they said," Mrs. Duckworth went on, turning from the window. "So that if you don't come out again in a reasonable amount of time, your friend can help you."

She took the glasses off, rubbed a finger wearily over one eyelid. The vulnerable moment underlined her resolute look.

"And do you follow that advice?" I'd seen no one with her in Eastport.

She shrugged minutely, a what-does-it-matter shrug. "No."

It was my move, and I was pretty certain she hadn't poisoned my tea. "Why don't I call her in now?" I suggested. "Ellie would probably want to hear what you have to say, also."

So I did. Ellie relaxed in the well-kept parlor and as quickly as I had. It was so comfortably unpretentious you felt you could kick your shoes off, yet spotless and smelling sweetly of houseplants and furniture polish.

And as usual, Ellie noticed something I'd missed. "Jake," she breathed, peering at something on the wall, "look at this."

Glancing at it earlier without really seeing, I'd thought it was a painting; instead, it was a large, very detailed piece of needlework, mounted and beautifully framed. Embroidery, I thought, but to call it that didn't really do it justice.

Nothing could. "Look at those stitches," Ellie marveled.

Fine as hairs, and in every possible color on the finest of ivory linen, they depicted a rich scene of life in some long-ago royal palace, with courtiers, ladies, peacocks, fountains . . .

It was astonishing, and immaculately worked. I thought it must have cost a fortune.

Then I noticed another chair with a tapestry frame pulled up to it and a magnifying lamp set nearby. Beside the chair lay an open canvas case equipped with slots for the sharp implements it contained: needles glinting in every size, some curved and others straight, scissors whose long, short, and angled blades gleamed wickedly, and a variety of other small, bright tools that I couldn't identify.

In its organization and the obvious quality of the things it held, it was like Victor's case of surgical instruments. Ready to hand, too, stood a tall wooden rack filled with dozens of spools of colored thread. Lydia came up behind me as I turned from it.

"Did you . . . ?" I began, gesturing at the framed tapestry. She nodded in reply.

"For a while after my husband passed away, I didn't do much else," she replied evenly. "Every time I finish one, I'm certain I never want to start another."

Each stitch was a tiny marvel, a molecule of color capturing the green iridescence in a peacock's tail, the purple of a grape.

"But as you see," she added with a modest little laugh and a wave at the tapestry frame, covered now with a new linen as white and fine as a blank page, "my resolutions don't last."

Then she got her first close-up look at Leonora. "Come here, you lovely girl," she cooed delightedly at the infant, instantly gratifying Ellie, who was still smarting over Azenath Jones's neglect.

Even Leonora, who was ordinarily not a big fan of strangers, cooperated. She accepted a remarkable amount of cuddling and baby talk before allowing herself to be put down on a soft, crocheted afghan that Lydia supplied, on the floor by our chairs.

And only then did Lydia speak frankly. "When I heard Jim Diamond had been murdered I confess my first thought was, good. Good for whoever did it."

"Probably you weren't the only one," Ellie responded gently.

"Perhaps. But that doesn't make it right. Only he did ruin my husband's business and hasten his death," Lydia went on, "so I can't seem to shake that last bit of vengefulness in my heart."

I thought she was being too hard on herself, and said so. She smiled in return.

"You are kind. But I know my duty, and revenge isn't it, not even in my imagination."

She shook her head ruefully. "Besides, Diamond was as much a victim as my husband, I've come to believe."

"Really? How so?" I asked, bewildered.

"When the check forging began my husband was still fairly well, and still in charge of the computer. But Howard—my husband's name was Howard—he wasn't at the top of his game anymore. He was on medication."

"So someone could have...what? Lied to him? Tricked him?"

Lydia Duckworth shook her head. "That's just the trouble. I don't know. Jim Diamond never admitted how he got checks that he could forge. And the computer records were destroyed in a power surge during a storm, soon after he was caught out."

She sighed regretfully. "So it wasn't possible to reconstruct what he'd done to them. Or—what someone else had."

She straightened. "Then Howard's condition worsened. The business closed, the employees moved away for other jobs..."

Ellie's glance met mine: drat.

"...not that it mattered," Lydia Duckworth added, "because the police had questioned them all."

"So you couldn't find out what had been done, or where the money got to," I concluded.

She sipped from her porcelain cup. "That's right, unfortunately. But what I do know is, no salesman had the kind of access Jim Diamond had to have gotten, to do what he did. Someone else had to steal those checks and give them to him, and someone who did have good access to the computer—authorized or not—had to help cover his tracks afterward."

She set the cup down carefully. I got the feeling she'd have liked to smash it. "Jim wasn't," she finished, "smart."

Ellie tipped her head thoughtfully. "So it's a stretch to think he'd have known how to fiddle the computer at all?"

"Precisely," Lydia Duckworth replied, looking grateful. "You have no idea how hard I tried to get that idea across to all the investigators at the time. But they just kept insisting that he'd forged the checks and cashed them, and that *that* was the crime. A helper, a brain for the operation, wasn't on their wish list."

"Besides, he insisted he didn't have one," I said, thinking again about the usefulness of a silent partner in such cases. To, for example, hang on to the loot until such time as the fall guy finally got out of prison.

Whereupon the fall guy would naturally want his share of the stash.

"Could your husband have done it?"

To her credit, she didn't look offended. Instead she seemed relieved to be talking about it, even about the parts that might reflect badly on her late spouse.

"I've wondered myself," she answered without hesitation. "Steal money from the business, avoid paying taxes, spend it on luxuries? Or some such notion. But as I say, he was ill by then. Luxuries were the last thing he wanted."

The dark, hollowly knowing eyes in the photograph agreed. By then, ordinary life would have been the luxury.

She went on. "Besides, once he was in the hospital I had to do all the financial things. Make the final payroll, pay off all the suppliers, and so on. And I never found evidence that he had money hidden, or that he'd spent any I didn't know about."

"And after his death?" I inquired gently.

"In the house, you mean? Among his things? I'd looked before he died." An edge of pain came into her voice.

Which made sense, too; of course she'd have searched the place. And while none of it could have been pleasant, trying to find out if your husband is a thief while he lies dying must rank near the top of the hideous-chores list.

"Jim was arrested just about a month before Howard passed away. The minute I learned the details of what he'd done, I knew Howard could have been in on it even if I couldn't understand *why* he might have helped in such a scheme. He *could* have taken the checks, faked records, and so on."

Her voice thickened. "That's why I went over this house from attic to cellar. In the pockets of his old suits. Everywhere."

She met my gaze. "No bankbooks. No safe-deposit receipts. No secret credit cards or stash of gold coins. Later I even let the investigators look. They didn't find anything, either."

Her fingertips pressed together. "So if Howard had any of the money Jim Diamond stole from our business, all I can say is that he must have burnt it up in the fireplace."

"You didn't have hard copies of your accounts? Paper printouts, I mean?" I inquired.

Because it seemed awfully convenient that computer records should have been destroyed, just when examining them might have been productive.

She shook her head ruefully. "No. Of course the police all wanted to know that, as well. But it was another thing I learned the hard way, not to rely on electronic storage."

The old dog got up, stretched, and moved to lie down beside Leonora. Lydia Duckworth smiled sadly at the pair.

"We tried using the paper records we did have, the canceled checks, the bills from suppliers, and so on. But it was hopeless, and what did it matter, anyway? Money was gone, Jim Diamond had taken it, and no one knew a thing about what he'd done with it."

"And he wasn't saying," Ellie put in quietly. "And then your husband died."

Lydia Duckworth nodded. "Afterward, I didn't care. Or," she added, "I thought I didn't. Now, though..."

Outside the sparkling windows of the Duckworth house, the shadows of the big old maples lining the road slanted toward late afternoon. I got up.

But Mrs. Duckworth wasn't finished. "Now that Diamond's death has brought it all to the forefront for me again, I find I do care what happened. I care very much."

Ellie gathered the baby up. "How he did it? And with whom, if there really was an accomplice?"

"Absolutely," she answered, her voice grim. "I want to know, even if it turns out there's nothing anyone can do about it. The money...that's secondary at this point. I just want to *know*."

A notion struck me. "Had you ever met his wife before you saw her at my house? Bella Diamond?"

A look of doubt crossed her face as she hesitated. "I'm not sure I..."

"It seemed to me you knew one another, that's all," I added.

She appeared to decide. "That's an awkward question. She asked me particularly not to tell anyone, but I managed not to say I'd promise because I thought it was so strange at the time."

"Strange?" Ellie inquired. The baby woke up and reached out very tentatively to stroke the dog's ear.

"Yes," Mrs. Duckworth said, "Bella came to see me. It was around the time Jim died. The same day, if what I've read in the papers is true. A few days later I went to her house in Eastport, not knowing it was hers, to leave a blood drive card." She thought briefly. "So that's twice I've met her, other than the day she came here. First at your house, then at hers. She was at Jim's sentencing, too, four years ago. But we didn't speak then. That is, she spoke to other people near me, but not directly *to* me. So I guess that doesn't count."

"Bella came here? What did she want?"

"It was quite extraordinary. She showed up soon after I had finished my lunch, saying she wanted to apologize on Jim's behalf. For the trouble he caused me, she said."

She looked down at the floor where the dog had begun snoring again. "And oddly enough, her visit helped. It reminded me that I wasn't the only victim in the affair...."

Squaring her shoulders, she met my gaze again. "But that day it seemed my listening to Bella helped her. And it's true, you know: Helping others is the remedy for a lot of troubles."

Her smile returned. "So, is that all you wanted to ask?"

"Just one more thing. Forgive me, but... would you have known how to help Jim Diamond steal that money? And how much did he steal, anyway?"

"Oh, yes," she replied without hesitation. "It was over a hundred thousand dollars, and I could have done it *quite* easily. As I said, I took over once my husband was ill. I was familiar with the computer."

She paused. "But as I also mentioned, the investigation was thorough. Everyone's financial matters were gone over with a fine-tooth comb, including mine."

She looked straight at me. "Nothing was found. And it doesn't really matter anymore."

She accompanied us to the door. Behind her the neat, well-kept house gleamed comfortably in the afternoon silence, broken only by the slow, measured ticking of the big case clock and the old dog's snores.

"But for my own satisfaction I'd still like to know how it was done," Lydia Duckworth said. "And," she added, "who the snake in the grass was."

Ten minutes later we were hurrying home through the onset of evening. The sun hung low, glaring blindingly over the horizon when we emerged from thick stands of trees, casting patterns of bright and dark onto the road ahead of us.

"So, is she on the level?" Ellie asked, meaning Lydia.

"What?" I lowered the visor, shaded my eyes with my hands.

Besides the glare, I was preoccupied with the notion Azenath Jones had suggested, and Mrs. Duckworth had confirmed: that Jim Diamond would've needed help with the stealing *and* the stashing of that hundred thousand dollars.

And there was no evidence he had spent it. "Everything she said would be easy to check," I replied. "And wait till I get hold of that Bella. She never mentioned seeing Lydia Duckworth at all, and she certainly didn't mention being in Machias that day. Which in case you forgot is in the vicinity of Lubec. Or near enough that she could've taken a side trip." A blaze of sunlight blinded me briefly. "Here we are driving all over creation to try to help her, and *she* won't..."

"...tell us all the pertinent facts," Ellie finished for me. "You're right, it's infuriating. But let's let her try to explain before we condemn her. She might have a reason."

"Sure, like her reasons for not telling about the money she was giving him, or about having a key to his place. Or about that damned skillet."

We reached the straightaway between the small roadside businesses of East Machias: a pie shop, an auto body repair, and a bottle-and-can re- demption operation.

"Next thing you know," I fumed, "we'll find out Bella just happens to have a handy little diagram of the human brain, so she knew just *where* to hit him."

The road curved hard, up and into the real wilderness. "Not that she won't have a good *reason*," I added sarcastically. "Oh, sure, she'll have *that*."

Ellie turned to Leonora, who was starting to get fussy. "Just a little longer. I know, we're testing your patience."

But the whole thing was starting to test my patience, too. Fifteen minutes later, we slowed for the intersection at Lubec, barely managing not to allow a camper to pull out ahead of us.

"This means someone can say Bella was in the area when Jim was killed," I added unhappily. "She could've visited Lydia, then gone to Lubec on her way back to Eastport. Maybe she had that skillet along, meaning to *give* it to him and she ended up hitting him with it instead."

"But we still think maybe she didn't, because...?"

"The notes," I replied grudgingly. "And the money. Where'd it go?"

I pressed on the gas pedal again. "There's just too much going on that we don't understand. And until we do..."

As we entered the Moosehorn Wildlife Refuge, a large shape loomed ahead of us; I touched the brakes. By this time of day most recreational vehicles had pulled into campgrounds for the evening so we hadn't gotten stuck behind any, but there was one up there now, lumbering along at about thirty-five miles per hour.

"...until then, I'm still going to wonder if the answer is in what we *don't* know," I finished, pulling up behind the big vehicle so the driver could see me, then tapping the horn gently. All I wanted was to let him know I was there.

A quick pull-over to let me by, and I could be on my way while he went on loafing and looking. Instead, he took it as an insult. He slowed to twenty-five and pulled as far to the left as he could, blocking any possible view around him.

I dropped back, biting my lip to keep the curse words I was thinking unspoken. "But for now," I told Ellie, "we're right where we started. We don't know who killed Jim, we don't know why, and we don't know what those dratted threat notes had to do with it."

"Or what Maggie was doing there that day," Ellie added, as if I needed to feel any more discouraged.

I'd thought Azenath had put us on the right track. To my mind, stolen money was a fine motive for murder. And it had been a good idea, trying to track down someone from Duckworth's.

But now it seemed all we'd gotten for our efforts was a cup of Earl Grey tea. Also, we remained firmly stuck behind that blasted RV for the rest of the trip.

Every time the road straightened, the camper sped up. On hills or curves it crept along, emitting smelly exhaust. Soon we were in a wagon train, as more cars lined up impatiently behind me. No one else could get around the behemoth, either.

Finally at the Eastport turnoff the RV rumbled on up Route 1 and we bid it a not-so-fond farewell, many drivers to the rear gesturing energetically after it to communicate how sentimental they had grown to feel about the big vehicle.

"There's another complication, too," I groused as we zoomed toward town with the red sun setting behind us. In the gathering evening the shore birds were black cutouts on the shining water. We sped across the causeway. "It's not enough to find out Bella *didn't* do it, because if all we do is clear her, the next in line to be a suspect is—"

"Maggie," Ellie concluded. "Because of your car. But no one else knows about that, do they?"

I explained what Bob Arnold had told me, that the car was going to come out sooner or later and that the logical answer to who'd been driving it *wasn't* Maggie; that it could be Sam.

"So unless we get ahead of it, the whole mess could go in any number of bad directions," I groaned.

"Don't you think Maggie would tell the truth if push came to shove?" Ellie asked reasonably.

"Sure. But would they believe her? Or would they just think she's lying to protect Sam?"

The streetlights in Eastport were coming on, and at the IGA only a few cars lingered in the parking lot. Turning onto Key Street, I came to a sudden decision.

"Whatever Maggie's story is, we have to know it now before all this— whatever it is—blows up in our faces. And I think it might be better if I talk with her alone. Maybe she won't feel so ganged-up on that way."

Besides, Leonora's fussing threatened to become a tantrum; she was a good baby, but she had her limits.

"I'll do dinner duty at your house," Ellie said generously, "and take care of the animals. But promise you won't go anywhere else without letting me know?"

"No," I assured her. "I mean yes, I won't, and I'll tell you all about it later. With any luck," I added, "I'll have cleared up the whole Maggie thing, anyway, by the time I get back."

I believed it, too, as I drove away down Key Street again; that I could clear it up. Out on the bay the running lights of vessels coming in for the evening twinkled serenely. Every time one of them bobbed into the boat basin, it was a promise kept: that even in the face of danger and uncertainty things could turn out all right.

So as I drove toward the studio apartment Maggie had taken for herself in a small complex of remodeled industrial buildings at the south end of the island, I felt reasonably optimistic.

Passing the old salt factory whose massive, dark-windowed remains loomed silently against the night sky, I drove on until I reached a long, low trio of wooden buildings extending out over the water. In the old days, the labels for sardine cans had been printed here. A slag heap of other old equipment still hulked by the long dirt drive leading in to the parking area.

The air was cool, tinctured with the sharp smell of exposed seaweed as

I got out of the car. Below, a half-collapsed wooden pier staggered out over the shallows of low tide.

But the building itself had been sturdily reinforced, and the walkway out to it felt solid under my feet. Lamps burned behind the curtains at Maggie's windows as I crossed the deck leading to her door, then knocked.

Inside, music was playing and I smelled something cooking; it was another of the things I liked about Maggie, that she took good care of herself. When she opened the door, though, my optimism evaporated. She took one look at my determined face, then dropped her hands to her sides in a gesture of utter surrender.

My heart dropped, too, at what she said.

"Jim Diamond was already dead," she said desolately, "when I found him. Or I thought he was."

She burst into sobs. "Oh, Jake, what am I going to do?"

Chapter 12

Could it have happened the way she said?" I asked Victor a little while later, after I'd persuaded Maggie to come back with me to my house.

"Oh, sure," he replied, closing his medical bag. Maggie had seemed so distraught, I'd been worried about her, but by the time he arrived she'd calmed down enough to let him tend to her.

"People survive with iron bars in their skulls," Victor informed me. "They regain consciousness after dozen-year comas. Once in a while, they even wake up in morgue refrigerators."

He loved grisly stories like that. "It's amazing what brain-injured people can do," he said. "Diamond looked dead to Maggie, lingered on for twenty-four hours or so, went out with a bang. It's not," he added, "even that rare."

At which point he looked ready to supply me with colorful examples from his experience, but I cut him off with a gesture. My memory of the way Diamond had gone out was colorful enough.

"What was she doing visiting his place at all?" he wanted to know.

Just then Maggie appeared in the door of the front parlor, looking pale but resolute. "I thought if I paid him, he might go away," she answered.

She'd refused Victor's offer of a sedative, insisting she just wanted to lie down. But being all alone upstairs obviously hadn't set too well with her, either.

"I had a thousand dollars with me, everything I've saved. I was going to offer it to him, if..."

If he would leave, so his stepdaughter Kris might decide to get lost, as well. To go to beauty school the way she'd planned.

And leave Sam alone. Just as I'd theorized, Maggie had taken matters into her own hands. "How did you know he was there, *or* that his leaving might clear the way for Kris?" I asked her.

"Sam told me. Back when he was still confiding in me, trying to defend Kris, he told me about her stepfather. He said Kris hated him and wouldn't move away from her mother as long as he was around. Made Kris sound like a real martyr. But then I thought, hey, maybe it's true, and it *could* work. Me trying to get rid of him, I mean. I was ready to try anything, because by then I had found out about..." She stopped.

"Found out what?" I pressed her.

"Nothing." A pause, then: "I don't understand," she burst out plaintively to Victor. "He wasn't *breathing* when I found him, I'm sure that he wasn't. And he didn't have a pulse. I'd never have left him if he wasn't already..."

She'd found Jim Diamond's door open just as I had, and called out several times to see if anyone was there. Then she'd gone inside.

"He was breathing," Victor said. "Just not very often. You probably didn't look at him for long. And his pulse would have been too weak for a layperson to feel."

"So I left him to die," she said in tones of self-revulsion. "If I hadn't, he might've—"

"No." Victor pronounced it with authority. "It wouldn't have made any difference."

He pulled on his jacket. "The damage was already fatal. At the end something changed, a blood clot in his brain shifted or his pressure dropped enough for the swelling to subside a little. So he got one last hur-rah, lunging up at Jake the way he did."

He looked at Maggie. "The brain injury he suffered was terminal as soon as it happened. I saw it, Maggie. Afterward at the hospital. And be-lieve me, I'm the man who knows."

Deep sigh from Victor. "But under the circumstances I can't say I'm sur-prised you're not convinced. Try not to feel guilty."

"But I do! How can I *not*? I should have called the police! A man was killed." She gazed at us, distraught.

"But after I found him I didn't want anyone to know I'd been there. So," she finished in tones of self-disgust, "I ran, and I *didn't* tell anyone. All I could think of was myself."

Victor looked at her for a moment. "You know, Maggie, it's not so bad to think about yourself. You should do it more often."

That stopped her cold. We left her in the parlor looking miserable, as I followed Victor to the door. "Thanks," I told him.

He shrugged. "No problem. Poor kid, she's devastated."

"Yeah. She told me on the way here that it was Sam she was thinking of when she ran from Diamond's. That if Jim was dead, what did it matter who found him? And she thought Sam would be mad at her for trying to interfere."

"Yeah. Probably he would." He paused uncomfortably, leaving a good deal unsaid between us. As usual.

I hated seeing Maggie so hurt and made a fool of by Sam, in part be-cause I'd been made very much the same kind of fool years earlier by the man standing before me.

So I knew how it felt. And I had a funny intuition that now Victor did, too.

But this wasn't the time to explore it. "G'night, Victor," I said finally, closing the door.

Back in the parlor I found Maggie sitting quietly with her hands in a praying gesture, fingers pressed to her lips. Her long dark hair hung loose about her shoulders; she looked beautiful, and utterly wretched.

"Maggie," I ventured, "are you sure you don't have anything more to tell me?"

But she said nothing, having derived I supposed a measure of relief, however incomplete, from telling the truth about what had happened.

And not wanting to start lying again now.

"I never," Bella denied vehemently a few minutes later.

I found her in my kitchen, where she'd insisted on staying to wash up the dishes after Ellie had cooked dinner for everyone.

"I don't know what that Duckworth woman is talking about," Bella declared.

She had a dish towel in her hands, an apron around her waist, and a look of apparent incomprehension on her face.

"I just treated her friendly, like I would anyone doing a charity job," she insisted. "I didn't know her, and I didn't know who she was, either. She never said."

Ellie stood by the refrigerator with a Tupperware container of Maine shrimp in garlic sauce in one hand—by all accounts it had been delicious—and the baby's bottle in the other.

"Bella, she told us," Ellie said, sounding impatient. "We saw Lydia Duckworth and she told us you were there to see her."

The housekeeper shook her head, but as she did so a sly look flashed across her face. I glanced at the shrimp dish, thought about having some, and knew that if I did it would turn to shrimp wiggle in my stomach.

And on top of the other events of the day, Bella's look of duplicity was the last straw. "All right, Bella," I said. "Finish up, then, and go home. We'll talk about it in the morning."

Once Bella was gone Ellie reached into the refrigerator, got the bottle of beer George had brought along to drink with dinner but hadn't—perhaps feeling delicate about it at the table with Sam there—and handed it to me.

"Jake. Go take a hot bath," she ordered.

Which I did, and between the bubbles in the bathwater and the ones in that beer, I came back down an hour later feeling better. The situation was better, too, or so it seemed at first.

Everything was quiet. In the parlor, Kris and Sam sat on the sofa watching TV, Sam's arm tight around the girl's skinny, bare shoulder. The maid's room door was shut, Ellie in there changing the baby and settling her for the rest of the evening, while Wade and George had gone up to Wade's workshop where Wade was showing off a new shotgun, because if summer was here then hunting season couldn't be far behind.

And Maggie had taken the dogs out, no doubt feeling about as comfortable as I did in the company of the two lovebirds. She returned as I was putting the beer bottle into the recycling bag.

"You all right?" I asked her.

"Fine," she said quietly, hanging the leashes up.

But she wasn't, and what happened next proved it. I suppose I should have known better than to let Maggie get anywhere near Kris and Sam, but by then I was a little tipsy, and so exhausted I figured everyone else must be tired, too, and would call a truce.

Sure, and after that the lions and the lambs would lie down together. "Thief!" Kris shrieked moments later from the parlor.

"Slut!" Maggie shot back.

And those were just the nicer remarks. By the time I got in there, things were threatening to degenerate into a hair-pulling contest, with Sam backing away in horror as if his nice little harem situation—with himself at the center of it as the grand pooh-bah, of course—had turned into a nest of snakes.

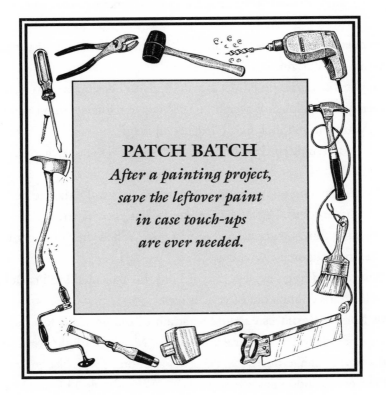

PATCH BATCH

After a painting project,
save the leftover paint
in case touch-ups
are ever needed.

What goes around comes around, I thought nastily at him, but of course I didn't say this. For one thing, I was too busy keeping Maggie and Kris from scratching each other's eyes out.

"I know you stole it!" Kris accused Maggie venomously. "My locket, you're always staring at it. Now it's gone, and who else would take it?"

"Who would want it?" Maggie shot back scornfully. "Piece of junk jewelry with something inside it that was anywhere near your scabby scalp? Yecchh." She shuddered dramatically.

I hadn't even noticed the locket was missing. But now I saw the cheap little gold-plated trinket wasn't in its usual annoying position, just above the girl's overexposed cleavage.

"Ohh," Kris exhaled, lunging at Maggie. "I'll make you tell me, you big fat..."

I stepped between them, seizing Kris's bony shoulders and sitting her down, hard. "All right, now, you just stop."

"Maybe if you put something in your body besides booze and birth control pills, you'd gain some weight, too," Maggie rejoined from behind me. "Then you wouldn't look like a drugged-up hag."

Kris tried to stand up. I pushed her down again. "I mean it. Sit down. And keep quiet."

"Which is what you're going to end up as, anyway!" Maggie persisted.

Sam left the room. His father used to do that, too; Victor was an expert at instigating things without ever seeming to. When the going got tough, however, he got going elsewhere.

I'd have liked to go myself, only if I did this pair might kill each other. "Maggie, that's enough out of you, as well."

But Maggie wasn't listening. The strain of the previous few days had been uncorked by Kris's unwise accusation. "Meanwhile," she went on, her voice lowering dangerously, "you'd better start being a lot nicer to me."

A flicker of caution crossed Kris's face. "Why should I be nice to you?" she demanded sullenly.

But from her look I thought she really wanted to know. *And,* I thought, *wasn't* that *interesting?*

"Because I know something about you," Maggie answered, her words confirming my sudden suspicion. "You just think about what it might be, and I bet you'll guess."

Kris shifted uneasily on the couch. "You're lying. You're just jealous; you want to get Sam back. So you'll lie about me."

Maggie laughed grimly. The gloves were off now, and though Kris was managing to put up a good front, I thought Maggie had her on the ropes.

"Sure I am," Maggie retorted. "You keep telling people that. But *you* know, and *I* know. We've got a little secret, the two of us."

This was it, I realized suddenly: what Maggie hadn't wanted to talk about. It was something about Kris, who was now staring at Maggie with real fear in her eyes.

"And sometime," Maggie steamrolled on, "when you think you've got everyone where you want them and you're least expecting it—"

"Stop!" Kris shrieked, putting her hands over her eyes in a theatrically childish gesture. "Sam, make her *stop*!"

But Sam wasn't there and Maggie didn't stop, leaning past me to tower over her victim. Her final words came in a singsong whisper so cruel, it raised the hairs on my arms.

"...*I'm going to tell!*"

Much later that night I lay in the crook of Wade's arm while he read shotgun-shell reloading specifications.

"I wonder what it is," I mused aloud, averting my eyes from paragraphs containing words like CAUTION, EXPLOSIVE MIXTURE, and my own personal favorite, SERIOUS INJURY MAY RESULT.

Wade glanced down at me over his reading glasses. "What *what* is?" he asked distractedly.

"What Maggie knows about Kris."

Wade nodded slowly, returning his attention to his reading material. "Could be a lot of things. Maggie went to bed?"

"Uh-huh. She wanted to go home, but I insisted she stay. I'm worried about her, Wade. Something's still eating her. And she feels so guilty that if she hadn't stayed here, I'd be concerned she might do something...I don't know. Something foolish."

Sensing my unease, Monday shoved her glossy black Labrador head under my right hand, while Prill resettled her enormous red Doberman pinscher body on my leg. Winter had favored us with a goodly number of two-dog nights, and the canines wanted them to go on right through summer.

"Why don't you just ask Maggie what else is bothering her?" Wade suggested. The dogs never seemed to want to crush him, maybe because they knew he would dump them unceremoniously to the floor the moment they tried it.

"I did. She wouldn't say. It might be something about that locket Kris made such a fuss about, but I can't imagine what. I do think it's got to do with Kris somehow, though. The way Kris reacted..."

"Sounds like that might be just something between the kids. Maybe you'd better let well enough alone?"

"Mmm. Maybe." I loved him madly, but his calm disposition was annoying sometimes. Also, his habit of being right; the enmity between Kris and Maggie was a side issue.

"You poor thing, though," he sympathized, turning a page of the reloading manual.

"Yeah. And on top of that I'd like to know what the deal is with Bella and Lydia Duckworth," I groused, sitting up.

Despite my fatigue I couldn't sleep, and there was no point pretending I'd be able to. Sam and Kris had gone out who-knew-where and would be back who-knew-when, and of course George and Ellie had gone home.

So I was alone, since a husband who is perusing a shotgun-shell reloading manual does not qualify as company. Ten minutes later, as I was sitting in the front parlor with a glass of milk and a headful of still-unanswered questions, Sam came in, whispering in the doorway with Kris for a long time. Finally she left and he went upstairs, and the house was silent again.

After that I wandered around for a while, trying and failing to figure out what was going on while at the same time performing a variety of useful household tasks just to keep my hands busy.

In the kitchen, I fixed the latch on the door to Wade's shop. It wasn't perfect—I'd have had to jack the end of the house up for that—but afterward it only took me leaning my whole weight on the door—instead of two or three people—to close it securely.

Next I worked on a squeaky floorboard. I'd tried putting talcum powder between the boards and it had worked for a while, but now I tapped small finishing nails at an angle between them; when I was done you could step on that spot without it sounding like a cat was being stepped on.

Finally at around two in the morning I pulled a jacket on and went outside, hoping a sky full of stars would make me and my problems seem unimportant. But it only reminded me of how alone we all were, and how we needed one another.

Shivering, I went back in and decided to call Ellie. If she was up she'd have her phone turned on, and if not, not. But as I picked up the handset, my own phone emitted a short *brinng!*

"I'm here," I said, expecting it to be Ellie calling me.

Only it wasn't. "Jacobia? This is Lydia Duckworth. I'm very sorry to be calling you at such an outrageous hour, but . . ."

"That's all right, Lydia." I imagined her in her tidy parlor in the house next door to her late husband's failed business, maybe with the aging Irish setter asleep by her feet.

"I'm up," I said into the telephone. "What's going on?"

"I'm examining my conscience." She sounded unhappy. "There's something I didn't tell you today. I kept telling myself that it couldn't matter, that the police looked into it all very thoroughly at the time, so how could it be important now? But in the end I couldn't convince myself."

"I see." I didn't, but if I let her talk she might explain it to me. A car went by outside, its lights casting the shapes of leaves onto the darkened dining room windows.

"They said he wasn't involved," Mrs. Duckworth murmured as if to herself. But she was slurring a bit, and it occurred to me that the pleasant Red Cross volunteer lady had been tippling.

Not a lot. Just enough to loosen her tongue. "Who did they say wasn't involved?" I pressed.

A pause. Ice clinked in a glass. Then, "Bill Imrie. That bank teller. They said they looked into him, and there was no reason to believe it happened any way other than the way he said. He was so young and terribly inexperienced.

He didn't realize Jim Diamond shouldn't have been depositing those checks."

"But you think otherwise?" From upstairs I heard the faint thump of a dog jumping off a bed, and then another. Moments later, the two canines padded downstairs into the phone alcove to check on what I was up to.

"It's not what I think, it's what I know," Lydia Duckworth said with the slightly excessive vehemence of the vaguely inebriated. "It was hushed up at the time, you see. People liked the father so much, they put a lid on it when it came to the son."

That was what Ellie had said, too, that Pops Imrie's great popularity had benefited his son, Bill. Satisfied, the dogs went out to the kitchen and lay down together in their dog bed.

"A lid," I asked Lydia patiently, "on what?"

"Why, on his gambling," she replied. "I wouldn't even know, but my grandson went to college with Bill Imrie and *he* told me. Said the Imrie boy played cards and kept a . . . a game book?"

"A sports book," I corrected her gently.

"That's right. A sports book. Only the bets he took kept winning, and his own bets kept losing. So he ended up owing a lot of money. Students' parents finally complained to the school."

"Oh, dear. That must have been inconvenient for him."

"Well, I should say. My grandson said Bill Imrie's father paid them all off, the debts, I mean, and the school didn't want any bad publicity. So it was all kept very quiet."

"So the gambling was before Bill came home and went to work at the bank. Did you mention this to the police?"

"Yes," she confirmed, sounding more sozzled now. "It was before he started work at the bank. The gambling, that is. But I didn't tell the police about it. I only learned of it after the investigation. By then of course they'd questioned Imrie themselves."

"So you assumed they already knew his history."

"I don't know what I assumed," she replied impatiently. "I understood they'd questioned him, that's all. And Diamond himself had said Imrie didn't have anything to do with it. So I guess I thought, well, if there was something there, the police would surely have found out about it."

There was a long pause; more ice clinked. Finally she came back to the phone. "And by then I felt sorry for him myself. For Bill Imrie, I mean. The story around here was that the police had given him a bad time."

"But now?" I asked, trying not to feel excited.

This might not mean anything. She'd gotten a little tipsy and decided she wanted to talk on the phone, that's all.

"Now," Lydia Duckworth replied sadly, "I guess I just wonder if maybe they should've investigated him more."

There was a last small tinkle of ice, after which she began apologizing for bothering me. I assured her it was no trouble, thanked her for calling, and was about to hang up.

At the last minute, though, something stopped me. Maybe it was the thought of her sitting there alone, then calling someone else on impulse the way she'd called me.

I'd known a few drunk dialers back when I lived in the city; they were always the loneliest kids in town and they never seemed to realize how obvious it was that they were loaded.

"Lydia," I said, "put the bottle away and go to bed."

I heard her short, surprised intake of breath. "Yes," she replied in a small voice. "I think I'll do that. Good night, Jacobia."

After she hung up I sat there listening to the dogs snoring peacefully together out in the kitchen. By now it was past three in the morning, so I changed my mind about calling Ellie.

Instead I cleared up the few tools I had been using, then slid my sock-clad foot over the floorboard I'd nailed down to be sure the nail heads didn't snag.

Finally I went back upstairs. In the hall window the sky to the east showed the faintest hint of gray, the roofs of town just a collection of cutout triangles against it.

I paused at Sam's doorway, hearing nothing from within, and then outside the partly open door of the guest room where I had put Maggie.

Nothing from in there, either. Nothing at all.

Not even breathing. "Maggie?" I whispered.

No reply. I tiptoed into the guest room. "Maggie?"

Silence. Moving slowly in the dark, I approached the narrow twin bed. From behind me in the doorway came Sam's voice, quietly but with some impatience.

He hadn't been asleep after all. "Mom? What are you doing?"

Ignoring him, I snapped the bedside light on. The last thing I needed was *him* questioning *me* about *my* activities. Then...

"Oh, hell," I said distinctly into the lamp's sudden glare.

The bed had been slept in, the pillow dented and the covers rumpled. But Maggie wasn't there.

Or anywhere else in the house, either.

Maggie was gone.

I went to her place first, thinking maybe she'd just walked home from my house. But she wasn't there, and neither was her car, an old blue Honda Civic. Alone in the little Fiat I scoured the island looking for Maggie. Her car wasn't outside the Waco Diner where the pickups of tradesmen and fishermen already clustered, the air scented with bacon and coffee. It wasn't outside her apartment when I went back a second time, either, or at her mother's, or anywhere I thought she might go to think.

And if she was already off-island I had no idea where she might be. But finally as the charcoal sky lightened to pale gray I returned to her place a third time, spotted the car, and found her there, sitting at the end of the deck looking out over the glimmering water.

"Maggie! You scared the living hell out of—"

Then I stopped. She wasn't weeping and she didn't look as if she had been, recently. She just looked...emptied out.

"I'm sorry," she said. "I didn't mean to frighten you."

Gulls cried in the early-morning silence, the first rays of sunlight turning their wings pale pink. I angled my head toward her apartment. "Are you going to be able to sleep?"

"No." She shrugged, looked across the water where the *Fundy Clipper* was beginning its first ferry journey across the channel. "But I didn't want to be at your place."

With Sam. Of course she didn't. "I'm sorry, Maggie. Last night was my fault. It was a really bad idea bringing you to—"

"No. You were trying to be nice. I thought I could slip out and not bother you. I should've left you a note, though."

"Where'd you go? I've been looking all over the—"

"Just driving around," she replied, gravel crunching beneath our feet as she followed me back to the parking area. Her tone was flat with sorrow, with guilt over the Jim Diamond fiasco, and with misery over Sam, I supposed.

And maybe if I hadn't seen so much of my own younger self in Maggie—and so worrisomely much of Victor in Sam—I'd have just left her on her own to deal with it somehow.

Hey, people do. I had. But suddenly I didn't see why Maggie should have to. Because standing there by the water with the seagulls crying and the sun hauling itself redly up from behind the hills of New Brunswick, it occurred to me that maybe what *doesn't* go around has to come around sometimes, too.

That maybe the help you *didn't* get is the kind you know best how to supply, and it's your job to start putting it out there.

Since obviously, there's some kind of a shortage. "Come on," I told Maggie. "You're coming with me."

Starting the Fiat, I lifted myself over the center console into the passenger seat. "Get in," I said, gesturing her behind the wheel.

Her face brightening cautiously, she looked at me to make sure I meant it, then snapped her seat belt on and put the little vehicle in gear expertly. "Where to?"

"Ellie's." The sky was full light now and in the distance I could already hear the concussive *rap!-rap!-rap!* of nail guns.

Wade and George hoped to finish the roof work today. "I've got an idea, and you're going to help," I said as the house came into view.

Wade stood on a scaffolding a couple of shingle-rows down from the roof beam, gripping a clawhammer. With his shirt already off and the hammer raised purposefully, he looked like a handsome weather vane.

Too bad looking hunky wasn't getting our guest rooms done. The thought of the relatives arriving very soon shifted ominously in my head, like one of the brain aneurysms Victor was so good at repairing.

But that situation couldn't top my agenda now; for one thing, I wasn't about to go up that ladder to nag Wade about it.

"Whatever you want, you just tell me and I'll do it," Maggie said earnestly as we pulled into the drive.

That's the spirit, I thought, gratified. She needed what I always needed when I was in a funk, and couldn't see my way out of it: something to do.

And someone to do it with. I felt better, too, since at the time what I meant to propose really seemed like a good idea.

At the time.

Chapter 13

Bob Arnold's squad car was parked outside the Country Corner restaurant on Route 1 when we all arrived there twenty minutes later. We knew it was Bob's because the perp screen bore a little cartoon sticker of Yosemite Sam, waving his shootin' irons.

Maggie saw the vehicle, too, and looked alarmed. "Don't worry, I haven't dragged you out here to be grilled," I reassured her as Ellie lifted the baby from the car seat and we approached the green wood-frame building.

Behind the restaurant a tidal salt marsh spread serenely to where the river turned under an old railroad overpass. Beneath that a couple of mallards paddled, circling their nest protectively.

"Maggie, I haven't told anyone what you said last night—besides us, only Victor and Wade know about it—and I'm not going to."

I hope, I added silently as we passed the restaurant's big front windows. We'd have to see how this all turned out. But I was sure of one thing:

Maggie's distress over her encounter with Jim Diamond was genuine, and her story about it rang true.

"I'm glad to see Bob's car, though," I added. "I've got some questions for him this morning."

We took a table in the back room and gave our orders. Then I briefed Maggie on all that had happened so far—Bella's threatening notes, Diamond's crimes and punishment, everything but what I wanted Maggie to do.

I hadn't brought Ellie up to speed on that part yet, or on Lydia Duckworth's late-night call, either. But I did so while Maggie went to the ladies' room to splash water on her face; even at nineteen, a night of weeping and no sleep had taken its toll.

"Why, that little weasel," Ellie said indignantly when I was finished. "Just imagine Bill Imrie letting his father pay off his gambling debts. So much for being the golden boy."

"Yeah, funny how that works out sometimes, isn't it?" Back in the city if somebody was a golden boy you counted your fingers right after you shook hands, in case he'd stolen a few.

"But the thing is, Imrie's not going to talk to me again, or to you, either," I said. "He made it clear last time I saw him."

Around us in the comfortable little diner the breakfast rush was in full swing, with a trio of waitresses serving booths and tables so fast they appeared to be on roller skates.

"I don't get why anyone has to talk to him," Ellie said as our coffees arrived. "We know now, so what's the point of asking him about it?"

Leonora, looking lovely in a polka-dot playsuit and gingham bonnet, seized a teaspoon and waved it happily. "That's not what we'd ask," I told her mother.

The coffee was fresh and I needed it badly. After I'd drunk half a cup I felt brain cells opening for business. "Because the thing is, coincidences happen and maybe this is one of them."

I drank the rest of it. "But has it occurred to you that Imrie runs his late father's custom sawmill, and the place Jim Diamond victimized was among other things a lumber-supply yard?"

"Pops Imrie could've bought wood from Diamond," Ellie mused.

"Correct. And even if not, they could've known each other. That's how Diamond could've met Bill Imrie, even though Imrie's saying otherwise."

"The police wouldn't have ... ?"

I shrugged. "If they both denied an association and no one else ever saw them together ..."

"I guess," Ellie replied. "But—"

"And now we find out that Imrie had gambling problems? Maybe he even still had them when he came back here? So maybe he needed money. And it could be that Jim Diamond found out about that somehow."

"I'd think it was a lot more coincidental if Bill had a history of writing threatening notes," Ellie countered. "Plenty of people need money."

The waitress poured more coffee. If I'd had a needle I'd have just mainlined the stuff into a vein.

"Sure, but as far as we know not ones with these other possible Jim Diamond connections. I'm just saying, that's all."

"So it's back to the idea that the notes might have been a way to frame Bella, set up a motive for her to murder Jim. And if Bill had a way to get those notes into her house, he'd have also had a way to get that skillet *out*," Ellie said.

She frowned. "But then why the final note? *After* Jim Diamond was dead?"

"Not quite dead," I pointed out. "And I don't know. I do think whoever hit Diamond with that skillet made the same mistake Maggie did, though. They thought he *was* dead. And I just think Bill deserves another good hard look."

"So you want ..." Leonora banged the spoon on the tray of her high chair.

"Right. We can't talk to Imrie. He won't talk to us. But Maggie could. If she met with him at the bank, she wouldn't even have to be alone with him," I said.

All I wanted was to give Bill a chance to trip himself up. If he didn't...

Well, if he didn't, we'd reevaluate the whole situation. But surely it couldn't hurt anything if Maggie merely chatted with him, with the safety net of some other people around.

Just then she returned. "What'd I miss?" she wanted to know.

But Ellie wasn't quite ready to answer that question. She liked Maggie. She even trusted her with Leonora, which was like saying she trusted the girl with her own beating heart.

Now, however, Ellie fixed Maggie in her pale green gaze, the intensity of which had been known to make strong men refuse the last piece of pie and offer to wash dishes instead.

"Put your hand on the baby's head," she said.

Because maybe I was persuaded of Maggie's innocence in this mess. But Ellie wasn't like me. When push came to shove, my friend Ellie could be as tough as Maine granite. And now she wanted *proof.*

Or the closest thing to it that she could get. "Look me in the eye and swear that every word you said to Jake last night was true, about the way you found Jim Diamond," she told Maggie.

If Maggie was surprised she gave no sign. "I swear," she said at once, smoothing the infant's silky hair. "I swear on this baby's head."

A moment passed. "All right," Ellie replied at last. "I'm satisfied."

Just then Bob Arnold got up from the counter and strolled to our table. "Morning, ladies. Mind if I pull up a chair?"

As he did so, I realized I hadn't wanted to see the squad car outside after all. Because Bob was smarter than the average bear, and noticing the four of us there, he'd just figured something out.

He looked at Maggie and then at me and a fact dropped neatly into a slot in his head with an almost audible click. He knew who was driving my car in Lubec that day.

Time for a distracting maneuver. "Good morning, Bob," I said hastily. "Just who I wanted to see. Do you know if Bill Imrie got *thoroughly* looked at, back during the Jim Diamond investigation?"

I didn't care anymore if he knew I was interested; suddenly I had the feeling that push was coming to shove real soon, now. And that when it did I'd better know everything I could.

Bob looked surprised but answered with certainty. "Oh, yeah. They went up one side of Imrie and down the other on that. Credit card records, bank accounts, any way he might've gotten a payment on the sly from Diamond. He came back clean."

"Great," I said. "And one other thing–the notes Bella was getting. You're pretty sure no one else knew about those? Other than your guys, I mean, when they were watching her house."

Bella had told Azenath Jones and Dinah Sanborne, at the Gopher Baroque agency. But she'd insisted she hadn't told anyone else, and Azenath had assured me they'd kept the information to themselves, not wanting the story associated with their business.

Bob glanced curiously at me, but his reply was equally sure. "No. Told you before, Jake, I ordered 'em, keep their yaps shut."

He eyed me evenly. "Didn't want anyone copycattin' that little prank, hear about Bella's threatening notes and decide to start writin' their own. Pretty soon we'd have an epidemic. 'Cause that's what it was, seems like. A prank."

He was telling me in his quiet way that this was the theory the prosecutors were going on, that Jim hadn't sent the notes but Bella thought he had, and that was her motive for going to Lubec and braining him with her skillet.

And considering who the fallback suspects could turn out to be, I decided not to argue it.

Yet. Maggie finished her orange juice and started working on her last slice of toast. Ellie took Leonora to the ladies' room to change her.

"So," Bob said, and I could see him deciding whether or not to bring up Maggie and the car.

Around him the breakfast rush was starting to slack off. Men in boots and work clothes were downing the last of their coffee and lining up at the register to pay their checks.

"That take care of your questions for me, for this morning?" Bob said at last.

I nodded. "That's it. Thanks, Bob."

He wasn't going to ask. Not immediately. But we both knew he was just giving me enough rope to hang myself, should I feel so inclined. He didn't like it that I was keeping something from him, and as he departed his backward glance at me said I'd better end up having a good reason for doing so.

That wasn't the only thing fueling my unease, though. As I'd sat there with my brain cells popping open under the influence of all that coffee, I'd had the growing sense I was missing something.

Something important. And now as I waited at the counter to pay the check, whatever it was I still *didn't* know felt like an open trapdoor.

Gaping wide, just waiting for me to put my foot through it.

Outside the sun had climbed higher in the sky, turning the salt marsh to a mirror of pale blue, each duck neatly doubled and each cattail growing out of its own reflection. Maggie gave the Fiat's black top a yearning glance, but left it up out of deference to Leonora's complexion.

"You still haven't told me what you want me to do," she said as the little car's engine growled to life.

I looked at Ellie, curled in the rear beside the baby's car seat. "We want you to visit Bill Imrie," I said.

Maggie let the clutch out too fast, nearly stalled, but recovered smoothly and pulled out onto Route 1.

"Does that idea bother you? You don't have to, if..."

"No," she responded quickly, taking the turn to Eastport. "My foot slipped."

She looked straight ahead, jaw taut and hands tight on the wheel. "Why do you want me to talk to him?" she asked.

Ellie spoke up. "He won't talk to us anymore. Still touchy about his reputation." Briefly she explained Imrie's connection to Jim Diamond's old crime. "That makes him want to avoid a pair of snoops like Jake and me."

"Right," Maggie said. "His reputation." She seemed privately amused by something. But that could have been my imagination.

"Okay, then," she agreed. "What should I talk to him *about*?"

She actually sounded eager. Suddenly I wondered what it was that had her so intrigued.

"The notes, right?" she went on. "You want to know if maybe Imrie sent them?"

Good pickup; the girl was talented at this. She slowed for the speed zone at Pleasant Point, then accelerated onto the causeway between the bay and Carryingplace Cove.

An eighteen-wheeler roared by, buffeting us hard. "Right," I said when my ears quit popping from the burst of air pressure. "Because the thing is, Bella swears she hasn't told anyone about them."

"Bob Arnold says no one from his shop would have been likely to talk about them, either," Ellie added.

Officers from Bob's cop shop disobeyed his instructions at their own peril; besides, it wasn't the kind of assignment they'd have been interested in gabbing about.

"Which means that for practical purposes, no one else knew about those notes," I said. "Except the person who sent them."

"So what we'd like you to do is work the conversation around somehow, not mention the notes, but give him a really good chance to bring them up himself, if you can," Ellie finished.

"To see if he makes a mistake," Maggie concluded correctly. "See if he says something about them, when he's not even supposed to know about them. Sure, I can do that. I'll go to his place."

"Wait a minute," I objected at once.

Her tone was reasonable. But her calm act was a fake. I knew from her taut posture, her grip on the wheel, and the way her lips parted that she wasn't merely willing to go interview Bill Imrie.

She was *dying* to do it. Suddenly I wished I hadn't suggested this idea. "Talking to me, he might forget himself, speak without thinking," the girl went on.

"Maggie, I don't want you going to his place. I want you to talk to him at the bank, during business hours, or maybe at the Blue Moon. But not all alone."

She ignored me. "If he doesn't mention them and I can't get him to, it won't prove anything. But if he does . . ."

She paused, her brow furrowing. "Hey, wait a minute, what if someone else *did* know? And the someone *else* told him about them?"

"Then find out that," Ellie said before I could come up with anything useful to add.

I was trying to think fast, but apparently I still had a coffee deficiency. One conclusion was jumping out clearly at me, though. Maggie was eager to meet with Imrie at his house, when it would've been perfectly easy for her to see him elsewhere.

"Listen," I said, annoyed, "if you can't do this our way—"

"What? Then I can't do it at all? How are you going to stop me, Jake? Tie me up in your basement?"

She laughed merrily, curls of her dark hair flowing back from her face as she drove my little car fast. If I hadn't known better I'd have thought it was the old Maggie, mellow and sweet.

But it wasn't. Maggie had thought of something, and whatever it was had made her . . .

Well, not lighthearted, exactly. But way too close to it for my comfort. The Imrie plan fit in with some wish or scheme of her own.

"Look, I'll be fine. He won't connect me with you and Ellie. Why should he? He's not in my social circle and I'm sure no one he knows ever talks to him about me," Maggie assured me. This thought made her chuckle again. "And he'll be way more relaxed at his place, you know he will."

Probably true. But I still didn't like it. "Jake," she said. "I'm not a little kid anymore. Now do you want this done or not?"

It was her voice that clinched it, suddenly devoid of humor and all business; she could do it, all right. If only her whole manner weren't screaming *ulterior motive* so clearly . . .

I looked back at Ellie, whose gaze said, *You opened this can of worms. You fish with 'em.*

"Fine," I told Maggie. "Do it your way. But don't," I added, "even *hint* that we sent you."

She shot me a sideways look. "Of course I won't. I'll tell him it's for the local history project, get him to talk about his dad's sawmill and so on."

Her eyes returned to the road. "He might really have useful information, too. I don't know why I didn't think of it myself."

Damn. This girl had an agenda, all right, and it had nothing to do with the Historical Society. But I knew better than to think I could pry it out of her now.

"Because if Bella didn't tell him, and a cop didn't tell him," Ellie recited . . .

Correct. There was another way Bill Imrie could have found out about those notes. It all added together: that maybe he had written them himself.

I just wished I knew why Maggie had apparently done the same arithmetic and come up with something else.

For the rest of the morning I had the kind of jitters you are only supposed to get before your wedding, or major surgery. I'd been so certain Maggie's assignment to interview Bill Imrie posed no risk to her.

That is, I had until she'd changed it. Half a dozen times I picked up the phone to call her and cancel, then put it down again.

Because I'd warned her. I'd told her to make him aware that other people—although of course not me or Ellie—knew she was there. I'd told her not to let him get between her and the door, and not to eat or drink anything, assuming he invited her inside. And to be sure she could reach me in an emergency I'd even lent her my cell phone, with my number programmed into it.

Not that any of it would be necessary. She was just checking out a coincidence—

—Imrie's gambling history, and thus his possible ongoing need for money, combined with the fact that Jim Diamond could've known Imrie or his father, on account of that custom sawmill—

—and she would call me, I told myself firmly, when she had something to say.

Meanwhile I went on reminding myself of all the reasons why the coincidence—I didn't *know* that Bill Imrie had needed money and so might have been a silent partner in Diamond's scam, nor was I *sure* that Diamond and Imrie had been acquainted—was probably meaningless.

But the argument in my head kept going the other way. "If Imrie was the bag man for the money Diamond stole, then when Diamond got out of jail and wanted his share, it would give Imrie a reason to kill him," I explained to my father.

"But for framing Bella to make sense, he'd have also needed to know the domestic history, that the notes would be perceived as part of a pattern of harassment," I added, pouring coffee.

I sat at the kitchen table. "Jim demanding money and so on," I went on. "Not to mention all the rest of it—that Bella had the skillet, and a key to Jim's apartment. He'd have had to get hold of the skillet, too, and kill Jim at a time when he knew Bella didn't have an alibi—"

My dad washed his hands at the kitchen sink. He'd been down in the cellar trying to make the washing machine hose straighten out, so he could stretch it across the ceiling instead of along the wall where it froze up promptly every December.

"And," I went on, pushing a plate of doughnuts across the table at him as he sat down, "he'd have had to get *into* her house to deliver the notes without being discovered."

"Which," my father pointed out, picking up a doughnut and examining it, "someone did. Neatly avoiding the trap you'd laid."

"Yes," I concurred unhappily. "Someone did, to leave that final note. Someone did all those things, and it *could* have been Imrie. Unless this is a fool's game and Bella really did kill Jim."

"You think so?" He bit into the doughnut.

"I don't know anymore," I answered miserably. "She's lying about other things. About seeing Lydia Duckworth, anyway, though I can't imagine why."

Maggie had said she was going to get right on the job, but the phone wasn't ringing. "What do you think?" I demanded miserably.

My father chewed his doughnut, drank some coffee. "I think," he pronounced slowly, "that if I was about five feet tall, and I wanted to kill someone about six foot two who I knew pretty well, then I *don't* think my first plan would be bonkin' 'em on the head with my own skillet."

He ate some more of the doughnut. "Or," he added after a reflective pause, "any other over-the-head-type weapon, either."

The simplicity of it took my breath away; the *over* part.

"Too tall," I exclaimed, remembering how Diamond had towered over me. "He was too tall for her to have hit him that way easily, and she would have realized that ahead of time for the simple reason that she'd been married to him."

My father nodded. "So why not do it some other way, right? Not sayin' it couldn't happen, o' course. There was an overturned chair, remember? In the apartment when we found him that day."

Right, there had been, and Diamond's killer could have stood on it. But would *he* stand there cooperatively and let you hit him?

I didn't think so. "Versus someone who didn't know him well enough to picture him clearly, or was taller," my father added.

Rats. Bill Imrie was about six feet tall, and that telephone still wasn't ringing. As I pondered this, Sam came in and saw me, then went on into the dining room, demonstratively silent.

Great. Another difficulty for an already complicated day: My son wasn't speaking to me. And as if I didn't have plenty on my plate already, the whole family reunion thing was still hanging over my head like an unexploded water balloon.

"Good doughnut," my father commented.

"Dad—" I began as he got to his feet.

It was bad enough that there was still no progress on the disastrous guest rooms. Worse was the fact that when the guests did get here, I had a feeling my father might take one look at them and head for the hills.

"Yes?" he inquired mildly.

I thought about asking him to turn his attention to building a doghouse out in the backyard. A nice roomy one, since if this all kept on the way that it was currently going, I'd be living in it soon.

Even more than I was already. Sam's silence hung in the dining room like a big, black cloud, the kind that threatens to go on raining on you for weeks, possibly even months.

But my throat closed as if one of those doughnuts had gotten stuck halfway down it. Because even though in the old days I'd faced titans of industry so aggressive they should've been quarantined for rabies, the truth was that I was terrified of my father's reaction to the upcoming family gathering.

And his reaction to me, too, for allowing it to happen. And now that I'd let all this time go by *without* telling him . . .

"Nothing," I mumbled at last. "Nothing important. If you need help with that washing machine hose, just let me know."

He nodded, heading back to the cellar while I, screwing up what little I did have of courage, headed for a talk with my son.

"How're things with the ice ship?" I began lightly. What I needed, actually, was an icebreaker. But for starters maybe we could have a conversation, just to raise the temperature a little.

"I'm kind of busy here," he replied flatly.

Oh-kay. Let's try this again. "Look, I realize you're pretty angry with me," I said.

"Yeah." Eyes on his notebook. He was ticked that I'd brought Maggie home the night before, and no doubt he blamed me for the fight between her and Kris, too.

Right, like it was my fault Kris was a witchy little—

No, start again. "But you know, that's not really fair," I said reasonably. "I don't insist that you enjoy all *my* friends."

No reply. It was like pounding on the door of a steel vault. "I don't see," I went on, "why we can't just agree to disagree."

He looked up. "Because I don't *criticize* your friends, for one thing," he said, closing the notebook decisively. "And what was the idea having Maggie here, anyway? She's not my girlfriend anymore, Mom. Were you *trying* to embarrass everyone?"

"Sam, Maggie's a *family* friend. And she needed our help. Don't you think—?"

"A family friend?" He looked incredulous. "Mom, what're you talking about? The only reason Maggie was ever around here was because of me." His gaze bored into me. "That was it, Mom. Don't you get it? Not you, not our family. *Me.* End of subject."

And with those few words, everything changed again. Doubt assailed me. Because maybe what he said was true.

Maybe Maggie had only been tolerating me all along; maybe she still was. That could be why she'd seemed so eager to interview Bill Imrie; not to be helpful, but because she'd figured out some way to use her helpfulness in her battle to recapture Sam.

By, for instance, staying on good terms with me. Suddenly it seemed more than possible; it seemed *likely*.

"Mom," Sam began, seeing that he'd wounded me more than he'd intended.

I just looked at him. He wasn't going to give Kris up. I saw clearly, now, that Ellie and my father had been right. With his eyes wide open, my son was making a mistake and there was nothing I could do about it.

Simple as that. Then I made one; a mistake, that is. "Forget it," I told him. "I'm just worried about your health, is all."

His face clouded abruptly. "No, you're not. That's just an underhanded way of saying you think I'm going to drink."

Oh, brother. "Sam, I . . ."

He shoved his chair back, grabbed his books. "If you didn't, Kris wouldn't be a problem. But you don't trust me."

And then what could I say? That my strongest sense of Kris was that she'd love to see him stumble again, even harder than before, just to prove she could make him do it?

But he didn't give me a chance. "Maybe she is a little rough around the edges. Not like Maggie, always sweet as pie." He put a bitter twist on the words.

"But I'll tell you what Kris doesn't do," he went on. "She doesn't say one thing to me if what she really means is something worse, the way you just did."

"Sam, I didn't mean to imply . . ." But of course I had, and he knew it as well as I did. So I said nothing more.

He did all the talking. "She doesn't look me in the face and lie," he said slowly, as if explaining this to someone whose IQ didn't quite reach the cubic zirconia level. "Kris may have her faults, but there's one thing I always can count on."

He paused in the doorway, about to turn his back on me. But first he fixed me in the pitiless gaze of a young man who—for the moment, anyway—has the upper hand and intends to shake it.

"Kris *always* tells me," he declared, "the truth."

Yeah, I thought, *like that's a major selling point.* Victor used to do it all the time, and I had the scars to prove it.

Besides, I didn't believe it. But I didn't get to say so because the next thing I heard was the back door slamming.

So there I was with nonfunctioning guest rooms, imminent guests, an angry son, and a father who might at any minute become long-lost again, once he got a look at those guests and found out who had invited them.

Not to mention a housekeeper who was threatening to become a home-wrecker; while I was talking to Sam, Bella had come in and—contrary to my precise instructions—launched into a cleaning project without so much as a by-your-leave from me.

She was in the kitchen, and by the sound of it the inside of my refrigerator would never be the same. I imagined Sam's half-finished fruit juice bottles, Wade's cherished hoard of leftover pizza slices, and my box of ancient but still delicious chocolate-covered cherries, all swept into the garbage with the liquefying cucumber, the leathery cheese.

On the other hand, once she was done maybe I could crawl in there. "Bella..." I began. I found her disposing of a bottle of pineapple-grapefruit juice.

The juice didn't look bad. "Bella, I want you to confirm something for me."

She was peering at a bottle with three furry stuffed olives nestled at the bottom. "Yes, Missus."

She looked just awful, her pasty complexion and Mixmaster-styled hair testifying to her distress. I didn't have the heart to stop what amounted to a siege on the Frigidaire.

But I was about at the end of my rope. "I want you to tell me again whether you visited Lydia Duckworth the day Jim died."

I was giving her a chance to change her story. If she didn't, I was ready to tell Ellie—and Maggie, too—that I was done with the whole affair. "Bella?" I persisted.

She turned, the olive bottle still in her hand. If it had held poison lozenges I thought she might just have downed them on the spot, she appeared so distraught.

Instead she put them back into the refrigerator, which was when I realized that the worst had happened.

From the second shelf of the refrigerator the fresh lettuce was gone, but two ancient pizza slices were still there alongside a green half-sandwich in plastic wrap and a moldy hot dog.

She was throwing out good things and saving spoiled ones, which meant that even her whacked-out, self-protective shell of supercleanliness was starting to give way under the pressure.

"No," she replied, settling the olive jar behind a grapefruit so shriveled it resembled a shrunken head.

"I didn't," she said, holding up a plastic container of feta cheese floating in something liquid. Not fresh whey.

Not even close. Slowly she put it back, too, dazedly as if not quite seeing it. And at that moment, it was right on the tip of my tongue to tell her that she could go home, now, that I was finished with her.

That I was finished, period. Let someone else sort out the lies, conceal-ments, and evasions; I was tired. But then, still staring into the chilly re-cesses of my refrigerator, Bella began weeping—silently, hopelessly—into her hands.

And the phone rang.

"He knew, all right," Maggie pronounced at the Blue Moon that evening. "He didn't want me to *know* that he knew, but when I sprang it on him I was watching his expression."

I recalled Bill Imrie's inability to hide his unease that morning when I'd met with him at the bank. He'd have been okay in a formal interrogation setting where he could prepare.

But Bill was not exactly a master of the spontaneous poker face. Which could account for some of the gambling difficulties Lydia Duckworth had reported, I realized. Maybe some of the bets he lost had been on card games.

"So what did you say?" Ellie asked Maggie.

It was past ten o'clock; we'd have met sooner but Maggie had insisted on sleeping first, then eating and taking a shower, and all that had suddenly sounded so irresistible, I'd done it, too.

Now Maggie's face glowed with the success of her interview with the bank manager. "Well, we were talking about his dad's sawmill—did you know some of the parts in it are nearly two hundred years old?"

I didn't, and I averted my mind's eye firmly from the idea of Maggie's getting anywhere near any of Imrie's big sharp blades.

She went on. "And while I was looking at the saw, out of the blue I just said hey, I heard somebody in town has been getting these weird threatening notes, and wasn't that, like, spooky? And he just about passed out."

"Really," I said evenly. "So he gave you the tour, did he? *Inside* the sawmill building?"

Her glance at me was triumphant. Too much so, even for the coup she'd scored.

"Yep. The house, too, upstairs and down. I know, I know," she added at my look of disapproval. "Don't let him get between me and the door. But I was supposed to be interested in history, and it is an *old* house."

Late at night in the Blue Moon there was jazz on the sound system and the rich aroma of espresso floating darkly in the air. Across from Ellie and me in the booth, Maggie looked lovely. But there was a hectic flush in her cheeks and her eyes were full of smug, I've-got-a-secret happiness.

I didn't like that. It was out of character for her. And I liked what she said next even less.

"Anyway, he recovered pretty fast and I went on to something else, so he'd think I didn't really care about the notes. *Or* who'd told *him* about them," she added with sudden glee.

"He told you that?" Ellie's slim fingertips pressed together.

"No. I figured it out. From this," Maggie replied, digging into her satchel. She produced a small glittery object and dangled it from its chain with a triumphant flourish. "Know what this is?"

I couldn't believe it. "Where'd you get that?" I asked when I found my voice again.

She shrugged carelessly. "I spotted it," she answered, a mean little suspicions-confirmed edge creeping into her voice, "on the floor beside his bed."

"Good heavens. Is that what I think it is?" Ellie wanted to know.

"Open it," I told Maggie.

She obeyed, prying at it with her fingernail until the top popped up to reveal its contents.

"Satisfied?" she asked, a touch resentfully now, as if we didn't quite understand the implications of her discovery.

We did, though. Maggie was the one who didn't.

"Yeah," I said distractedly. "We're satisfied, all right."

Then I looked at Ellie, and she looked at me, and the two of us got to our feet as if our nervous systems had been hot-wired together. Which in a way they were, by the object Maggie dangled before us.

It was Kris Diamond's famous, supposedly stolen locket with the curl of her own hair in it.

"I knew she'd been out there," Maggie revealed as we quick-stepped toward my car. "I've followed her there plenty of times."

Yeeks, two more bombshells. Kris was cheating on Sam, and Maggie's penchant for driving around late at night wasn't just a harmless habit, something to soothe her soul.

She was turning into a stalker. "And I really doubt Kris and Imrie were out there balancing her checkbook together. Not that she could do it alone. Anyway, where are we going?"

"Have you still got my cell phone?" I demanded.

It was a clear, chilly night with the stars like ice pellets littering the sky. Across the bay, the lights on Campobello lay in a long row, reflecting on the still dark water.

"Yes," Maggie said, producing it, "but why–?"

I took it from her, punched the button that dialed my home number.

"Didn't it occur to you that Kris might have mentioned you to Bill? That you could be in real danger?" I asked angrily.

But of course it hadn't. Maggie was only nineteen, and nineteen-year-olds are immortal in their own eyes. Besides, the one I was really mad at was myself, for letting her do it.

Ellie pursued another thought. "Kris and Bill," she said. "That's how he could have gotten the notes into Bella's house."

"And how he could've gotten the skillet," I said, listening to my phone ringing.

"Kris could've told Imrie when Bella would and wouldn't be able to alibi herself, too," Ellie added as we reached the parking lot across from Wadsworth's Hardware Store.

"He could've done it at lunchtime when he leaves the bank," I agreed. "We never really suspected Kris because she *did* have an alibi, and probably *couldn't* have written the notes—"

"All those big words...but what we never considered was that she could have been someone's accomplice," Ellie concluded.

Both tugboats hunkered placidly at the pier, lines as thick as a man's forearm looped over the wooden pilings. Nearby, the enormous landmark fisherman statue loomed over us.

All familiar, but all now disorientingly different in light of what I'd just learned, that Kris Diamond was in close and probably even regular contact with Bill Imrie.

Wade finally answered the phone, reporting that the baby was asleep; he and George had been upstairs in the shop. Sam was there but Kris wasn't; according to Wade, she'd blown Sam off at the last minute to do something else.

Summoned, perhaps, by Bill Imrie? Because maybe Maggie thought her comment about the notes hadn't alerted Imrie, but I wasn't so sure.

"Okay," I said, and hung up before Wade could ask questions; there wasn't time for them.

"Wait a minute," Maggie objected suddenly. "I'm no fan of Kris's, but one thing I do know. Even she wouldn't get her mom in this kind of trouble on purpose. Besides," she went on, "Kris *depends* on her mother. What'll she live on if her mom goes to jail?"

Sam, maybe. Or Bill Imrie. But Maggie had a point. It had seemed to me that Kris was genuinely worried about Bella. Would she deliberately set her own mother up to be blamed for a murder?

"Yeah," I said as we piled into the car. "You could be right about that. But she's no rocket scientist, remember?"

The Fiat's tires squealed as I pulled out. But the hell with it, I was in a hurry.

"That's why I'll bet Kris had no idea what she was really doing," I went on as we roared up Washington Street and out onto Route 190, headed for Imrie's place.

"But now," I added as we took the turn onto Kendall's Head Road, climbing the steep curves until the whole of Passamaquoddy Bay spread darkly out below, "now she could be the only one who knows what Imrie's really been up to."

And if I were Imrie, once it occurred to me that Kris was my weak spot, I was pretty sure I knew what I would do about it.

And soon. Maybe even tonight. When the lights of his place came into view, I slowed the Fiat until its engine was a mild purr.

"Whatever she knew, though," I went on as we pulled to the side of the road, "and whatever Bill told her, by now Kris could be figuring out the truth."

"Maybe he said Bella would *think* Jim was behind the notes, and that would help get rid of Jim somehow?" Maggie theorized aloud.

"Sure. And later, when Kris knew different, her complicity in delivering the notes would keep her silent," Ellie added. "The fact that she was involved in Jim's murder whether or not she'd realized it...that would probably be enough to scare her into shutting up. For a while..."

"So she'd be afraid to tell the truth about what she'd done, once she understood it?" Maggie said slowly. "Maybe hoping it would all work out okay without her having to confess her part?"

From her face I saw that she could relate to this notion: her own recent experience with Jim Diamond's body had made it terribly vivid for her.

"Yeah, something like that," I said.

I got out, taking care not to slam the car door. "But Imrie must have known from the start he couldn't depend on Kris to keep her mouth shut forever. And now that *we've* been asking questions..."

"He'll be getting nervous," Ellie concluded grimly.

Quietly we walked toward Bill Imrie's farmhouse. Ahead in the darkness its windows beckoned, glowing warmly like the lights in a cottage out of a familiar fairy tale.

Kris's car wasn't in the driveway. We made our way down it anyway, and across the path to the front door.

Inside, music was playing. It was Funkhouse II, the same CD I had admired at the Blue Moon. But now its impressionistic keyboard/percussion sound had a sinister tone, like the score of some particularly literate post-ironic slasher film.

I just hoped we weren't walking into one of the really scary parts.

The door stood open about an inch.

Chapter 14

U h-oh," Ellie said softly.

The inside of the house looked like one of Imrie's saw blades had ripped through it. Chairs were overturned, dishes shattered, and a leaf from the dining room table had been smashed right through one of the windows.

Ellie went over and turned the music off. But the resulting silence wasn't any more pleasant. "Kris?" she called.

No answer. Nothing moved. A sheet of white paper lay on what remained of the table.

"It's a note," Ellie said, snatching it up. "I think..."

Swiftly I scanned the thing over her shoulder. "This is a confession."

"That sneaky little bastard," Ellie said. "All this time he's been playing the goody-goody..."

"But what's it say?" Maggie demanded.

"It says he *was* in on the check-forging scheme with Jim Diamond, that he told Kris so, and then Kris threatened to tell on him unless he got rid of Jim Diamond for her, that's what it says."

I thought a moment. "But that doesn't sound right."

Ellie agreed. "He didn't even want to talk about how he was *innocent* in the check fraud. So why tell Kris he was guilty?"

Our eyes met. "So maybe," I postulated, "he *didn't* write this?"

Maggie caught on. "Maybe *she* did?" Then, "Oh, my god," she breathed, pointing at the floor. "Look!"

It was blood, smeared on the floor in a path leading ominously to the kitchen. There it pooled briefly by the phone, then led out the side door, where the trail disappeared in the darkness.

"Switch a light on," I called back to Ellie, who stood behind me in the doorway.

The yard light mounted over the door blazed suddenly across the lawn, revealing the faint blackish shine of more blood on the grass. Maggie appeared beside me.

"I looked upstairs," she said. "No one's there. But from the window you can see Kris's car behind the barn. That's where she always puts it when..."

When she's here. Which she was now; maybe hiding, because she was guilty of all this.

But maybe hurt. Or worse. Something bad had happened here, that was for sure, and the blood trail suggested that afterward someone had been trying to get to the barn, perhaps to the car.

"We should call Bob Arnold right now," I said, turning to go back inside. "Somebody needs an ambulance."

But Maggie had gone ahead of me down the barn path. "Oh!" she cried. Ellie ran with me to where the girl bent over something.

No. Not some*thing*. It was Bill Imrie. And from the amount of blood spreading blackly out around him, I knew he must be dead. Even so, I crouched hastily by him, hoping against hope.

But a small hole darkened his shirt, more blood staining it. He had no pulse, and his throat when I touched it was cool.

"He's been shot," I reported. And he'd been here a while. Which didn't make sense, either. If Kris had shot him, why was *she* still here? And...

"Where'd she get a gun?" Ellie wondered aloud.

I wondered that as well. I was even more curious as to whether she still had it, and was aiming it at us from somewhere in the darkness.

Out in the fenced yard the goats milled uneasily as if they too knew something was wrong. "Ellie," I began nervously. "Maybe we should..."

But before I could finish, we heard it: machinery running in the barn. Next came a metallic *whang!* I recognized from Wade's workshop: the sound of a big round blade starting to turn.

Someone had turned on the circular saw in Imrie's sawmill. "Go," I ordered Maggie. "Call Bob Arnold, tell him we need him out here *immediately.*"

She ran toward the house as I looked down at Imrie again. A dozen possibilities ran through my head. Had he tried to silence Kris and had the tables turned on him? Or had she been behind Jim Diamond's death all along, with Imrie as her fall guy?

Then it hit me: Ellie. She'd already crept to the open door of the barn, and was peeking in.

And she didn't belong here. "Ellie, you get back to the..."

Car, I intended to say. *Out of danger.* But she just waved me urgently closer, then slipped inside.

The noise of the machinery in the barn was shockingly loud. Hearing protectors dangled on a hook by the door, but I ignored them. The last thing I needed was to know even less about what was going on here. Anxiously I scanned the interior of the barn, looking for Ellie.

The saw mechanism and the conveyor belt feeding the blade were on the far side of the big, open-raftered enclosure. Above, a set of fluorescent tubes flooded the place with harsh white illumination, turning the spinning saw blade to a disc of silvery light.

The barn smelled sweetly of sawdust and, faintly, of something else. Ellie appeared beside me so suddenly I gasped. I waved her out but she shook her head stubbornly. So together we moved among the piles of sawed hardwood.

As Ellie took another step into the maze created by the lumber, a sound came from behind us. A loud sound, but that saw was still running and in the thunder of machinery I couldn't identify it.

"Maggie?" I began tentatively over my shoulder.

Then I stopped. Two new thoughts hit me and neither of them was cheerful. One, that the smell I'd been noticing was gun oil.

And two, that it wasn't Maggie standing behind me.

It was Lydia Duckworth, her neat pageboy hairdo disheveled and her lower lip, devoid of lipstick, beginning to swell. Imrie had slugged her, it looked like, in their struggle.

But .22-caliber beats a knuckle sandwich just about every time. Lydia had already fired once; that was the sound I'd heard. Now she smiled unpleasantly, waving me toward her with the gun.

"I guess you're not here to protect us," I shouted over the roar of the saw. I kept my eyes on the gun she held. "Or have I got that wrong, too?"

I couldn't have said what kind of gun it was. One of those rocket launchers I'd been wishing for a few days earlier, maybe.

Right now it looked big enough to be one. And her hand was surprisingly steady. "You weren't really drunk when you called me, were you, Lydia?" I asked.

Amusement tinged the gleam in her cornflower blue eyes. She shook her head. Behind me the machinery continued roaring. Ellie turned, got the unhappy drift of the situation.

"Next time I ask you to get in the car . . ." I began to her.

"Shut up," Lydia Duckworth snapped.

Shutting up wasn't an option, though, because I was sure she intended to kill us. Our only chance was to get her talking, keep her interested until Bob Arnold could arrive.

Or so I thought until Maggie appeared silently in the barn doorway, unnoticed by Lydia. I had to force myself not to look at the girl again, so Lydia wouldn't realize something was up. But the urge to glance past Lydia at Maggie, to latch onto her with my eyes as if the mere sight of her could save me, was nearly overpowering. At the same time something shifted in the machinery, quieting it a little.

Or maybe my ears were just getting used to being hammered by the racket. Blurred in my peripheral vision, Maggie pantomimed a snipping motion with her fingers: The phone line had been cut.

Oh, terrific. My cell phone was in the Fiat, but Maggie didn't seem to remember—*phone, car, phone, car,* I thought at her—and there was no way to tell her.

"Jake," Ellie said from behind me. "The saw blade . . ."

Right: still spinning. And I had a bad feeling that we were going to have to deal with it soon.

If we could. But for the moment I kept my eyes on Lydia and the gun. Now that the first unpleasant shock had faded I could see that it was a horrid little item, the kind of thing that in a childless home could get tossed into a drawer and forgotten.

Probably that's what Lydia's late husband had done with it, and after he died she'd found it. "So I suppose the story about Bill Imrie's gambling problem was a lie, too?" I asked her.

She nodded minutely. Oh, what a sap I'd been.

"Back up, please, Jacobia, and don't make any sudden movements. My husband kept this to use on burglars, but I'm sure it would work just as well on you," she said.

Yeah, probably it would. Just the way it already had on Bill Imrie. "Both," she emphasized, "of you."

Ellie took a step back. I did likewise. The saw's whine ratcheted up into a metallic snarl as it began cutting something.

"Why, Lydia?" I asked.

She stepped nearer. "Howard," she began over the din, "was such a straight-arrow. Good service, fair prices..."

I only caught every other word. But it was plenty.

And I'd have nodded to keep her going even if I hadn't been able to hear any of it.

"Not enough. Not in this day and age," Lydia said.

She was right; those old-fashioned notions didn't work when you were up against chain stores, mega-competition. That this was a funny place to discuss commerce didn't seem to occur to her.

Fine by me. "So you decided to do something about it, didn't you? Without telling Howard."

She looked satisfied. "Of course. I couldn't let that happen. So I enlisted that fool Jim to help me."

Which was when it all began to make terrible sense. Diamond hadn't had an accomplice; Lydia had.

I glanced back over my shoulder. The saw's conveyor belt was creeping forward, the blade biting into a block of wood still out of my view. Sawdust sprayed, but I couldn't see what was on the conveyor belt with the hardwood.

Something, though. Oh, I'd wager anything on that. Lydia's eyes shone with grim purpose tinctured with a glint of madness.

"But then," I guessed, "Diamond got caught. Because your husband found out?"

Another nod from Lydia, accompanied by another implacable step nearer. But not near enough for me to do anything about her.

"And maybe," I improvised hastily, "to save your reputation your husband promised Jim Diamond money if he would take the blame? Go to prison, not mention your involvement?"

Because if you were a good guy like Howard, and you knew you were dying, and you could do one last thing for your wife, wouldn't *you*?

Her face said I'd guessed right. But there was more. "Not just my reputation. We had stockholders. Angry stockholders."

So she hadn't just stolen from herself. She'd stolen from others with a financial stake in the business, and she would have been prosecuted, probably even jailed.

From the corner of my eye I glimpsed a big red switchplate mounted on a support beam a couple of inches from my right hand. If I could reach it, I might be able to shut down that saw....

Because my suspicions were growing about what was on the conveyor belt, headed for that deadly blade. Or rather, *who* was.

Lydia Duckworth took a final step toward me. Maggie still hesitated behind her, unable to help; if she made a sound Lydia might fire that damned weapon, and Maggie realized it.

"Howard promised Jim Diamond a payoff when he got out of prison. But I...I never promised anything," the old woman finished.

With the result that Jim became incredibly inconvenient when he did get out...My fingers nearly brushed the switch, the whirling blade connected to it eating slowly but remorselessly forward.

I fought down a pang of nausea at the thought of what would happen next. Then all at once with a fresh surge of fear I realized that I couldn't see Maggie, and I didn't know where she'd gone.

"So when Jim demanded his payment, and threatened to expose you if you *didn't* pay..."

"I dealt with him," Lydia agreed flatly. "Exactly as I will deal with you." Her hand tightened on the gun.

Ellie spoke for the first time. "I don't understand."

"Why kill Bill Imrie?" I asked, even though I knew. "And Kris, why would you..."

Lydia's eyes narrowed. "Because he'd figured it out. I saw him on the street here in Eastport. I saw his *face* when he looked at me. He tried to hide it by turning away. But I knew."

She hadn't, actually. She couldn't have, because Bill hadn't figured anything out. It was only guilt that made her think he had.

Her fresh guilt, because she'd just finished murdering Jim Diamond.

And later our visit to her had confirmed her notion that Imrie was onto her, that he must have told us something.

How she would have dealt with us if we hadn't shown up here tonight I didn't know. But I had no doubt that something would've come to her.

"So you came here, wrote that fake confession, and..."

"To make him look guilty, yes. And it can still work. My car is down the road. I can dispose of all of you..."

It would be a big job, but the sad part was she was probably right. There'd clearly been a struggle in the house, and Bill was bigger and younger, but she'd had the gun so she'd won.

She could win again. Maybe she'd get away with it and maybe not. But it wouldn't matter as far as we were concerned. . . .

My fingers brushed the switch. Maggie was still nowhere in sight. But I couldn't worry about Maggie now. Time was running out for us.

In the instant when the saw's snarl stopped, Lydia would be startled. Distracted for a moment...and whatever else happened at least I would halt the progress of that blade.

I pulled the switch.

But the saw didn't stop. Instead I got a glimpse of a frown on Lydia's face, then of Maggie appearing suddenly again, raising something in both desperate hands...

...before all those long white fluorescent overhead lights went out at once, throwing us into pitch darkness.

The darn switch didn't run the saw. It ran the *lights.*

With a harsh grunt of pain Lydia fell on top of me. Something heavily metallic—the gun, I thought, my hand scrabbling for it—clattered to the floor near my head but I couldn't find it. And over it all the howl of that awful blade went on, cutting in the dark.

Ellie scrambled behind me, fumbled for the switch I'd hit. Bright light blazed down onto Lydia Duckworth's crumpled body. Whatever Maggie had hit her with had knocked her out cold.

"Maggie, keep looking for the gun," I said desperately. "She could—"

But Ellie cut in urgently. "Never mind her, both of you come here and help me! *Hurry!*"

She was running toward the saw mechanism and we ran, too, but once I got there I almost wished I hadn't. I'd known what I might see but the ghastly reality nearly dropped me to the floor again, filling me with fright.

Kris Diamond lay atop the moving conveyor belt, strapped to a thick board with what looked like adhesive tape. Her mouth was taped but her eyes rolled in fear.

Inexorably, inch by slow inch, the conveyor moved her headfirst toward the massive whirling blade. "Can we cut her off?" Maggie shouted.

"No. Way too much tape." Impossible to get enough of it off in time. "Where's the freaking switch?" I yelled over the din.

All around us stood a variety of tools, crates, shelves full of lubricants and boxes of spare parts, in an order that probably had made perfect sense to Bill Imrie.

But it didn't to me. And I saw no other power switch. Still, it *had* to be here somewhere. . . .

"Find something to cut off as much tape as you can," I yelled to Ellie. "If we can't get the saw stopped, maybe we can—"

Ellie grabbed a pair of shears from a shelf and attacked the tape. But that didn't work, either. It was wire-reinforced tape, the shears struggling fruitlessly against it.

Meanwhile the conveyor belt just kept chugging steadily along. Beneath the table its gears rolled together, meshing like metal teeth.

"I'm going outside," Maggie said into my ear. "There's a power wire to the barn. I think I can throw a wooden ladder I saw out there against it, to break it."

"Okay," I hollered back. It was a glimmer of hope; we didn't have time now to hunt for circuit breakers or a fuse box. Hell, we couldn't even find the switch. "Go for it," I added.

But then I stopped, because there behind Maggie loomed Lydia

Duckworth again, her eyes dazed and her gait staggering, a trickle of blood running down her forehead.

And that dratted little gun in her hand. Damn, I'd *known* we should've stopped to look for it....

Lydia grinned hideously. One of her front teeth had gotten chipped when she fell, and her lip was bloody and swollen, but she didn't seem to be having any problem aiming the weapon.

At me. And for a long terrible moment that I firmly believed was my last one, I couldn't speak.

But then Ellie did, from behind me. "Oh, screw this," she pronounced distinctly, then hurled the shears she was holding at Lydia Duckworth and rushed headlong at her.

"Ellie!" I cried, but it was too late. The gun discharged, a bullet caroming with a metallic *ker-whang!* off the spinning saw.

Ellie drove both clenched fists hard into Lydia's solar plexus and I heard the breath go out of the older woman with a pained-sounding *oof!* Both of them fell backward, Lydia's head smacking the floor as Ellie got a knee in her midsection and finally—finally!—snatched away the gun, prying it from Lydia's still resisting fingers.

"Tie her with something," Ellie gasped as I searched Lydia roughly, alert for another weapon. But she had none unless you count trying to spit in my face. I jerked my head aside just in time; in the next moment my fingers found something in her sweater pocket.

It was a roll of reinforced tape, probably the same stuff she'd used to tie Kris. But there was plenty left.

"We should wrap it around your neck," I told Lydia, tossing the roll to Ellie. Instants later Lydia Duckworth was hog-tied.

"Oh, God," Ellie breathed, hauling herself up. "Jake..."

"Yeah. Maggie, get that ladder and *get out there—*"

But Maggie wasn't going anywhere. "No," she said. She held a crowbar, a big one. "There's no time."

Before her lay her enemy, at the mercy of the blade. Twenty seconds remained, at most; only a sliver of light showed between the teeth of that relentlessly advancing monster and the top of Kris's head.

Kris squeezed her eyes shut, her body straining uselessly at the tape. I wanted to shut my eyes, too. Then...

Maggie hefted the crowbar. "I have no idea how to do this," she said. "Or if it will work. But back off, because I think it could be *bad.*"

Then, lunging forward decisively, she thrust the flat end of the crowbar into the space between the meshing gears under the conveyor belt. And the result was like...

Well, it was like the end of the world. Metal chunks flew, sparks spewed wildly from the machinery's innards, the wooden supports shuddered as if they might bring the barn down around us, and a hideous grinding protest of steel on steel tore out of the mechanism's viciously clashing guts.

And then, with a series of booming thuds, the conveyor jerked backward as the motor howled, groaned in dying anguish, and failed with a sudden hot stench of burning electrical components.

Finally... the conveyor belt stalled and halted.

The shriek rising up in my throat dissipated, too, as Lydia Duckworth moaned. A chunk of something had hit her in the cheek, opening a horseshoe-shaped wound leaking bright red blood drops.

But no one else had been struck. In the near-silence that followed, Ellie pulled a fire extinguisher from its mount and activated it toward the smoking scrap wood the sparks had ignited.

Meanwhile I spotted another switch, this one underneath the saw. Oh, sure, now that I *didn't* need it...

I pulled it. The humming of the motor under the saw table ceased. The blade slowed with a descending whine, its blurred teeth resolving into sharply nasty, distinct hooks.

And then it really was quiet, except for the faint tinkling sounds of hot metal cooling.

"Maggie," I said breathlessly, but she wasn't listening. She was staring down at Kris. I started toward her; Ellie put a hand out to stop me.

"Let her do it," she told me.

So I just stood there as Maggie stepped toward the conveyor belt. She'd found a pair of tin snips and, as Ellie and I watched, she used them to cut the strips of wire-reinforced tape from Kris's body.

Shakily, the other girl sat up, her eyes dull and only half alert, as if she'd begun shutting down all the important systems in advance of the killing blade.

"This is going to hurt," Maggie said ominously, then ripped the tape from Kris's mouth.

Kris didn't scream. She just sat there a moment as if stunned by a hammer blow before her body sagged sideways.

Maggie caught her, looping an arm firmly around her. Then, frowning as if this part took concentration, she put the locket with the curl of Kris's hair in it around Kris's neck.

"Here," she said, "it's yours. You should have it back."

Once we got Kris down off the saw table I muscled Lydia to her feet. "So, Lydia," I asked her, "how soon after your husband caught onto you did he die? And if they dig him up will they find something in his body that shouldn't be there?"

She stumbled; I hoisted her. Not gently. "Painkillers, maybe?" I went on, hearing the coldly furious edge in my own voice and not bothering to soften it. "The potent kind he might've overdosed on, accidentally-on-purpose?"

Her answering look was venomous.

"Or," I continued, "that you might have given him? And since he was already terminally ill, the doctors assumed that it was suicide? Hushed it up for the family's sake?"

Because promising money to Jim when she would've preferred a more permanent solution was bad enough. But God forbid her sick, meddlesome husband should add insult to injury by, for instance, becoming even more ill, maybe even lapsing into a semiconscious state.

A *talkative* semiconscious state. And in her gaze I found a look of such virulent rage, I knew my theory was correct.

She'd killed her husband, too.

"Okay, Lydia," I said, suddenly dead tired. We reached the front lawn of the farmhouse where the reek of burnt wires overlay the sweet smell of fresh-turned earth. In the distance sirens whooped, coming from town. Cherry beacons whirled on Route 190, speeding toward us.

Bereft, the tame goats muttered sadly from inside their wire enclosure. "It's over now," I told Lydia.

But it wasn't.

Not quite.

Much later—

—after Bob Arnold had arrived and had summoned an ambulance and the state police, and after Wade and George had been phoned and reassured that we were quite fine and didn't need reinforcements, and after a great number of questions had been asked and answered, many of them several times over—

—we drove home again to my beloved old house in Eastport.

I'd put the top down, the salt air scouring the burnt taste of fear mingled with fury from my mouth. A full moon was rising, the night sky a milky bowl over our heads and the bay a sheet of silver.

"I don't understand," Maggie said. "If it wasn't Jim Diamond or Bill Imrie or Lydia, and it wasn't Kris, then who wrote those dreadful notes?"

I glanced in the rearview. Hollow-eyed, Kris met my gaze, then looked away. She'd refused medical attention, and the police had their hands full with the murder scene and Imrie's body.

So after consultation with Bob Arnold, they'd let her come with us.

"Think about it," I said. "Lydia stole the skillet the day she came to my house."

The sheer audacity of it still amazed me. "She saw Bella working there, recognized her from having seen her at Jim's trial, and realized that Bella's own house might be empty."

I stopped a moment, imagining the plan springing almost full-blown into Lydia's mind. A truly ruthless solution to the Jim Diamond problem...

"As it happened," I told them, "Bella's house *was* empty; Kris was out with Sam. Lydia knew just by looking at it that there would be a key under that statue on the porch, the same way I had. And she needed a weapon that belonged to Bella."

What she must've been feeling when we showed up at *her* door, I couldn't imagine. But she'd carried it off beautifully.

"So she went in," I continued, "found one, and took it. She knew that combined with those notes, if the police could track the weapon back to Bella, they'd figure she was guilty."

"That still doesn't explain who wrote the notes *or* how Lydia knew about them," Maggie persisted. "If...wait a minute, was that the same day Bella *told* you about them?"

"Correct. Lydia had come up onto my back porch that day—she really was doing volunteer work, that part was true—and she recognized Bella's voice, again from the trial...remember? Lydia said Bella spoke within earshot of her but not directly to her."

"Yes, and Bella does have a distinctive voice," Ellie put in.

"So when Lydia heard that voice again at my house, she stopped to eavesdrop," I went on.

Lydia had told me this part and more while we waited for Bob Arnold, relating it distantly and a bit wonderingly as if it had happened to someone else.

"So that's how she found out about the notes *and* that Bella thought Jim was behind them," I finished.

At the foot of Kendall's Head Road I stopped for an eighteen-wheeler loaded with particle board, headed for the freighter Wade had piloted into harbor that afternoon.

"As it turned out, Bella had no alibi for the time when Lydia went to Jim's place," Ellie added.

Improvising skillfully to get in, Lydia had told Jim that Bella had given her the skillet to give to him. And while his back was turned, she'd hopped up fast onto a chair and clobbered him from above, before he had time to react.

I pulled out behind the big truck. "But that was just luck. Even if Bella'd been able to place herself somewhere else..."

"Yes," Maggie interjected, "what then? If Bella *had* an alibi..."

The truck's backwash buffeted us. I slowed, letting it pull away. We were in no hurry now, and that felt like luxury.

"Even then, *Lydia* wouldn't be suspected," I said. "The only real risk she took was getting in and out of his place unnoticed. After she got past that hurdle..."

"Which she'd have *known* she had, once the body was found and no one started looking for a woman fitting her description," Ellie put in.

"Exactly," I finished. "Lydia knew then that no suspicion was likely to fall on her. That she'd gotten away with it. Bella being blamed was just going to be an extra layer of insurance."

That is, until Bill Imrie did a U-turn away from her, that day in the street. "So who...?" Maggie asked again.

The truck's taillights vanished around a curve. "Think. Who else had the ability, opportunity, *and* the motive to write those notes?"

It was the ability part that had flummoxed me. I'd paid too little attention to those crossword puzzle books in Bella's house. But Maggie had seen them, too.

She let out a breath of sudden realization. "Bella thought if people believed Jim was threatening her, then he might get sent back to jail? Is that it? Bella wrote the notes *herself*?"

To our right, islands lay on the water like mute animals, their humped shapes distinct against the shining ripples.

"I think so," I replied. "Bella knows a lot of words, but she's real-world naive. She thought her story might be enough to make the police get rid of her ex for her. When they didn't cooperate, she tried the story on me, hoping I'd somehow scare Jim enough that he'd leave town. The last note was just window dressing, to keep me interested."

Because by then, Bella really had needed me. As for the ash trap I'd laid on her porch steps, no one had stepped in it; no one had needed to. Bella had taken that final note from her bag, again merely pretending that it had been left by someone else.

Suddenly Kris spoke, jammed with Ellie into the backseat. "So I guess you're going to tell Sam," she uttered bleakly.

Maggie turned to her. "About the locket? That you were cheating on him with Bill?"

Bill Imrie had been only a backup for Kris, I guessed, nothing more, in case Sam didn't work out. I remembered her impassive expression when she'd seen Bill's corpse.

"No." Maggie said it firmly. "You can tell Sam if you want to. Or don't. Whatever."

As we crested the final hill toward town, the full moon broke suddenly free of the horizon, suspending itself over the bay.

"He wouldn't believe me," Maggie added. "And anyway, I don't care."

Below us lay all the little houses of Eastport with their windows aglow, the tugboats hunkered together alongside the fish pier, and a few last small boats puttering into the boat basin, running beacons alight.

Maggie took it in with the soft, wondering expression of a person who is seeing it for the very first time.

Or the last.

Chapter 15

As we turned the corner toward home, I noticed something odd going on at the top of Key Street.

There were lights up there, lots of them, and the shapes of many vehicles, their brake lights winking on as they maneuvered out of the traffic lane and parked.

Bob Arnold was there, too; he'd left the scene out at Imrie's to the state police and departed before we had. I slowed beside the squad car as he finished waving the last big vehicle over to the side.

"What's up?" I asked when he came over to the Fiat's driver-side window.

"Better find a parking spot. You got yourself a traffic jam here," he said.

Yeah, no kidding. I pulled over. Then another thought hit me. "There are animals at Imrie's that need taking care of," I said to Ellie. "But I guess you and I can do that."

"And do something about Lydia's dog, too; the poor old thing," she agreed.

"No, I will," Maggie volunteered from inside the car. "You have company."

I'd been trying not to notice. But I couldn't ignore forever the people getting out of the enormous vehicles, or the sound of their voices as they spoke in the excited tones of travelers who have completed a long journey.

Nor could I mistake their long-unheard yet familiar accents. They were flocking into my yard now, carrying tote bags and suitcases, exclaiming softly to one another and to my father who stood there alone, his hands in his overall pockets.

The relatives were here. "Jacob," said one and then another of them as they flocked around my father. It was his name: *Jacob.*

But hearing them say it made it new again for me, as if I'd never really known it, before. Their voices were twangy, some scratchy with age and others youthful. But all carried that same dissonant note of odd music, like an old fiddle being played lonesomely with an unwaxed bow.

Reluctantly my father drew his hands from his pockets, hesitantly extending them to a small wiry woman who stood waiting before him, her own hands clasped. Carefully, as if one or the other of them might break, the two embraced.

Then the rest crowded around, too, uttering his name again in soft, glad tones. It was as if, instead of them being the ones arriving, they were welcoming him.

"Your dad," Ellie observed, "isn't running away."

"Right," I murmured through the lump in my throat.

Someone in the house turned a yard lamp on. My father smiled in the round patch of light it threw, peering into one long-lost face after another, embracing women, gripping men's shoulders.

Knowing full well, of course, that he was the long-lost one. But I could see they were all much too tactful to make reference to that. And . . . they had come in recreational vehicles!

"Beds!" I said aloud, realizing the implications of this. "Little kitchens and bathrooms. All the comforts of home."

So they wouldn't need the guest rooms. Somehow Wade must've reached them and told them...but then the next thing hit me.

They hadn't seen me yet. Ellie hugged me hard, released me as the music of their voices mingled, my father's the deep bass note among them. He sounded surprised, overwhelmed.

And happy. Mostly he sounded happy.

Ellie gave me a little shove. "Go on, now, silly. Go on over there and say hello to them. They're your *family*."

Whereupon, at her gentle urging and after a last, almost-but-not-quite-paralyzing moment of fear, I stepped from beneath the dark canopy of the maple leaves into the circle of light.

Moxie doughnuts are made very simply by substituting boiling Moxie for some of the liquid in the doughnut recipe. Achieving a *good* batch of Moxie doughnuts, however, is something else again.

For one thing, you first must make ninety-nine *bad* batches, each only a fraction less heavy and indigestible than the one before; mine resembled grease-sodden hockey pucks with holes in the middle.

But Bella Diamond had mastered the art of the light, tasty, crisp-on-the-outside and cake-on-the-inside example of this unique Maine delicacy. For our Fourth of July picnic, she also assembled pounds of fresh crab salad, a cooler of potato salad, red hot dogs, and enough cold drinks and scalding coffee for an army.

Which was what we resembled as we all gathered on the hill behind the high school on Fourth of July night, to eat and watch the fireworks.

"Looks like they're having a good time," Wade observed, carrying his plate over to sit beside me on a blanket. "You ever hear your dad play the mandolin before?"

"I didn't know he could." Right now my father was ripping through a tune called "Blackberry Blossom," while a nephew accompanied him on a pennywhistle and a niece kept time on a washboard.

I bit into my second red hot dog. The sizzling skin popped tastily under my teeth. "I've never heard him laugh that hard before, either," I added.

Under the influence of his long-lost relations, my father had reacted like a creaky old door hinge that has suddenly been supplied with grease. "And I've never seen him *dance*."

Which he was doing now, his booted feet astonishingly sprightly. "Thank you," I told Wade, and meant it with all my heart, "for all the arrangements."

The recreational vehicles, I meant. Wade had called the town hall in the little mountain community Dad's relatives all hailed from, got a cell phone number for one of them, and presto, talked to my aunt Eunice.

And of course she'd understood. After that, he'd called the fellow in Limestone who owned the Harper's Ferry rifle that Wade was restoring. The fellow wasn't short of money; Wade had been doing the guy a favor, that was all, simply because he could.

And *that* fellow owned an RV dealership. Wade grinned, his eyes twinkling in the light of the bonfire we'd built.

"Least I could do for my best girl," he answered. Then, "You know, Jake, what I still can't figure out is where that woman stashed all the cash."

I glanced at him, surprised. "Lydia Duckworth? Well, it's a funny thing."

Not ha-ha funny, precisely. "But back when I first talked to Bill Imrie about the Jim Diamond mess—that Bill was terrified his reputation had been ruined, I mean, on account of him maybe being in cahoots with Diamond..."

I took a breath. "Well. Bill said he thought people would rather put their money under a mattress instead of in his bank."

Wade looked puzzled. But then his face cleared. "And that's where she...?"

"Not under it. But *in* it. Diamond always took the stolen cash out of his account as soon as he could, took his cut, and turned the rest over to her."

A snapshot of Lydia's elaborate needlework projects rose in my mind's eye. *Stitches fine as hairs...*

"Each time he did that, she opened her mattress and tucked the cash in, then stitched it back up again so perfectly that you'd never know it had been done. And no one did, even when she let the police investigators search her house."

"Huh," Wade remarked appreciatively. "Some stitchery."

Right, that and the same kind of fearless, take-no-prisoners *chutzpah* Victor had every time he delved into someone's brain. Like Victor, Lydia had the arrogant confidence to know she could do it and believe it would work.

Which in large part were the reasons that it had. Meanwhile, cleared of murder and not charged with anything else—

—when he heard the whole story, Bob Arnold looked severe, but decided to let the whole authorship-of-the-threatening-notes question wither away quietly, and I agreed—

—Bella Diamond had settled down very satisfactorily in the housekeeping department, so much so that the word-puzzle books strewn on my kitchen table now seemed always to have been there. We all wondered how we'd ever gotten along without her, especially Lydia Duckworth's old dog, whom Bella had adopted and whose comfort had become Bella's special mission.

"Hey," Wade said, angling his head at Sam, who sat apart from the rest of us, staring out across the bay. As we watched, Victor went over and sat beside him.

"He okay?" Wade asked. Near the musicians, Ellie and George danced with Leonora held up between them, all three laughing.

"I guess," I replied. "Just that he's pretty quiet."

Kris wasn't here tonight; she'd split up with Sam the morning after the events at Bill Imrie's, and we hadn't seen her since.

Maggie wasn't here, either; the message on her answering machine said she'd decided to go away for a while, and would be in touch when she got back.

I wondered if she ever would be. But at the moment she was the least of my worries.

YOU CRACK ME UP
To fill hairline plaster cracks,
mix a little powdered patching
compound from the hardware
store with some of your touch-up
paint, and brush it on.

"Wade, do you really think Sam ought to go?" I asked anxiously. "Do you think it's even safe for him to be living away from us?"

Sam was moving in the morning to Wade's little house on Liberty Street. Everybody else seemed to think it was a great idea, Sam being on his own and responsible for himself at last.

Everyone but me. "Jake," Wade told me, "he's got to go sometime. You don't want him living with us when he's thirty, do you?"

Actually, maybe I did. But before I could reply, Aunt Eunice put down her ukelele and came over to me. "Hello, honey," she said, laying a finger along my cheek.

My father swung into a fast, jazzy rendition of "Billy in the Lowground." "Don't you want to dance?" Aunt Eunice asked.

I looked over at Sam again. Victor had disappeared somewhere. "Yes, I'd love to, but first there's something I need to do," I told her, and went to join my son.

The two of us sat for a while in silence, watching the fading light as it re-flected off the water between us and the mainland.

"How's the pykrete boat coming?" I asked finally.

He shrugged. "Okay. Not a lot of demand for 'em, though. I mean, un-less you're Winston Churchill."

He laughed a little when he said it, which encouraged me. "Uh-huh. I suppose that's true."

Another silence. Then: "I was wrong," Sam said. "About Kris."

I decided not to mention the ring he'd bought. "Yeah, well. So are we all, pretty often. Wrong, that is. Don't worry about it too much, but try to do better next time. That's all," I added, "anyone can do."

He absorbed this. "Okay." A pause, then, "I mean, unless you told her to break up with me. Did you?"

I have to admit I thought about lying to him; I really did. Saving his pride, giving him the chance to make it all about me just one last time.

But I couldn't. "No. She did it on her own."

He nodded. "Yeah. I guess I knew that."

Hesitantly, I put an arm around Sam's shoulders, and after a moment he did the same, there on the final night that we would be living under the same roof together.

He pointed into the distance. "Hey, what's out there?"

Something was in the water; something big, moving toward the far shore. Near the bonfire, Wade got out the field glasses and peered through them.

"I don't know what it is," I said, squinting, too.

"Hey, you two, come on over here," my father called. "You want to see this!"

So we went, and the others gathered around as well, paper cups of hot coffee steaming in their hands as dusk fell.

"Wow," Sam murmured, peering into the field glasses before handing them to me.

"Wow," I echoed, because through them the creature swimming to the mainland was clearly identifiable.

It was the moose, a shining wake swirling behind the hump on his back as he neared the pale stretch of beach between water and shoreline forest, then clambered out onto it.

Wade put his hands on my shoulders. Ellie leaned on George, whose neck little Leonora had made a pillow of. From a few things Ellie had said I got the sense that once the adrenaline quit pumping, she'd been considerably sobered by our narrow escape.

That despite her earlier protestations, things were going to be different. But we could talk about that later.

Around us the relatives exclaimed together about how lucky they were: Maine, a family reunion, and as an extra-special bonus a real live moose. Somehow they seemed to feel I had arranged it all, especially my father, whose glance at me was surprisingly tender.

Suddenly to the east an orange-white chrysanthemum unfolded on the sky, each bright petal opening in a series of sharp pops that showered sparks down onto the bay.

The fireworks had begun. "Oh!" Ellie said as Leonora's eyes widened in wonder.

"That were a good 'un," Bella enthused over the boom.

"Mighty fine 'splosions," agreed Aunt Eunice. She put her arm around my father's waist and hugged him energetically.

And they were fine, too; big, showy, and loud. But as the last gleams of evening faded in the west I couldn't quite stop looking through the field glasses instead, passing them to Sam and taking them from him again at intervals.

"Why do you suppose that moose ever came to Eastport in the first place?" I asked, not expecting an answer.

"And where's he going now?" Sam wondered aloud, not sounding as if he expected one, either.

With fireworks erupting over our heads we watched the moose's majestic antlered silhouette dissolve into the night, unable to guess what further adventures might be in his future.

Or in our own.

ABOUT THE AUTHOR

SARAH GRAVES lives with her husband in Eastport, Maine, where her mystery novels are set. She is currently working on the ninth novel in the bestselling *Home Repair is Homicide* series. Visit her website at www.sarahgraves.org.